Mafia Captive

MAFIA Captive

KITTY THOMAS

Burlesque Press

Mafia Captive
© 2013 by Kitty Thomas

Printed in the United States of America

ISBN-13: 978-1-938639-09-8
ISBN-10: 1-938639-09-X

Wholesale orders can be placed through Ingram.
Published by Burlesque Press

Contact: burlesquepress@gmail.com

For M, as always.

Acknowledgments

Thank you to the following people in no particular order for their help in making *Mafia Captive* happen:

Robin Ludwig for cover art!

Natasha for copyedits and developmental edits and help with Catholic and Italian stuff.

Annabel, Claudia, Michelle, and Matthew for beta reading.

Thanks also to Matthew for his help with medical expertise and Italian stuff.

Tiffany for blurbing.

M for all his emotional support and for digital formatting. Love you!

Disclaimer

This is a work of fiction, and the author does not endorse or condone any of this book's content in a real world setting. This work is intended for an emotionally mature, adult audience. Do not try this at home.

Prologue

Leo Raspallo regarded St. Stephen's from across the road, overwhelmed by the grandiosity of the architecture and all its history. It was a building one could believe the creator of heaven and earth might actually deign to live in.

He pulled out his cell and pressed Angelo on speed dial. He'd spoken rashly to his brother. Whatever must be done, Leo mustn't play a role in it. He cursed when the call went to voice mail. Angelo never checked his voice mail. He didn't want to be reached, and there was no telling when he'd turn it back on.

After the first human life on his conscience, Leo vowed never again. His face was scarred forever by that night. He knew people must whisper. *How did he get that scar? He deserved it, no doubt.*

Leo had hoped the reminder of his sin would keep him on the straight and narrow, but there were too many roads that wound around him, all leading into Hell.

This time, it was a woman on his conscience, and there was no physical scar to carry. He'd used her and broken her, and in the end, he was responsible for her death.

But they say confession is good for the soul.

One

Seven months earlier . . .

Faith huddled in a dumpster surrounded by garbage, her breath coming in quiet, desperate gasps. Heavy boots thudded nearby. *Please keep moving. Please please keep moving.* Her face was wet from silent tears gliding down her cheeks.

I should never have gone this way. She'd almost stayed home, snuggled in bed with her cat, a sappy movie, and a bowl of popcorn. But it was too pathetic for a Friday night—especially so close to Christmas when she was all alone. The general holiday malaise and depression had already started to set in, and it was only the first week of December. Grudgingly she'd gotten dressed and met some girlfriends at a club. But the others had wanted to party later than she had.

It was just a few blocks to a subway station. She'd comforted herself with knowledge of the pepper spray tucked away in her purse—the pepper spray her pursuer now had possession of.

Faith closed her eyes, trying to shut out the sound of the shot, the image of the body falling, her stupid gasp that had turned sharp eyes on her.

She hadn't had the presence of mind to retrieve the mace before he'd grabbed her purse. But with the way the wind was blowing tonight, it would have just as likely blown into her eyes as his. And then where would she be? Another corpse.

The footsteps stopped. His breath sounded as if it were blowing right in her ear. His cologne put him in the cramped, dark space with her, drowning out the scent of rotting food and alcohol. He was a professional, not some random street tough. Poor, desperate people didn't bother with cologne. And if they did, it wouldn't have been such an expensive brand.

She bit back a scream until it rattled around and echoed so loud in her mind she feared he'd hear it. There was a snick of a lighter and then cigarette smoke filled the air.

It was as if he were trying to smoke her out, as if he knew she couldn't stand the stench. He took drag after drag as she watched the faint light through the cracks of her metal cage. He was toying with her.

She heard the pull of a zipper, and for one sick moment thought it was his pants, but the sound that followed was the snap of a wallet being opened. Her wallet.

"Faith Jacobson. 580 Flatbush Avenue. Brooklyn." His voice was relaxed, casual, because murder was casual to him.

She didn't want to stereotype, but a nicely dressed Italian man in Brooklyn standing over a dead body required no leaps of logic. This guy had mob written all over him. Letting go of the purse had been necessary to save herself, but now he knew who she was and where she lived. For a moment she continued to pretend he didn't know she was in the dumpster. She tried to think about where she could go, how she could stay safe from someone who would no doubt relentlessly pursue the only witness to his crime.

"Pretty. Brunette, though. Too bad." He must be looking at her driver's license photo. She'd dyed her hair right before that was taken. Now it was back to her natural red. She didn't know what he meant about her hair color, why it should matter one way or the other.

He let out a heavy sigh. "All right, come on out. If you make me come get you, I might have to play with you first."

That was it. She'd held it together as long as she could, been quiet as long as she could manage. "Please, let me go."

"Sorry, I can't do that. You've got too much information in that pretty head."

"I don't know anything. I don't know who you are. I don't care. I won't get involved. I swear to God. Walk away. Please. Whatever happened back there, it's not my business. I don't care about it." All Faith wanted was to be safe in her bed at home with her cat.

The silence stretched on like he was considering it.

"Sorry. Your number's up tonight, baby."

Although he'd made vague reference to torturing her first if she inconvenienced him, she couldn't make any part of her body move. Everything had shut down. How could a person step outside their hiding place, knowing a bullet was waiting on the other side?

She was frozen between a rotting burger and a bag of empty beer bottles. Faith squeezed her eyes shut and willed herself to be in her cozy apartment.

The lid of the dumpster flew back, and she screamed for a savior she knew wasn't coming.

The Italian aimed the gun at her. "Shut up, bitch. You want to be responsible for someone else's death, too? I can shoot witnesses all night."

No one would reach her before he pulled the trigger. "Please don't hurt me. I swear I don't care what happened back there. I just want to go home."

"Fuck it. I shoot you in the dumpster, and I don't have clean up. Works for me." He took a step to the side, lining up his shot as light from the opposite wall hit her in the face. Instead of pulling the trigger, he just stared. "If you want to live, get out here right now."

"I thought you said . . . "

"What I said was to get your pretty ass out of the dumpster before I change my mind."

He might torture her. Might rape her. There was no way this could end well. Wouldn't it be better to stay where she was and die quickly? The logic of the situation didn't matter. She couldn't help holding onto the thin hope that she might survive the night if she complied with his demands. In spite of the warnings shouting through her brain, she hoisted herself over the piles of trash and clumsily climbed out of the dumpster.

She had to grip the brick wall to hold herself upright.

"Stand over there in the light."

Faith wasn't sure how she'd managed to run in three-inch heels, because now she could barely walk in them, wobbling as she did, a few feet to the left to obey his order.

"Please . . . "

"If you say please once more I'm clipping you."

She shut her mouth.

"Tell me, baby . . . does the rug match the drapes?"

Out of the million horrible things he could have said, "does the rug match the drapes" wasn't in the top thousand. "I'm sorry, w-what?"

"Are you deaf, honey? It's a simple enough question. Are you a natural redhead?"

"Y-yes."

"Show me."

She turned to run again, but he was too fast. He pressed her against the wall and pulled her panties down while he shoved her skirt up and awkwardly aimed her body into the light. She thrashed and fought him. She expected he'd throw her down and violate her, but after he found proof of what she'd said, he covered her back up.

"You may be the luckiest dumb slut in the world." His arm went around her throat, pressing, pushing her consciousness down a dark well until the world shrank to a tiny pinpoint of light, then blinked out of existence.

Faith didn't expect to wake up. She especially didn't expect to wake up unclothed in a bathtub of water, with her pursuer, now captor, sitting on the closed toilet lid, staring down at her. She struggled to cover herself.

"You don't gotta worry about me. You're not my type." He motioned to some soap in a dish on the rim of the tub. "Clean yourself up. If you smell like a sewer, even Leo won't have mercy on you." He flipped open a cheap prepaid cell phone. "Pray this goes in your favor."

His eyes didn't waver from Faith as he dialed. The call connected, and his features softened, breaking out into a smile that made him almost attractive. If he hadn't been trying to kill her, that is.

"Leo!" he said.

Faith took the soap from the dish, too scared not to do whatever he asked. She tried to ignore her nudity, focusing instead on the man's conversation.

" . . . yeah, it's been awhile. I've been busy. Listen, I have something here you might be interested in— think of it as an early Christmas present. Remember what you told me last time I was out there? That thing you'd have if it weren't for your moral code? . . . I'm not suggesting that . . . Stop and listen for a goddamn minute, Leo. I had to fire one of my crew tonight. I wasn't as careful as I should have been, but I've got someone out there doing cleanup now. There was a witness. She's your type. Redhead. Slender. Big green eyes. I don't know what it is with you and Irish bitches, but she's perfect for you. You can have what you wanted. All you have to do is come collect her."

There was a long pause where Faith heard indiscernible shouting on the other side of the phone.

"Calm the fuck down. Look, what you do with her once you get her is up to you. But if you don't take her, she's dead. If you let her go, you know I'll find her, and once again, she's dead. Her life is in your hands, and once you see her, I know you'll take her. I'm doing you a favor, giving you what you want, and saving her life. I'm a regular saint. I could have shot the slut . . . yeah, I'm at the house . . . Yeah, well don't pretend your hands are clean. You may not be in the family business, but you know where the money came from. Don't forget that . . . Honest business my ass . . . You couldn't have started that business without your family. Now get down here."

Awful images flashed through her mind, even worse than the scene of the murder she'd witnessed or the recent threat of death. He was going to prostitute her out. What then? Would she be passed around until she was used up and then left in a gutter? Faith wrapped her arms more tightly around her body. Despite his personal lack of interest, she'd never felt so sexually exposed.

He closed the phone, his gaze raking over her, assessing her like a horse he might sell. "You're a lot more trouble than you're worth. My brother is an ungrateful ass."

The bathroom door opened and another attractive man in a slick suit walked in. Faith rushed to cover herself.

"The fuck?" the man said, spotting her in the tub.

"Relax, baby. She's for Leo."

"Oh."

He chuckled. "Did you think I'd switched teams?" He turned hard eyes back on Faith. "Get out. You're as clean as you're getting."

He held out a robe and she stepped into it, trying to figure a way out of this mess.

If this guy Leo *saved her*, it wouldn't make her safe.

Two

L eo stared at the phone in his hand, not sure what to think. Myriad emotions rolled through him: disgust, guilt, excitement. The guilt was premature. The disgust was warranted. The excitement was the problem. As repulsed as he was by his brother's twisted gift, his cock had twitched in his pants the moment the scenario had unfolded over the phone. He hadn't seen her yet, and already he was fantasizing about his very own slave, existing only to please and obey his every sexual whim.

Angelo ran a crew out in Brooklyn now. He wasn't bluffing. He would kill her. The family didn't like having to kill women and avoided it whenever they could, but Angelo's dick didn't swing in that direction, which made a woman just another man to him. He was the least likely to hesitate, the least likely to give a shit what kind of genitalia his victim had. Bad luck for the girl.

Leo was the first person Angelo had come out to. His brother had worried the others wouldn't follow him if they knew, but it had turned out to be a nonissue. He was so brutal, his orientation didn't make the slightest difference in the level of respect he could command. And Uncle Sal hadn't blinked when he'd promoted him. All he cared was that Angelo was a big earner and family.

In a drunken moment of twin-bonding and secret-telling, Leo had confessed his own alternative sexual leanings—a choice which in hindsight may have been a mistake, given the way his brother's mind operated.

Leo had had a few long-term kinky relationships. They'd gone okay, and they'd ended without much trouble, but the thing he wanted was the thing he'd never been able to have: a true slave.

Could he do the things he fantasized about? It was one thing to wank to it; it was another to do it. She was a living, breathing human being. Frightened. Losing everything in her life. Could he be that callous and cold? Did he have a strong enough moral leash to stop himself?

Angelo's words echoed in his mind: *What you do with her once you get her is up to you.*

Easier said than done. Once she was in his care, dependent on him and vulnerable, would he be able to resist training her? Taking her? He doubted he had such saintly self-control. Going to his brother's home guaranteed he'd become as amoral as Angelo. But if he didn't show up, she'd be in the harbor before dawn.

Angelo opened the door on the first knock and Leo stepped inside. Chaos greeted him: a broken vase, smashed bottles on the floor, upturned tables. In the midst of the maelstrom, sat the girl in a white bathrobe, bound, gagged, and blindfolded. Bruises were forming at various points on exposed flesh, while blood dripped onto a towel from her feet.

"For God's sake, Ange, what did you do to her?"

Her head jerked in the direction of his voice, and a sharp pain jabbed at his chest. Even so, seeing her bound state aroused him. It shouldn't, but it did. How could he go through with this? His brother had backed him into a corner, and a part of him wished Angelo had killed the girl without Leo ever knowing of her.

Angelo shrugged. "She struggled. I almost thought, 'to hell with it', and clipped her, but I knew you'd be upset. Look her over, see if you want her. Makes no difference to me one way or the other."

Of course it didn't.

Leo sat beside her. Her hair was a brilliant red, his favorite. He couldn't stop himself from running his fingers through it. It was still damp and must be even more vibrant dry. She shrank from his hand and whimpered.

"Shhh. I'm not going to hurt you."

Was he going to hurt her? He didn't know yet. Everything inside him laughed in triumph at what he had. A real slave. A woman at his complete mercy. And yet, he hadn't taken her from her life. His brother had orchestrated the scenario so Leo could play the hero, rescuing her from certain death.

"Did you or Davide touch her inappropriately?"

"Of course not. She's got the wrong parts for our taste."

But not for mine. His fingers itched to stroke every inch of her, to feel her surrender beneath him.

Leo pulled the blindfold from her eyes, unsurprised to find a luminescent green shining out at him. She was so young it made his heart hurt. Obviously legal, but at least fifteen years his junior. Probably more. Too young to lose her whole life.

There was a muffled scream from behind the gag as she tried to escape his touch. His hand pressed against her cheek. "Shhhh. I'm not him. Look." He motioned toward his brother. "We're twins."

Leo was always conscious of his scar, but perhaps it wasn't that obvious. Or maybe she was so scared that the idea of a twin hadn't occurred to her.

She was perfect in every way. The right thing was to take her to the police where she'd be protected and turn his brother in, but that was never going to happen. Family came first.

His attention went back to her feet. They were long and delicate with raspberry polish on her toes. The blood dripped steadily. It must have happened moments before he arrived.

"Get me a first aid kit. Why the fuck didn't you clean this, Angelo? It could get infected. What kind of gift is she if you break her before I arrive?"

"I didn't want to waste my time if you weren't taking her. *Are* you taking her?"

"I don't have much choice, do I?" Leo didn't bother hiding his disgust.

Angelo smiled. "Well, if you don't find her appealing, if she's not everything you've ever wanted to tie up and dominate, then all you have to do is say the word and she's gone."

The girl flinched at that. Whether her reaction was about the tying up and dominating or the implication of her death, he couldn't be sure. Likely equal parts of both.

"Just get the first aid kit." He couldn't bring himself to remove the gag. Not with an audience. Later, alone in the car he would, but not here. Whatever words would pass between them wouldn't be witnessed by Angelo and his lover. From here on, what happened between them was private.

His brother returned a moment later with the kit, and Leo pulled the girl's legs onto his lap. He didn't care about the blood getting on his pants. All he cared about was getting her bandaged so he could get her out of here.

Faith was glad to escape Angelo, but now she had another man to fear. She tried not to look at the brutal, angry scar on his face. As if she needed more evidence this man had known violence.

A new bruise formed on her wrist, chastising her for her escape attempt. She couldn't see it in the dark, but she knew it bloomed and burst across her flesh like an erupting volcano.

"I untied your hands as a kindness, and you try to attack me as soon as I start the car?"

"What the hell did you expect?" Was it not normal to try to save yourself from captivity?

Minutes ticked by in silence.

"I can understand your reaction, but I told you I didn't want to have to hurt you. You forced my hand."

She tried not to think about how gently he'd bandaged her wounds back at Angelo's place. There had been glass embedded in her skin. He'd spoken quietly to her and told her exactly what he was doing through the process. Then he'd put a topical antibiotic on the wounds and wrapped her feet in gauze.

Even if she'd managed to get away from him, how far could she have gotten on bandaged feet before he—or something worse—caught her? She hadn't been thinking that far in advance. The only thing she'd been able to think about was how she couldn't surrender. She had to fight. Sitting quietly was the worst thing she could do. It would only allow her too much time inside her own head to imagine what might lay ahead for her and later to regret not taking any opportunity to save herself.

While she'd noticed—in a purely clinical way—the attractiveness of the brother, Leo's small acts of kindness and his tenderness had created an unexpected, visceral reaction that made his matching physical beauty come into sharper focus. It was a physical beauty that even his scar couldn't mar. In fact, the imperfection brought the rest of his perfection into starker contrast. She didn't want to admit she could see herself doing anything this man wanted. Her only fears were that he might hurt her, not that he might fuck her. The realization made her feel sick inside.

"Just let me go," she whispered. "I told your brother I don't care who you are or what you're doing. I'm not interested in being a hero. I just want to go back to my life. Please. I swear I won't say anything to anyone."

She'd seen enough movies about crime families to know talking got you killed, that these people were omnipresent. It hadn't escaped her notice that Leo might be her only safety, the one person who could keep her from having to spend the rest of her life running.

"I won't take that risk. What's your name?"

"None of your business." If he thought they were going to sit here and have some polite conversation as if he weren't committing a felony . . .

Leo pulled the car onto the shoulder and turned the engine off. The interior lights came on, casting his face in shadows and light that made him look demonic. Anger twisted his features in a gruesome tableau of barely constrained violence. Before Faith could react, his impossibly large hand wrapped around her throat, pressing her against the glass.

"This. Will not work," he practically growled. "I saved your life. You belong to me now. You keep show-ing me attitude and see where it leads you. I can make your life the darkest hell imaginable. Or I can show you kindness. Your choice."

Faith clawed at him as his hand tightened. She wanted to beg, but she couldn't squeeze words out of a throat already being squeezed. Leo was no less lethal than his brother.

"Are we clear?"

Faith nodded frantically. He released her, straightened his suit, and started the car. She coughed as she tried to get air back into her lungs. Leo appeared unconcerned with her struggle as he pulled back onto the road, quickly accelerating to the full legal speed.

"Let's try again. What's your name?"

"F-faith."

"Was that so hard?"

Her mind screamed *yes* while imaginary finger-nails ripped at his skin, but the reality was more muted. She looked down at her hands and quietly whispered, "No."

"No, Master," he corrected.

Her eyes widened and her lips pressed into a firm line. She couldn't be his slave. Thinking of herself as his prisoner had been bad enough. She was a human being. The fact that he could demand so demeaning a title from her meant everything she suspected he'd take from her would happen, and if he didn't hurt her, she wasn't sure how hard she could fight someone so overwhelming and seductive and experienced. He was quite a bit older than her, a grown, mature man, whereas the guys she'd been involved with were silly boys by comparison.

"Are we going to have to pull the car over again?"

The threat had the intended effect. The lesson was too fresh in her mind. She recoiled as she heard herself say, "N-no, Master."

"Good. Now, there are servants in the house. Don't take that as hope. They will not help you. The phone goes through a switchboard. The operator won't help you either. If you seek their help, they will report it to me and you'll be punished."

She flinched at the warm hand on the back of her neck, but he wasn't there to hurt her. Instead, he massaged the tight muscles, a feeling that was comforting in spite of everything. She shouldn't want his hands anywhere near her, but if she was stuck with this man, she much preferred kindness to cruelty or pain.

"I can't let you go, and I won't be able to resist taking you. But I'll be good to you if you let me, Faith. Are you going to let me?"

Each time her name rolled off his tongue, it was as if a piece of her will broke off from her and floated away. She wanted to argue about belonging to him but knew that wasn't the way to get to the kindness he offered. She nodded, not wanting to have to call him master again. He let it slide.

"That's smart." He took an exit and the city began to disappear behind them as buildings became fewer and trees more common. "Are you married?"

"No. I-I'm just twenty-two."

He cursed, and she worried he'd take her back to Angelo.

"Way too fucking young." He shook his head. "Boyfriend?"

"No."

"Faith . . . I'll pull the car over, and I'll do much worse. I am your Master. You are my property. Now say it. No ,what?"

"N-no, Master," she forced out.

"Good. Family?"

"No M-master." Not anymore.

"Friends?"

"A few girls at work." She was beginning to be thankful she was alone. At least there was no one in the world he could use to hurt her further.

"You've got less to leave. That'll make it easier on you."

He didn't know what he was talking about. Having nothing to leave was never easy. She'd been thrown into Miami's foster care system when she was twelve. Her foster father had beaten her, and as she'd grown into a young woman, he'd attempted other things. A college scholarship in New York had been her escape hatch before he'd gotten a chance to succeed. Now her earned freedom felt unreal because this man would bring to fruition her foster father's sick desires. Why else would he take her? Why else would he emphasize that he owned her? Leo wasn't the first man to make such a claim, and this wouldn't end any better. Only there was no ready way out this time.

She didn't know how to be around people. How to talk to them and make real, close friends. She'd never learned how trust worked. Now all she was leaving was a too-small apartment and a few shallow friendships. Fresh tears flowed down her face, and she thought she might never exhaust her supply of them.

"I have a cat. She'll starve without me." The only being she'd miss was reliant on her for survival. She couldn't stand to think of Squish suffering and dying alone in the studio apartment. That cat had seen her through her senior year of college and getting her first real adult job.

Leo's hand was still at the nape of her neck. "I'll send someone to retrieve your cat."

Faith's head snapped up, and she stared at him a moment, trying to determine if he was playing with her. "You'd do that for me?"

"I told you I can make your life easy or hard. Give me what I want, and I'll make it so easy. When we get to the house, you can write down your address and make a list of anything else you want from your former residence." He stressed the word *former*.

"My key is at Angelo's. He took my purse."

Leo nodded. "That's no problem."

Faith tried not to think about the price he'd extract from her for all this kindness. A tab had started, and there was no doubt he'd take it out of her body. Even so, she couldn't help the instinct that made her want to cling to him for his protection, however irrational or foolish such an instinct may be.

When they arrived at the house, Faith's mouth fell open. *House* was an understatement. It was like calling an ocean a quaint body of water. She was glad he'd gotten rid of the blindfold, ropes, and gag. With all the guards and household staff, it would be mortifying to be brought in like a prisoner, though that was her status. *Slave*, her mind whispered.

She tried not to look like a starry-eyed tourist outside a celebrity home as they made their way inside.

Leo exchanged a few hushed words with a man that looked like head of security while Faith looked around the entryway. It was decorated for Christmas, and there wasn't a nook or cranny that didn't have an ornamental flourish or a string of glittering white lights. A high-quality sound system played Christmas carols just loud enough to notice if you paid attention, but still unobtrusive enough to go about your day without undue annoyance.

"Faith. Come with me." Leo took her hand and led her through the marble-tiled foyer, up a grand staircase, and down a hallway.

Her heart was in her throat as he urged her inside a room with a large and ornate bed. A fire roared in the fireplace, and a Christmas tree stood near the windows. A golden retriever hopped off the furniture to greet them, tail wagging and tongue lolling out.

"Hey, Max," Leo said, bending to pet the dog.

How monstrous could the man be with a golden retriever? Though Faith knew this wasn't a real marker of a man's overall goodness or evil, it gave her a spark of hope.

The sitting area in front of the fireplace had a small coffee table, a couple of high-backed chairs that looked comfortable despite their opulence, and a love seat. A bathroom led off to the side, and Faith had no doubt the closets alone were probably the size of her studio apartment. At the back of the room was a large set of three bay windows with thick drapes that reached the floor. In front of the windows was a writing desk with fancy stationary and pens.

"Sit and write down your address and make a list of everything you need. There's a heated pool here, so you might factor that in."

Faith didn't say anything. She couldn't say anything. She just sat, uncapped a fountain pen, and stared dumbly at the paper. Was she a prisoner or

Cinderella? Had she experienced the worst luck of her life or the best? What he was doing wasn't okay, but here she was, surrounded by people in a nice place with a man who, despite realities she couldn't yet cope with, was prepared to . . . what? Take care of her like she was his girlfriend or wife?

"Leo . . . " she said, forgetting herself for a minute.

He patted the dog one last time and straightened, his face stern. "Master. Not Leo to you. Ever."

With that pronouncement, her silly little-girl fantasy came to an abrupt and screeching halt.

"I'm sorry, Master." She'd never get used to the title. "Why are you doing all this? I don't understand why . . . " It wasn't a question of why he was doing something so immoral. The real question was why was he wrapping it so nicely, making it a seduction that part of her couldn't help wanting to fall for?

Aside from the slavery aspect, wasn't this what most girls fantasized about from childhood—Prince Charming swooping in and taking care of all their needs, showering them with safety and security, and living happily ever after?

Despite escaping her foster family, things hadn't gotten much easier. The brief party of college and dorm life had been fleeting, only to give way to a cold world that demanded she produce or sleep in a gutter. She'd barely been eking out a living, squirreling away every spare penny she could, hoping it would be enough to keep surviving. Because what if she lost her job? She had to have a safety net.

It had taken a lot of nagging from her friends to get her to go out drinking, but she needn't have worried.

There had been plenty of men to buy her drinks so she didn't have to dip into her own funds.

Leo strode over to her and she couldn't help cringing, afraid of what he might do. So maybe it wasn't such a dream-fantasy after all. She was still bone-chillingly terrified of him.

He stopped at the other side of the desk, regarding her calmly. "I have specific requirements in a relationship. Certain . . . kinks and desires . . . "

Faith's mind immediately flashed to images of whips and chains. But with the title he'd demanded, hadn't that idea drifted through her mind already, no matter how much she'd tried to push it away? She might not be into that, but she wasn't oblivious.

Given her current circumstances, it would seem most appropriate that such things would happen in a dirty, dank basement where she'd be fed crumbs and kept in a cramped cage, but she imagined whips and chains with this man would be dressed in refinement.

"A-are you going to hurt me?" Plenty of women lived in abusive relationships that looked like pampered luxury on the outside. Faith didn't want to be one of those women. Give her a simple studio apartment with an uncertain financial future any day over riches that obscured a nightmare of ongoing torment behind closed doors.

"I don't know what I'm going to do yet, but if you obey me and honestly seek to please me, you'll remain safe and may even come to be happy here. Now make your list."

She tried to quiet the whirring questions and relentless fears. His word meant nothing. He could promise anything he wanted, but trusting in such a promise would be too naïve—no matter how much she wanted to. Her only desire was to find safety here. All thoughts of rebellion and escape left her in light of the hope she had of garnering his favor.

Faith scribbled down her list, hoping it wasn't asking too much, and handed the sheet to Leo. He looked it over briefly and nodded. "I'll take care of it. Stay here."

Three

Saving Faith from Angelo's bullet had given Leo an irrational sense of entitlement. But the girl wanted him. In between her moments of fear and indignation, he'd glimpsed the half-starved glances she'd aimed his way. It was the effect he'd always had on women. The combination of danger, money, and looks was too irresistible for most females of the species—even a captive like Faith.

He intended to make this as easy on her as possible, if she'd let him. Each tiny step toward complete submission would be rewarded. Each misstep, punished. By the time he was finished with her, she would crave him so deeply, she wouldn't remember this had all started with her forceful loss of freedom.

It had been a long night, especially so close to Christmas. Though he couldn't imagine the men in the family caring one way or the other about how Faith had come to be here, the women and the children didn't need to know. He'd have to come up with a cover story before family started streaming in for the holidays.

Once he'd made the choice to get involved in Angelo's warped offer, he was committed, the course of his life irrevocably changed, his own options narrowing. Her death wouldn't only be a sin on Angelo's soul, but on Leo's as well.

He couldn't get bored with her or decide it wasn't working out and send her packing. Not without the price of her life. He'd been kidding himself if he'd thought he could be in this family without being tainted by his environment and pulled into an increasingly amoral world.

Leo dropped the list off with one of his men and went to take care of some business. When he returned a couple of hours later, he found her on the love seat with Max's head resting on her lap. The dog had an uncanny ability to sense distress and bring comfort, and right now he was doing what he did best. Her hand trembled as she stroked the dog's fur.

"Faith."

She looked up, startled. The fear in her eyes pulled at him. He wanted to lock the door, toss her down on the bed and ravage her within an inch of her existence. But instead he rolled the cart in, letting it come to stop next to her.

"Are you hungry?"

Her gaze drifted to the floor as if she couldn't look into his eyes while she acknowledged her status with him. "Y-yes, Master."

There was a hesitance in her reply, though Leo guessed the hesitance wasn't about the title he'd insisted on. From the look in her eyes, she was afraid of what she might have to do to earn the food. He brushed a stray tear off her cheek and put a plate on her lap. Max repositioned himself on the floor beside her feet, looking up at Leo with accusation in his gaze. Or maybe Leo imagined it, needing someone to disapprove of his actions. No one else in the house would.

If a dog was to be his moral compass, so be it.

He sat across from her with a plate of his own, watching as she hesitantly brought the sandwich to her lips. God knew what kind of fears the poor girl harbored. And he couldn't promise that at least a few of them wouldn't come to pass. Though there existed sadists far worse than him, if she was a complete vanilla, any of it was going to terrify her. And on some level that excited him more.

"You'll share this room with me." Leo pointed to the far end of the room. "That closet is empty, so you can use it for your things when they get here. It shouldn't be long now."

Faith's hand shook as she raised the sandwich to her lips.

"Are you listening to me?"

She looked up, her face alert like a rabbit about to be pounced upon. "Y-yes, Master."

He smiled at the remembered title. She was so sweet. Given her attempt at fighting both him and his brother, he'd been surprised when so little pain and threat had resulted in obedience. He'd expected attitude and mouthiness at least, but she was surprising him. Even if she didn't classify it as a kink, there was a submissive current that ran through her like electricity, a deep need to appease a stronger party.

"You just want to stay safe, don't you? That's why you're being so agreeable."

"Yes, Master. P-please don't hurt me." She chanced a look into his eyes. "Please."

He tried not to let her pleading affect him. "Ignoring for a moment the circumstances of your presence here, do you find me attractive?"

"Please don't make me answer that."

"Because you're afraid to make me angry?"

She looked down at her hands. "No, Master."

"I see." So she *was* attracted. "I'm not going to fuck you for a while. Be a good girl and you have nothing to fear from me. And . . . you're allowed to speak."

"I don't have anything to say."

When Angelo had been assessing his type, he should have remembered Leo liked conversation. Before he could have much time to brood over this, there was a short knock on the door.

"Come in."

As the door pressed open, a gray cat with a face that looked like it had been flattened trotted into the room, meowing angrily at the sight of another animal lying at her owner's feet. Despite the flattened face typical of its breed, it was cute.

Faith looked up, relieved to see her pet. Instead of coming up to her, the cat bypassed her to sniff and rub up against Leo's legs. He picked her up and placed her in his lap, whereupon she began to purr as he stroked her.

"What's her name?" Leo asked.

"Squish."

He looked up, raising an eyebrow. "Squish?"

Faith shrugged. "Well, look at her face."

Leo glanced at his watch. "I imagine you're exhausted. Go ahead and do whatever you usually do before bed."

Faith let out a slow breath. She was safe for a moment behind the locked door of the bathroom, holding a pile of things from her apartment in her arms. Could she wash her face and brush her teeth and floss like nothing scary was going on? Could she slip into her pajamas and get into bed with this man?

She went back to the question he'd asked about if she was attracted. Hell, yes she was. But she shouldn't be. She was ashamed that she found him appealing on any level.

She should be kicking and screaming and fighting. She should be running. But she didn't want to die. It was easier to be his slave in a mansion than run and wait to be gunned down in the streets. It was hard to hold the idea in her head that he was her captor when he was also her rescuer. The roles were too different. If she let herself, she'd forget the captor part and latch onto the rescuer part.

When she'd brushed and flossed and scrubbed her face and changed, she sat on the edge of the tub. She should go back out there. He might get angry and take this fantasy away if she stayed too long. But she couldn't help it. She couldn't make herself leave the room. It was easy to pretend he could forget about her in here and she could stay, unmolested forever.

But the knock on the door burst that irrational bubble. "Faith. Are you all right in there?"

She held back the hysterical laugh as it danced in her throat. Was she all right? She was so not all right. But she could never explain the reason she wasn't all right was because none of this was playing out as she'd imagined it would. If he kept playing his hand like this, he might actually succeed in seducing her. The thought made her recoil.

When she opened the door, Leo blocked her path, wearing nothing but a sinister smile. She tried to avert her eyes from his impressive erection, tried not to hyperventilate. Not going to fuck her? Like hell he wasn't going to fuck her. The next thing he'd be saying was "Don't worry, I'll just put the tip in."

She was beginning to wish she'd gotten a lot more drunk tonight.

He gave her a once over then shook his head. "No."

She forced herself to look at his face and nothing else. "No?"

"I don't recall saying you could wear pajamas to bed. I want you naked."

She took several steps backward. "E-excuse me?" What happened to his promise to leave her unmolested for a while? Did "a while" translate into fifteen minutes in his world? "I-I thought you said . . . "

"I said nothing about sleeping attire. Take it off."

His words were clipped and hungry . . . nearly a growl. If she did what he said and took it off, what would protect her from him? Nothing. But what was protecting her from him now? Did she think her pajamas had magical powers?

"Leo, please . . . "

His eyes glinted dangerously as he gripped her wrist and pulled her closer, causing his hard-on to brush against her thigh.

"What did we say about that? Address me properly."

"Master. I-I meant Master, please . . . I can't . . . " How could she disrobe in front of him? She couldn't make herself do it. It wasn't that she wanted to enrage him or bring retribution on herself, she just couldn't do it. Spinning through her head were thoughts of her foster father with whiskey on his breath, cornering her in a back bedroom at a party, trying to pull her top over her head moments before they were thankfully interrupted.

Her foster father had only wanted to *look*, too. And yet she'd known that his horrible hands would be on her the moment her breasts sprang free of the shirt.

No one was going to rescue her tonight with Leo. And there was no scholarship with her name on it, paving a path to freedom in a distant city. This was the end of the line.

She let herself be led into the bedroom and didn't protest when he sat on the edge of the bed beside her. It didn't occur to her to try to struggle again until he'd put her over his lap and ripped her pajama pants down. Faith gasped as his hand landed solidly on her bottom. She reached back to protect herself, but he gripped her wrist and squeezed hard.

"Never shield yourself. Do you understand?"

She couldn't reply because he kept spanking her. It was painful, of course, but the pain was hard to process in light of the shock and humiliation of the event. She couldn't believe she'd thought he'd continue to be kind. Did every man in the world just want to hit and take advantage of her? "Please . . . "

"Do you understand?"

She wanted to claw or bite or kick him, but such acting out would get her hurt more so she whispered, "Yes, Master."

She shuddered in revulsion when a finger slipped inside her, but then he released her. She scrambled back to the head of the bed, huddling against the headboard, holding herself in a ball as if it would protect her from him. A few minutes passed before he spoke again.

"Why are you still dressed? I don't want to hurt you. I want you to obey me."

She couldn't contain it anymore. All of her resolutions to be agreeable and obedient and hope for mercy evaporated in the face of her recent humiliation. "You're already hurting me. You brought me here against my will with no hope of freedom and now you're stripping me and hitting me. It's too late to pretend like you're good. You intend to rape me, and you expect me to happily go along with it!"

He reeled back like she'd slapped him but quickly recovered. "You have exactly thirty seconds to be naked. If you fail to comply, I will show you what true pain is."

The only difference between this man and her foster father was his looks. If Leo would only be kind to her and give her some time, she could see herself willingly going into his arms, but that fantasy was gone.

Before he could unleash the wrath he'd promised, she peeled off the T-shirt and sweatpants and covered her bare breasts with her arms.

"Panties," he said, ignoring her attempt at modesty.

She wanted to beg again, but the look in his eyes told her it was pointless. She took off the last scrap of clothing and squeezed her eyes shut, waiting for the inevitable.

"Get in the bed."

Although she was afraid of what was coming next, it was at least an opportunity, however momentary, to cover her nudity with blankets, so she took it.

Leo shut off the lights and got under the covers.

She waited, her breath barely going in and out of her lungs. She waited for his hands to be on her, trying not to be horrified by the idea. She was too scared of him right now to be attracted. If he fucked her, he'd rip her, she was so dry.

"Are you going to cry all night?" His voice was gentle, in contrast to the content of his words. The words themselves were callous and unfeeling, but he delivered them with a kind of compassion that confused her terribly.

Faith had tried to be quiet, hoping he was already asleep and couldn't hear her. As each minute had passed, she'd become more hopeful that he'd stay on his side of the bed, but she couldn't help the tears.

"I'm sorry, Master."

He got up, and she tensed. But a few minutes later, a warm bundle of purring fur was in her arms. Then he got back in bed.

"Thank you," she said, not sure what to do with the odd gesture. It occurred to her that she hadn't thanked him for sending someone out after her things and her cat. She'd been too surprised by the action, too happy to see Squish. And it had been hard for her to think it was appropriate to show gratitude to this criminal.

"Go to sleep," he said.

Squish curled under her chin, and Faith allowed the rumbling purr to lull her to sleep.

Leo stared at the moon shining in through the large windows, gritting his teeth as Faith's breath evened out in sleep, the cat still purring in her arms. It was so simple. She was attracted to him. She was desperate to stay safe. That equation should have added up right.

But the amount of terror she'd experienced at a mild spanking told him all he needed to know. If there had been any doubt, when he'd slipped his finger inside her, he'd known. She'd been dry. No arousal. No reaction. She wasn't kinky. Not even a little bit.

In a perfect world, Faith would have had secret fantasies about being dominated her whole life. She would have tried to resist, but her body would betray her.

No matter how scared and upset she was, her cunt would have been at least a little wet. Her clit would be swollen. She'd be flushed and flustered. If she already found him physically attractive, which she'd admitted to, a mild spanking would have her body reacting to him in a favorable way. Instead it had upset her so much he'd thought she might hyperventilate.

Bringing the cat to her had been the one thing he could think of that might calm and settle her so she could sleep. And so he could.

Four

L eo woke late in the afternoon to find Faith sitting up in bed, her knees drawn to her chest and the blankets wrapped tightly around her. She cowered when he looked at her.

"Did you sleep okay?"

"Y-yes, Master."

An obvious lie. She was too afraid for truth. If anything, in the light of day her anxiety was heightened. Her eyes were red-rimmed.

"Go take a shower and get dressed. We'll go down to the kitchen for something to eat."

She remained frozen against the headboard, and Leo frowned.

"Do you want to start your day off with punishment?"

"P-please, Master, no. I-I . . . please don't look at me."

This was not going well. She felt violated just being naked in his presence. Even if he didn't touch her. It had been one night, nudity, and one spanking, and she already acted like some tormented refugee. If he pushed her farther, she might retreat inside herself and never come back out. The idea that he was damaging her with such small actions was another nail in the not-kinky coffin.

His fantasies meant nothing in light of the very real human being he was ruining with them. The slight weight of her body lifted off the bed, and she scurried into the bathroom and shut the door. The click of the lock snicked into place.

Leo opened his eyes. A moment later she shot out of the bathroom with a towel wrapped around her, into the closet to retrieve clothes, and then back to the bathroom like a frightened mouse.

While she was in there, he grabbed some clothes of his own and went down the hall to another bathroom to shower and get ready. During the night he'd dreamed of her. In the dreams she was sweetly submissive, obeying his every command, becoming aroused when he delivered pain, desperate to please him and getting off on it.

The gap between the dream and the reality was so disappointing he could kill his brother for doing this to him. Nevertheless, he closed his eyes and stroked himself in the shower, thinking of Dream-Faith, the girl he wished his captive could have been but so clearly wasn't. Even if he planned to torture himself today with an attempt to slowly draw her into his world, he already knew it would be fruitless. And the cost to her would be higher than he could stomach.

He found himself angry, not just with his brother, but with Faith. As if it were her fault she wasn't kinky.

As if she could be blamed for being afraid of him. His feelings were unreasonable, but still, the anger built as he jerked himself off.

After showering, he came back to the bedroom to find her on the edge of the bed like an animal caught in a trap with nowhere to go. His anger faded, replaced by a pain in the center of his chest. *I did this to her. And in only one night.*

She wore jeans and a T-shirt. Her feet remained bare except for the gauze which had gotten wet in the shower. Leo went to the bathroom and took a first aid kit from the closet.

"I need to look at your feet and change your bandages."

Reluctantly, she uncurled her body. But before he looked at her feet, Leo pulled her into his arms and stroked her hair. She resisted at first, her body tense and uncertain, then she let go of everything and sobbed against him. So young. With her whole life ahead of her. Or that was how it should have been. That was what his brother had stolen, what Leo had stolen. He held her until she settled. Then he took one of her feet in his hands and began to unwrap the bandages.

None of the cuts had been particularly deep, even though he'd had to dig some glass out of her flesh the previous night. She was walking on it okay, but her fears may have been drowning out any pain she was feeling. He carefully cleaned the wounds, applied more ointment, and rewrapped her feet in fresh gauze.

When he was finished, he stood and offered his hand. It took every ounce of courage she had on reserve to put her hand into his.

"We're going down for food, nothing scary," he said.

She didn't look reassured.

Leo led her down to the kitchen and found some leftovers in the fridge. He reheated them in the microwave and indicated a seat for her at the table. Usually the servants waited on him, but they'd honed amazing instincts over the years and had made themselves scarce. Whether they did it for Leo or for Faith, he wasn't sure.

"I hope you like lasagna," he said, growing more uncomfortable with her silence.

"Y-yes, Master."

He wondered if she'd ever be able to say it without the stutter or the tremble in her hands that accompanied speaking to him.

"What would you like to drink?" If he wanted to have any shot at all with this, he had to make small gestures, occasionally give her the illusion of choices.

With any other sub, he would have had her on her knees by now. He wouldn't have given her any food or drink options. But Faith wasn't any other sub. She wasn't a sub at all. She was his prisoner. His slave. And now the word felt dirty.

"C-can I have orange juice?"

"With lasagna?"

"I'm s-sorry. W-whatever you want to give me is fine."

He put a plate and fork in front of her, and put his food in to nuke it. Then he went to the fridge and, with some trepidation, poured the juice. "No, if you want orange juice, you may have it. It just doesn't sound very appealing." A horrifying thought struck him then. "Are you pregnant?"

Her eyes shot up to his. "N-no, Master. I just like the taste."

Strange, but if it would add to her comfort, he'd let her have it. Even if he had to fight not to be sick over the odd combination. At least it was simply a quirk and not a pregnancy symptom. The idea of having her here against her will would be worse with a baby growing inside her and then a small child running around.

The meal was silent. Faith looked lost inside her own fear and anticipation over what he might do to her, and Leo couldn't bring himself to make small talk. Finally he said, "Perhaps I should go over my expectations."

Her eyes darted up to his, and the fear was back louder. Leo tried to ignore it.

"As long as you acknowledge that you belong to me and as long as you obey me, your life doesn't have to be bad. I can give you a good life, but there are certain things I require. I'll be as gentle as I can be if you'll let me." Saying it out loud sounded monstrous, especially given her reaction to him.

He decided not to mention specifics. If she knew exactly what he was into, down to nipple clamps and violet wands, it would only frighten her more. If such a thing was possible.

"Faith?"

"Y-yes, M-master?"

Though she didn't seem to be kinky, he was intrigued that she hadn't slipped when it came to what he'd asked her to call him. It made him believe that somewhere deep within there was a spark of something naturally submissive he could awaken. Even if it didn't express itself directly as a kink . . . it could . . . given enough patience and training.

"Are you familiar with BDSM?" Perhaps he should be asking himself the same question—since the tenets of the lifestyle were safe, sane, and consensual—three things he wasn't offering the woman in front of him.

"N-not really. I-I mean I know what it is. Like spanking and stuff?" Her respiration grew faster. It was obvious the idea scared her. Which part of it scared her the most, he had no idea, but the general idea wasn't something she was into. But then he'd known that when he'd pressed his finger inside her to find her dry.

"Put your plate and glass in the sink and go up to my bedroom. I'll be there in a moment."

She gave him a pleading look, but did as she was told. He rinsed the dishes off and put them in the sink, then followed her.

He found her standing in the middle of the room, looking lost, like she didn't know where to go or what to do or what might happen. Leo crossed the floor to her and reached out to stroke her breast through her t-shirt. As far as sexual acts went, it was mild, but she cringed away.

"P-please don't make me . . . " The terror in her eyes was too much for him. This wasn't what he wanted. Yes, he wanted someone who couldn't walk out and leave whenever they wanted, but he was terrorizing her. He wanted a slave who couldn't get away, but he also wanted one who wanted to serve him.

"Fuck," he said.

The profanity made her more afraid, and she dropped to her knees. "I-I'm sorry, Master," she whimpered. "Please. I'll do whatever you want. I'm sorry. I'm sorry, I'll be better."

"No. This isn't working."

At that, her body stiffened. And he knew what she feared without her verbalizing it. If *this* wasn't working, would he kill her? Given what she must suspect about his family, it wasn't an out-there assumption, but he wasn't in the business of killing women.

"I'm not going to hurt you, but you're too scared of me. You don't have the same kinds of needs and desires I have, and while I think it's possible to train a body to want these things, I'm not a sick enough bastard to do it to you without your consent. Get up."

She pushed herself up off the floor, still trembling, staring at the ground as if she could become invisible and safe that way. If he went any further he'd break her beyond repair. He found he didn't have the stomach for it. Why couldn't she have been a sub? Why couldn't she have been wired so that they could both find happiness together? He could get his fantasy, and she could get hers. But this wasn't her fantasy. It was her nightmare.

"Get your cat, and come with me."

She looked confused and still afraid, so he added, "I'm giving you your own room in the east wing. You'll be far from me. I'm sorry I can't set you free, but I'll let you live here without having to be afraid I'll touch or hurt you. All right?"

She gave a quick nod and scooped up her cat.

The sound system played an ominous version of Carol of the Bells as Leo led her through his massive estate. Faith silently berated herself.

Why couldn't she give in to him? She'd dated a lot of guys and none of them were as attractive or rich as Leo. Though Italian men weren't a rarity in the city, Leo made it look exotic and wild. Why couldn't she do what he wanted? He didn't repulse her. Wasn't that something at least?

But she was too afraid. The things he'd hinted he was into . . . well, she didn't know a lot about them. But she knew they scared her. She knew the spanking he'd given her the previous night had scared, humiliated, and hurt her. She knew if that was the first thing he did to her, that things would become horrible. Whatever else he had going for him . . . this was too much. And then there was the *family of killers*. These people weren't like her. They'd kill anybody who saw too much, knew too much, or got in their way.

Still, if he followed through on his word to let her live in another wing of the house and not hurt her, she found herself extremely grateful—enough so that she wished that what he wanted was normal. If he wasn't into scary or painful things, she could almost see herself letting him touch her without cringing. If he'd only let her get used to the idea. Give her time.

Leo stopped in front of large, white double doors and pushed them open.

Faith followed him and set her cat on the carpet to poke around and wander, she'd have to go back for the litter box.

The room was nearly as big and nice as Leo's, with a bathroom and large closets and a fireplace. The difference in this room was the light. There was so much light, and more so with snow on the ground. Three-fourths of the wall space was taken up by windows.

A large Christmas tree with tiny white lights that dimmed and brightened in a slow pattern stood next to the windows. Green and silver ornaments decorated the tree, and a silver- and green-patched skirt was wrapped around the bottom. Squish was already burrowing underneath the tree skirt to take a nap.

"The rooms on the farthest ends of the house are like this, but this one is the best," he said. "You'll get a lovely sunrise each morning."

She knew she should thank him, but she was still too afraid he'd go back on his word, or that he would use all that he was giving her as justification for taking what he wanted later. The way he looked at her, she knew how badly he wanted it. That morning, his erection had pressed up through the sheets, and she'd been terrified he was about to force himself on her. She'd drawn herself tightly into a ball against the headboard, trying to keep her tears quiet so she wouldn't wake him, her breaths coming out ragged and panicked.

"I'll have someone bring your things. You can go anywhere in the house, except my room, the cellar, and the back of the house that contains my office and operating theater."

"Operating theater?" That sounded macabre.

"I'm a surgeon. At least that's a part of my work. I run a private practice here with a separate entrance in the back. We probably won't see each other a lot, but if you need anything, use the intercom system." He indicated a white box on the wall beside her bed. "Someone will come and take care of you. You don't need to be afraid of anybody who works for me. They've all got orders to leave you in peace."

Faith remained quiet, unable to bring herself to look into his eyes. She was afraid if she did, she'd see the devil trying to drag her into hell.

She'd seen crucifixes in various places about the house and a few other religious iconographies, like a Virgin Mary statue in the entry hall, so she knew he must be Catholic. She was a lapsed Catholic herself, and wondered if being taken was some kind of punishment for her sins. She hadn't been to church in longer than she could remember. She couldn't call this place Heaven, but if Leo stayed true to his word, it wasn't Hell, either. She silenced the voice in her mind that whispered, *purgatory*.

"I'm truly sorry you've been taken from your life and your friends. My brother has a bad sense for what is an appropriate gift to give someone. I'll leave you alone, now."

"Thank you," forced itself out of her throat after the door had clicked shut.

Half an hour later servants came through with her things. They'd put her stuff back in the bags and boxes they'd brought them to the house in and left everything on the floor beside her bed. No comments were made, but she wondered how much any of them knew.

Did they know their boss was sexually twisted? Did they know she was meant to be his slave to serve those needs? What would they think about her being moved to the other end of the house? Would they think he found her lacking or that he'd had mercy on her? Why did she care what they thought?

She stayed out of their way until they left without uttering a word to her. She went to work unpacking and arranging everything in the closet. Squish came out from under the Christmas tree to poke her nose into all the empty boxes and bags. Faith put the luggage in the closet, stacked and folded the rest of the containers, and put them outside her door in the hallway. Surely someone would take them away. It wasn't as if she'd need them ever again. She'd resigned herself to this large, ornate prison. He couldn't let her go.

Faith sprawled across her bed, and the cat hopped up to snuggle with her. What if Leo got tired of keeping her as a house guest when she wasn't giving him anything? What if he got tired of feeding her and taking care of any other needs that came up? Would he make her disappear? What if he couldn't maintain the self-control not to try again to make her his slave? What was she supposed to call him? Did he still consider her his property? It wasn't realistic to assume she'd never see him again. What would happen when she did?

She reached across the bed to find a remote on the night table. She didn't see anything it could possibly go to, but when she pressed the button, a large flat screen television rose out of a white chest at the foot of the bed. She pressed the button again to let the screen go back into its hiding space.

Would there be a story on the news? Probably not. In the grand scheme, she was a nobody and people disappeared in the city all the time. Still, she wondered about the reactions of her friends. They might not have been best friends but they'd notice her missing.

She imagined her boss would be angry at first, with plans to fire her when she returned, and then the slow, dawning realization that she wasn't coming back at all. Would they notice when her final paycheck wasn't cashed? Would they worry or care? Would anybody file a missing person report?

Her life might not have been much, but it was hers. It was a crappy apartment but she could pay for it on her own. She was frugal and careful with her money, and had some savings. She'd been proud of her ability to save so much . . . until Leo had taken her. If he knew what was in her bank account, and the fact that she thought it was a lot of money, he might never stop laughing at her.

But maybe, if he wanted . . . she could use her own money to repay him for what she ate . . . for a while, at least until it ran out. Maybe if she made an effort, he wouldn't resent her or grow angry. She couldn't imagine him being okay with this setup indefinitely.

Five

I t was a full three days before Leo saw Faith again. He'd been careful to avoid her as he was sure she'd been careful to avoid him. But it was inevitable they'd run into each other eventually. As it happened, they both went to the kitchen one afternoon at the same time for a late lunch.

She jumped when she saw him, and he had to bite back a curse. He found himself angry with her. He'd uprooted his routine to stay out of her way. He was letting her live. He wasn't molesting her. He was taking care of her needs and keeping her comfortable. He wasn't doing anything wrong. Except keeping her locked away against her will.

He'd seen her naked. Once. And touched her breast. Once. And spanked her. Once. None of that should be cause for this much anxiety or jumpiness, no matter who his family was. He glanced down, noticing his erection and knew she must have noticed it, too.

"I'm not going to hurt you," he said. But the gruff way he said it didn't sound believable to his own ears.

For the past three nights he'd fantasized about her, jerking off to the thought of her bound and helpless. Of whipping her. Of making her cry and beg and call him *Master* while crumpled at his feet. Even her fear turned him on in the fantasies.

He wanted to take her. She should be grateful and happy to serve him. He'd saved her life. If not for Angelo's odd early Christmas present and Leo's willingness to take her home with him, she'd be at the bottom of the harbor right now. And they both knew it.

She turned and scurried off back to her end of the house. She must be hungry so he made them both a sandwich. He ate his in the kitchen, then went to her room. He didn't have to, but he knocked.

"W-who is it?" She knew very well who it was.

Your lord and master. The man who owns you. The man you owe your life and your body to.

"It's Leo. I brought you something to eat." He didn't wait for her to invite him in or open the door. It was his fucking house.

Once inside, he placed a tray on a small card table. He'd brought her chips, tea, and a sandwich.

"Thank you," she mumbled.

He noticed that she didn't address him. But who was he kidding? If he couldn't bring himself to break and train her, he couldn't be upset if she changed the way she spoke to him. He found that he missed hearing that word fall from her sweet mouth.

He thought back to a few days ago when she'd been so scared he'd hurt her, when she'd dropped to her knees in front of him. He left her alone with her food before his hard-on could return.

When he got back downstairs, his butler, Demetri, held out a cordless phone. "It's your mother, Sir."

Leo took the phone. What fresh hell was this? "Hey, Ma."

He'd barely gotten the phrase out when she started blabbering in a nonstop string of excited sentences, some of them running on top of each other.

"Angelo tells me you've got a girl, now. Says you're getting married. When were you going to tell your poor old mother? When we all got there? The whole family is dying to meet her now. What's her name? Faith? Is she Catholic? Is she a good girl, Leo? What's her family like?"

"Ma . . . " Leo said, trying to calm her. This wasn't good. His family would all be here for a week for Christmas. He hadn't known exactly what he was going to do with Faith. As horrible as it would be for her, he'd considered locking her downstairs in the dungeon for the duration and having Demitri take her meals down. At least he wouldn't risk questions that way. Maybe by next year he could trust her enough to let her be with the family under one pretense or another, maybe as a new household servant or nurse for his practice.

But he'd already known sending her to the dungeon would terrify her and make him feel like a monster. He was almost glad hiding her wasn't an option now. Surely Angelo hadn't implied Leo had known Faith long enough to propose marriage? That had to be something that had gotten into her head from somewhere else.

The women in his family were a bunch of gossips. You could start out with the simplest story and end up with illicit affairs, murders, and a funeral with a missing body by the end of it.

"I mean it, Leo. I'm very unhappy you didn't tell me about this. And if she's living at your house like Angelo said, you *better* be marrying her! You know I don't like my boys living in sin."

He knew she was thinking of Angelo and Davide. He could practically hear her crossing herself over the phone. The shock of his brother coming out had about killed her and she still wasn't over it. Of course. *That* was why Angelo had told her Leo was getting married —to take the heat and attention off him this year.

He suppressed a growl. "Yes, Ma. We're getting married. I already proposed." If they knew about Faith, he may as well have a sham marriage. He'd never get his mother off his back if she thought they were *living in sin*. He wondered what she'd think if she knew Faith was being held here against her will? Nothing good.

"Without us meeting her!?! We raised you better than that! I can't believe you'd get engaged without so much as calling your poor mother! Is she Catholic? Please tell me she's at least Catholic."

He had no idea one way or the other, but what was another lie on top of the rest of it? "Yes, Ma. Of course she's a good Catholic girl."

"What about her family? Are they a good family?"

"She doesn't have any family," he said, injecting a drop of honesty into the conversation.

"Oh, that poor girl. Well she'll have a big family, now." It was all it had taken for his mother to switch gears. "Is she Irish? I know you've dated your redheads, but Sal won't like Irish blood in the family. Please tell me she's not Irish."

"Yes, she's a redhead."

"*Benedica la vergine Maria*," she whispered. Blessing the virgin mother was Gina's response to anything scandalous. If his mother knew the full weight of the scandal, she'd be praying the rosary nonstop until the New Year.

"Ma, I've got to run, but I'll see you next weekend."

They exchanged the normal end-of-conversation pleasantries and he disconnected the call. Demetri rose an eyebrow.

"Don't say it," Leo said. "Go to Tiffany and get me an engagement ring. Something that looks convincing . . . like I bought it for someone I deeply love." Of course, any ring from Tiffany sent that message.

"What if the girl won't go along with it, Sir?"

With Faith being moved to the other end of the house, the staff knew he'd gone soft and left her alone.

Leo's expression hardened. "If she won't go along with it, she'll spend Christmas tied up in the dungeon."

Demetri's eyes widened a fraction, but he left to carry out the order.

Faith sat at a writing desk near the Christmas tree, doodling on a pad of paper while a sitcom played on the TV in the background. She'd finished her lunch several hours ago and was hungry again. The sun had set, but she was afraid to leave her room to go to the kitchen—afraid she'd run into Leo. She wanted to use the intercom and send a servant after her food, so she could stay safely hidden away in her room. But no matter what he'd said about them being there to take care of her needs, she was afraid of making them angry or that it would get back to Leo and he'd be angry. Surely he hadn't meant for her to order room service with that thing.

She'd intended to offer to pay for her room and board, at least until the money ran out, hoping it might appease him. It wasn't as if her money could do her any good otherwise. But when she'd seen him standing in the kitchen, the reality of him came rushing back. He was so large and strong. She'd felt the evidence of his strength as he'd held her down and spanked her that first night. His intense eyes and the constant grim line of his lips made her afraid. And that scar on his face . . .

Although he'd been kinder to her than his twin had, that scar made him darker and harder around the edges, less approachable.

She jumped when the door opened—no knock this time. He stood framed in the doorway, like death had come to claim her. Faith tried to calm her breathing, but he never looked at her calmly. It was always with an intensity that made her afraid to breathe, to exist. As if she needed to be very still and quiet to stay safe.

He strode across the room so fast she couldn't stop herself from cringing. When he reached her, he placed a small box on the desk. It looked like a jewelry box.

"Open it," he growled when she just stared at it.

What could be inside a jewelry box? Jewelry was the obvious answer, but Faith couldn't think of a reason her captor would give her any kind of jewelry.

Her hand trembled as she reached out and opened the box. She couldn't help the gasp. What a rock.

"W-what is this?"

"Haven't you ever seen an engagement ring before?"

"Y-yes, but . . . "

"My family will be here next weekend for the Christmas holidays. You're going to pretend to be my fiancée during that time. Put the ring on." It wasn't a request.

"I-I . . . w-what will happen? W-what will you do?"

"Do you find me that repulsive?"

"N-no." She shrank from the disappointed look on his face. Every time she ended a sentence now, he got that look.

"You'll continue to sleep on this end of the house. My mother is pretty religious and wouldn't be pleased with us sharing a room. You just have to pretend you're in love with me when we're all together. The most you'll be subjected to is holding hands and a few kisses."

"I . . . "

"Put the ring on. Now."

His voice had taken on that edge again, and she scrambled to obey his request. She was surprised when it fit.

"T-this must have cost a fortune," she breathed, almost caught up in the fantasy. For a brief moment, she could see the room and the tree and the ring and imagine this was some romantic proposal from a rich boyfriend right before Christmas. But only for a moment. Then she was brought back to the reality of her situation—this man she didn't know and couldn't trust, who might snap and do anything to her at any moment.

"It was quite expensive, yes. But my family would never buy the ruse if it wasn't. They know me too well. Now will you do as I asked and pretend we're engaged? I should warn you, if the true nature of your stay with me should come out, you will disappear. Do you understand what I'm saying?"

"Y-yes," she whispered. The casual way he spoke of killing her was exactly why she was so afraid. His moral compass had a crooked arrow.

"Yes you understand or yes you'll do it?"

"D-do I have a choice?"

"Of course, you have a choice. If you don't want to pretend to be the love of my life, or if I feel you can't do it convincingly, you'll be kept in the dungeon until they leave."

"Please, no!" The words flew out of her mouth with such force, it embarrassed her. But the idea of being locked in a . . . dungeon . . . was too much to cope with. It hadn't occurred to her that he might have such a thing, but now that he'd spoken the word, she had no doubt as to the truth of it. "I-I'll do it. I'll d-do whatever you want, just p-please don't do that."

"You'd better not screw up." His cold words terrified her, but beneath them, she could see the fear that she might do something that would lead to him having to kill her. She wished she could reassure him there was no way she'd cross him.

"I-I won't. I promise."

"You understand the consequences if you do?" Desperation edged his words.

"Y-yes."

Her life had hung in the balance since she'd first seen Angelo pull the trigger in that alley and the body hit the ground. And she was far from out of the woods —if there *was* a way out. She wasn't sure that there was.

"I'm glad you're being so agreeable." He reached into his jacket and pulled out two stapled stacks of papers. "You will fill this out, and you will answer as honestly as you can. I'll need to study your answers so we know each other well enough when my family gets here. The other packet contains my answers to the same questions. You will learn all my likes and dislikes and enough about my work to make it look like you belong here."

He hovered over her, which made her more nervous. The simplest questions like her favorite food became hard to answer in light of the pressure that grew the longer he stood there.

"In the back of the other packet is the story I concocted of how we met and how I proposed. That will be one of the most important things to know since everyone will ask."

After several minutes, he went to the door. "You'll join me for dinner in half an hour, and bring your papers with you. You have to get used to being around me and me touching you. If you cringe every time I come near you, they'll think I'm beating you."

He closed the door quietly behind him, and Faith went back to the questions, trying not to stare at the gigantic rock on her hand. The trouble with pretending was . . . if he was a decent actor, if he was kind and gentle while his family was here, she'd start to want it to be real, but when they left everything would go back to the way it was, the spell broken.

At least with his family here, she'd be safe. He was going to a lot of trouble to not make waves with them.

When she finished the questions, she took the papers and went to the kitchen. Two plates had already been set along with salad bowls and wine glasses. One of the servants unobtrusively filled the plates and bowls. Dinner was Caesar salad, chicken Parmesan with risotto, and some red wine. Leo drank wine with practically every meal and seemed keen to break her of her orange juice habit.

Faith ate while he looked over her answers. Occasionally he said "hmmm" in between bites. She tried to stay focused on her food. She just wanted to get through the meal and then go hide again. When they were finished, she started to get up to go back to her room, but Leo stopped her.

"No. We have less than a week before they get here. We have to practice. Come with me."

He left their papers on the table and led her down the hallway to a sitting room. The absence of the questionnaires left no doubt as to what they would be *practicing*. She tried not to have a panic attack as she trailed behind him.

He'd left her alone for three days. He hadn't tried anything. He hadn't killed her. Nobody had done anything to hurt her. But the threat of the dungeon loomed large. If she pulled away from him too many times, would he lock her up? She couldn't help how his intensity frightened her. She was used to less intimidating guys, guys who let her take the lead, though she didn't like that much. Were there no happy mediums with men? A man who would take some control but not be so overbearing and terrifying?

She tried to imagine how she'd survive being kept tied up in the dark for a week if Leo got fed up. Would someone feed her? They'd have to. At least give her water or she'd die. Would he care if she did? She wanted to believe he wasn't a monster, but she couldn't bring herself to let her guard down to trust even something so basic. Not when their worlds were so different.

Leo sat on a brown leather sofa at one end of the room. "Come sit beside me, Faith."

It was odd that she should have been given such a name when she'd never had much faith in anyone or anything. Even religion had been something that had inspired little more than doubt. Each time her name was spoken, it mocked her and her inability to trust.

She sat at the other end of the couch, and he quirked an eyebrow. "Really? This is how an engaged couple sits? As if they are afraid of spreading a contagion? Sit *next* to me." He patted the cushion beside him and reluctantly she scooted closer.

When she was within reach, he pulled her close so her thigh pressed against his. His arm went around her and she was forced to lean against him.

"Relax," he soothed, his fingers trailing through her hair.

She only stiffened more. If he started touching her, what would make him stop? She'd seen his arousal whenever he was near. He wanted to fuck her. Whatever stopped him from doing it, could break down at any time. Silent tears slipped down her cheeks. And then they were less silent, causing her shoulders to shake as she tried to keep her emotions within her control.

"You can't do this when my family arrives. You have to stop now or I'll have no choice but to keep you in the dungeon."

"No, p-please, M-master. I'll try to do better. Please give me a chance."

This time, it was Leo who stiffened and went still. Faith wasn't sure why she'd called him that. She was so confused. Ever since he'd mentioned the dungeon and the threat of being kept down there, she couldn't think of herself as a house guest anymore—if she'd ever been able to maintain that delusion in the first place. She wanted to appease him, make him happy enough with her so she could stay alive and safe.

"You can't call me that when they're here. And you can't accidentally slip. So start calling me Leo."

A burning flush came into her cheeks. It was humiliating enough being forced to call him Master when he'd demanded it, but to say it unbidden and have him correct her made her want to die.

"I-I'm sorry, L-Leo."

"And you've got to get rid of that stutter."

It was so much pressure. No stuttering. No cringing. No fear. How was she going to make people believe they were engaged, let alone in love? She'd have to if she wanted to survive in this house. She'd have to make herself believe it if she wanted them to believe it. She'd have to let go of all her reservations and try to embrace the fantasy, however briefly it lasted.

"Tell me something I don't know about you," he said.

She wracked her brain trying to come up with something. He didn't know a lot about her, even with the questionnaire, but she couldn't pull an important enough piece of information out of her head. At least not one she felt safe sharing.

"It can be anything. I want to get to know you better." But it wasn't the words of a boy on a date with a girl. It was the words of a man hell-bent on acting out a Machiavellian play.

"Until a few months ago, I had two cats. The other one was older and sick a lot so she had to be put to sleep. I thought about getting a kitten because Squish got lonely and depressed, but . . . "

"But?"

Faith looked down at her hands. "Your brother happened."

"I see."

He was quiet for a long time, stroking her hair until she started to relax against him. She closed her eyes and pretended it was a boyfriend or a date— someone she'd gone freely with. Someone she liked and trusted. Her breath slowly began to even out. If he wanted her to do this acting job for his family, he wouldn't hurt her before they got here.

"Good. That's much better," he said. "Now sit up for me."

She sat up, and the back of his hand brushed against her cheek. She pulled away—on reflex more than anything. Her survival instinct said *danger*, and she responded the only way she knew how . . . shrinking back, becoming smaller . . . trying to fade away until she was forgotten by the predator.

"No," he said firmly. "You'll let me touch you."

Faith fought with herself to stay still and accept the way he petted her cheek. It took another couple of minutes before she could will her body to unclench and take the gentle caress.

After a few more moments of this, he took his hand away from her cheek. She leaned forward, feeling bereft at the absence of the touch she was beginning to feel comfortable with. Then he linked his hand with hers, his thumb stroking over the back of her skin.

It made her feel like a teenager, her stomach going all fluttery and nervous. Though her fears were very different from the childish fears of a girl holding hands with a boy for the first time.

Without warning, he pulled her to him with his other hand, a firm grip on the back of her neck, angling her head how he wanted it, and he kissed her.

At first she froze, afraid he wouldn't stop with kissing, but after a few seconds of his lips caressing over hers, he pulled away.

"We've got to work on that. No one will believe that kiss."

The heat rose to her face, and she looked down at her hands. "I-I'll do better."

"Yes, you will," he said. "Go get your papers. You can go back to your room. I expect you to study and know everything in that packet by tomorrow evening."

Faith got up without a word and retreated to the kitchen. When she got back to her room she locked the door. He might be mad if he found it locked to him, but it was the only way she'd feel safe enough to sleep.

Leo contemplated the enigma that lived in his house. She *had* to be a sub. Somewhere deep down. He'd been surprised from her answers that she wasn't a virgin. Her level of fear toward him had led him to believe she might be. She'd in fact had several boyfriends in college, and was what he'd call *experienced*. Even so, she didn't feel experienced to him. Not in any way. He imagined the college boys she'd been with were just that . . . boys. Perhaps she wasn't yet ready for a mature man with an established life and any discernible power.

He tried to see things from her perspective, and admitted he might feel as she did, but he'd never encountered a woman who behaved this way. Of course, he'd never held one hostage, either.

The women who came to his bed knew his requirements. They knelt and obeyed and served or they went home. Most who'd attempted to seduce him had found the scar on his face attractive. They'd been excited by the evidence of darkness etched down his cheek.

When Faith had called him Master again, Leo had been stunned. It made him want to break her and train her. If he had more time . . . if his family wasn't breathing down his neck, he might do it. He reminded himself she'd shown no physical signs of kink-wiring.

Even completely vanilla activity with him distressed her.

Maybe she had a need to serve, in a nonsexual capacity. But he wouldn't be happy with that. He wanted a sub who would warm his bed. Hearing the word *Master* fall from her mouth because she'd thought that was what he wanted to hear, only made him want to assert his ownership. She had no idea the fire she played with, and the real trouble was . . . she'd done it innocently, with no idea what she might awaken.

Six

A t dinner the next night, Leo grilled her on the questionnaire, surprised she'd studied so much. "Tell me what you know about my work," he said, as he sliced into his New York Strip.

She took a deep breath. "Y-you went to medical school and became a s-surgeon, but you felt the heart lung machines you needed c-could be improved upon —"

"Faith?"

She looked up like a rabbit caught in a trap—a mixture of pain and fear on her face. Or perhaps the anticipation of pain.

"No more stuttering. I mean it. It's gotten tiresome. We have four days. You have to break out of this fear by then or I have to put you in the dungeon."

Leo placed a hand over hers; she jumped and stared at her plate.

"Look at me."

She looked up, her lip trembling.

"I don't want to put you down there. If I did, I wouldn't waste this time on you. But I care about my family. The women don't need to know about this nasty business. Do you understand?"

She nodded.

"Now try to speak naturally and tell me the rest."

With great effort, she pushed the words out of her mouth, working to keep the stutter out. "Y-you designed an improvement on the m-machines and got a patent, and now you sell them to hospitals and surgeons all over the country, which is where your money came from." She gathered steam as she spoke. "You still do surgeries two days a week, and with your money, you opened a private clinic here when you had this house built."

"And? What about the blood?"

"Oh," she blushed at her oversight. "You got involved with consulting on artificial blood, and you've been engaged to run clinical trials, which you'll do in a lab you've set up next to your operating theater. They'll start bringing you regular shipments of the blood late next spring."

He didn't expect all of this to come up, but if anyone started talking about his work, it was the type of thing they'd expect him to discuss with his fiancée, particularly since he wasn't involved in the family's business. It would be suspicious if she looked clueless. You couldn't slide a lot past his family.

"Very good. What about the household staff?" Leo asked, going back to the questionnaire.

She was confused for a minute. "Oh. You sent some of them through school to be nurses and assist with surgeries and recovery, allowing them to take care of the house and help you with your business."

"How many recovery rooms are there on-site?"

"Three."

Her voice came out so small when she talked to him that he couldn't decide which he wanted to do more: tie her down and whip her, or comfort her. As noble as he wanted to believe his gesture of letting her live in another wing was, he couldn't be sure how long his self-control would hold. When *would* he take what was his?

"Tell me how we met."

"We met at a deli in the city. I had forgotten my wallet and you o-offered to pay." She took a deep breath. "Then you asked me out. And I said y-yes." She squeezed her eyes shut as if the lie were too painful to speak.

Leo stroked her arm. "I haven't hurt you, Faith. Trust me. All I want is to protect those I love. I won't allow Angelo to go to prison. And if you hurt the women—especially my mother—by letting them know the true nature of our arrangement, I *will* hurt you. That's the only reason you'd have to fear me. It's so simple here."

As she gazed up at him from beneath thick lashes, he knew she wanted to believe that if she played her role right, she'd be safe.

"L-Leo?"

He forced himself to hold onto his temper. She wasn't trying to annoy him with the stutter. "Yes, Faith?"

"What happens next Christmas? Am I still going to be alive?"

What kind of question was that? "Of course you'll still be alive. If I wanted you dead, I would have left you with Angelo."

There was a long pause while she gathered her courage. "What happens then? Or the next year? Will you lock me in the dungeon? We can't pretend to be engaged forever."

So that was where it was going. "I know," he said. "We'll have to get married. I was thinking next June. Everyone loves June weddings, and my mother will be in wedding-heaven. Shut your mouth when you chew your food, please," he said in response to her gaping fish impression.

"I can't do this," she whispered.

Faith raced down the hall to the entryway and flew up the stairs to her room. Once the door was locked, she pressed her back against the wood and slid to the carpet. Her sobs came out among strangled gasps for air.

What he demanded of her was too cruel. Pretend she loved him. Pretend they were a couple. Have a sham marriage. All the while she'd be a princess locked in a tower with no true love or life to call her own. She wanted to survive and stay safe, but what kind of life was this? What kind of safety?

The stupidest part of all of this was that she wouldn't have told anyone. She would have been too scared. And calling the cops wouldn't resurrect the guy Angelo had killed. But no matter what she said, there was no way they'd believe her and set her free. Especially now that she'd become their victim. They wouldn't believe she'd let that go, too.

She'd let anything go if it meant safety.

"Faith, unlock this door, right now!" Leo's voice boomed from the other side of the door, sending vibrations along her back as if his hands were on her.

She couldn't breathe. If she opened the door, he might hurt her. If she didn't open the door, he might break it down and hurt her. Her mind flashed to the night he'd spanked her for such a small infraction. Would he do it again? Or worse? *Why did I lock the door? Why did I leave the table?*

"A-are you going to h-hurt me?"

"I'll hurt you if you don't fucking stop stuttering!" he shouted.

She unlocked the door and rushed to shut herself in the closet, huddling in the corner. All she wanted was to get away from him. God, let her fall through some other magic dimension, away from this place. Why couldn't he leave her alone?

She hugged herself as his footsteps approached her obvious hiding place.

"Come out. Now." The anger was still there, but it was muted behind tenuous self-control.

"Please, Leo . . . "

His breath was harsh outside the closet as he got hold of himself. She prayed he could reign in his temper and that he wouldn't take it out on her.

"I'm sorry. I'm sorry. I'm sorry." She'd gotten caught on a loop and couldn't stop saying the words, hoping they would calm him.

His breath slowed back to normal, and then he seemed to move away. It was enough to give her the courage to leave the closet.

Leo sat on the edge of the bed, watching her. "Come here."

"Please . . . "

"Come. Here."

She joined him, and he wrapped his arms around her and held her. An attempt at comfort? He had to know, his touch couldn't comfort her. But somehow, it did. The more he touched her, the more she found herself desensitized to the fear of it.

"I'm sorry," he said against her hair. "I don't have any other choices."

"You could let me go. I swear, I won't say anything about what I saw, or about being kept here. I'll go back to my life and be quiet. I'll never speak of this. Please." Then she said something she hoped was true but wasn't sure. "I-I know you don't want to do this. You can trust me. I promise I won't talk."

He stroked her hair. "Family comes first. I won't take the risk. And you have no idea of the things I want to do where you're concerned. Pray you never know."

Despite the irrationality of the act, she found herself clinging to him, because he was the only thing to hold onto. He could protect her from Angelo. She had to get herself together if she wanted to keep his protection.

His voice was quiet when he spoke again. "Next summer you'll become my wife in name only. I won't force you. I won't hurt you. Things will stay as they've been the past few days. I know you're losing so much. I wish things could be different for you. Please believe that."

He pulled away from her and helped her to stand. "Come finish your dinner. We still need to practice and finish going over our answers on the questionnaire."

Faith placed a shaky hand in his and allowed him to take her back to the kitchen where their food had been left. He put her plate in the microwave and heated it for about a minute, then did the same with his. While she ate, he stroked her arm and she tried not to jerk away from him.

"Do you have any food allergies?"

The question caught her by surprise. "No, why?"

"It occurred to me that being Irish as well as not having big Christmases, you might not be familiar with our traditions. Our big meal is on Christmas Eve. We have mostly fish, including shellfish, and we tend to have a lot of cookies that have nuts in them on the Venetian table."

Faith made a face. "Fish for Christmas?"

"It's an Italian-Catholic thing. We call it The Feast of the Seven Fishes. Not all Italians do it, but it's been a tradition with my family in Brooklyn since before I was born. We have seven different seafood dishes: calamari, scungilli—which is a conch delicacy— baccala, shrimp, clams with pasta, often lobster with pasta and a red sauce, and then something like salmon or trout. And of course we've got other stuff that has no seafood in it like spaghetti without the meat and antipasto."

"What's antipasto?"

"Are you kidding? Lettuce, roasted peppers, olives, anchovies, and cheese mainly. Then on the dessert table we have *Baci DiDama,* which are hazelnut meringue sandwiches filled with chocolate. We have cherry-almond star cookies, and *pignoli*—those are pine nut cookies. My aunt Lily makes a mean rainbow cookie with an almond filling, even though she's not Italian. And of course you'll find some *cannoli* and various fruits."

Leo went into a sort of trance. No doubt he was lost inside holiday memories that Faith couldn't pretend to understand.

After dinner they went through the rest of the questionnaire. She knew all the answers. She'd read them over and over, the threat of the dungeon hanging over her head. The hard part would be pretending she loved him. The easy part was facts and figures. She'd applied herself doggedly to learning everything he'd written down, hoping it would keep him from locking her up during Christmas.

When he was satisfied with her knowledge, he led her to a different room. This one had a large, flat screen against one wall. He put a disc in the player, turned out the lights, and joined her on the couch. It was a mockery of a date: a chick flick and his arm around her.

The movie was a typical romantic comedy with the typical formulaic plot line. If you'd seen one, you'd seen them all. It might be nice to get lost in it, but she couldn't. She wondered if she might have watched this, or something similar if she'd stayed home with her cat that night instead of going out.

Midway through the film, Leo turned her face to him, and his lips met hers. She still froze when he did it, unable to bring herself to relax under his touch given the circumstances.

He pulled away. "Give in to me, Faith. All I'll take from you are chaste kisses. You can give me that. You'll be doing a lot of this when my family arrives. You'd better get used to it."

He tried again, and this time she forced herself to relax and pretend it was a date with a guy she'd said yes to.

"Better. We'll work on it."

Leo pulled her into his arms to finish the movie. He held her as if he was her boyfriend, but even under cover of darkness, he never tried anything. When the credits rolled, he turned on the light. "We'll try again tomorrow. Go to bed."

He didn't have to ask her twice. She couldn't get back to her room fast enough, the one place where she was moderately safe.

That night, Leo starred in her dreams. Except instead of being a scary horror-movie monster, he was her boyfriend, and he was kind and funny. When he kissed her in the dream, she melted against him and moaned, opening her mouth to accept his probing tongue. Her arms gripped his shoulders, trying to pull him closer, wanting to be consumed by him. Between her legs, a throbbing ache started until his hand slid underneath her panties to soothe it away.

"See, Faith? This is nothing," Dream-Leo said. "You can give me this."

When she woke, her own hand was between her legs, and she was aroused. *No!* If some part of her actually fell for him, it would be more painful. She didn't want to be like one of those kidnap victims who started sympathizing with her captor. She didn't want to start believing his lies. And she definitely didn't want to want him or like his hands or lips on her. She pressed her face against her pillow in an attempt to muffle her distress—though she knew Leo couldn't hear her from the other end of the house. Then she pressed her face against the pillow to muffle the sound of her orgasm.

Seven

L eo paced the entry hall, the usually unobtrusive Christmas music beginning to set his teeth on edge. His family would start arriving in less than an hour. About half of them were coming in from Vegas, and they'd be trickling in until dinnertime. The other half would be equally *laissez-faire* about their arrival times, though they were all in or around Brooklyn.

He still second-guessed the plan. Faith had improved. When he'd instructed her to do a better acting job, she'd delivered. He couldn't imagine how afraid she must be of the dungeon to be so compliant. And she'd never even seen the dungeon.

She probably imagined it as a far worse place than it was. In her mind, Leo had no doubt she saw damp stones with water dripping from some unknown source and algae growing through the cracks and crevices. There would be a dripping sound, a dank, putrid smell, a dirt or concrete floor, a chill that wouldn't leave the air, and heavy chains.

He'd not bothered to disabuse her of that notion. The scarier the dungeon was to her, the easier it would be to get her cooperation. In reality, the dungeon was none of those things. If what he'd been told by the servants who had gone to get her belongings was true, the dungeon was nicer than her apartment in the city had been. It was done in black and a tasteful deep red with occasional splashes of other colors like purples and greens and yellows. It had been an inside joke with his previous submissives that the dungeon was the color of death, blood, and bruises. But it had still turned out beautiful.

There was a comfortable circular sofa in one corner and a bed close to that. There was reading material because a few of his subs had lived down there. There was a small bathroom with a whirlpool tub and a separate standing shower. Nothing large or fancy, but Faith would consider it nice. There was thick carpet in the bedroom area and heat. Max had a habit of curling up on the couch down there for naps when Leo left the door open.

There were chains, of course, and a box full of kinky toys and whipping implements, and the standard and some not-so-standard BDSM furniture. But it looked like a high-end club for kinky people, not a snuff film.

Though maybe it wasn't the atmosphere that so terrified her. Maybe it was the bondage, the isolation. Maybe it was the fear that she would need something— and no one would hear her to help. Even a luxurious prison could be horrible. She was already living in a prison, confined to the house like an indoor house cat.

But chains would be necessary if he kept her underground. Though the dungeon was well-insulated and tucked away from everything else, if she banged on the door, there was always the risk someone might hear. He wasn't sure if he'd be able to kill her if she were to alert a sympathetic member of his family to her plight. And even if he could, it wouldn't stop the cat from being out of the bag.

She'd made such progress. Her lips had become pliant under his. She'd stopped cringing from his touch when he came near her. It had taken working with her every day, but they'd gotten to something resembling a believable relationship forgery. He still worried it wasn't enough. What if his mother saw through the ruse? What if the men did? They were too shrewd, able to spot a con because they knew how to pull one.

Maybe he should have locked Faith in the dungeon, but locking her up and isolating her for Christmas was too cruel even for his sadistic nature. He had to believe this would work. Then they could go back to the fucked-up dynamic the holidays had been so rude as to interrupt.

Leo smoothed his suit for the fortieth time. He'd dress more casually for most of the family holiday, but he liked to look nice when people first arrived, particularly on Christmas Eve. Jeans and a T-shirt would have made him look less nefarious. If his intent was to come off squeaky clean and sell this engagement story, perhaps greeting his family looking like Michael Corleone wasn't the best of plans.

He knocked on his captive's door. "Faith?"

When she opened the door, he was pleased to find her wearing what he'd laid out. He'd raided her closet for something to make a good first impression on his mother, but he'd come up short, so he'd had something brought in. It was a green sweater dress with a scooped neck. The dress came to just past the knees. It accentuated her figure without being too form-fitting. It was sexy, but classy and respectable. He'd given her a pair of brown boots to finish the look. A couple of small, gold chains adorned her otherwise bare neck.

Angelo was the real expert on fashion, but Leo had people, and his people assured him this was understated and stylish, that it would give the impression he wanted his family to have—of a girl who belonged here.

"Do I look all right?" She was so nervous, as if she thought he'd change his mind at the last minute before anybody got there.

"You look beautiful." And she did. He wished he was more like his brother—more ruthless, less conscience. Seeing her like this, with that gorgeous red hair, made him want to enforce the roles between them. "Come here." He wanted to devour her, prey upon her, possess her, and in some deep recess of his mind he knew it was only a matter of time before she broke him and he took her like some savage beast.

He frowned when she hesitated. This sign of his displeasure was enough to move her swiftly into his arms. Somewhere in there she *had* to be a sub. Leo was tempted to test it, to test her. He could have pushed her harder, he could have taken her and dropped her into the darkness with him. Every day that passed, he regretted his decision to be noble and give her space.

"You'll do fine," he whispered as he held her close and stroked her hair. "Nervousness is okay. If this was real, you'd be nervous. I have a big family, and they can be intense. It's a lot to take, even for a real fiancée."

Faith stiffened further at that, and he rubbed her back. "Shhh. It's okay. I'll tell them you're shy. This will work out. I'll keep you safe."

At those words, she relaxed against him. Perhaps some part of her believed in him. Though he was frustrated to have a beautiful captive he couldn't bring himself to defile, he'd begun to feel oddly protective of her. He might need her to believe he'd kill her if she tried to get help from his family, but holding her in his arms, he knew he'd never be able to do it or let anybody else do it, for that matter.

In his mind, he imagined smoothing things over so they would accept him keeping her. Surely they would approve of that outcome more than they would her murder. He could convince them he'd be kind to her. She had no bruises or marks. Such an idea was believable, especially with the way he always took care of everyone and shied from the uglier sides of the family business.

Leo thought back to a couple of nights ago when he'd asked her what she usually did for the holidays. The look she'd given him had been blank. She'd mumbled something about going out for drinks with her friends on Christmas Eve. And then something about an office Christmas party with a store-bought cake and a game that involved gag gifts.

And that was her Christmas experience. When he'd pressed her on her childhood, it hadn't been much better. She'd said her family hadn't had very much and she didn't always get a Christmas present. Some years they didn't have a tree. Sometimes a local charity would see to it that she got a doll or a game and a decent meal for the holidays, but it wasn't anything like his own memories of the season. Such sharp contrast between the memories they had made him feel guilt for all he'd enjoyed while she'd suffered or barely scraped by.

From the moment she'd told him all that, he'd become determined to give her a nice holiday. If she must be his prisoner, he would make it easy on her.

The more he'd learned, the more he'd come to admire her, not just for the way she looked and the way she made his dick hard, but the way she'd fought for what she had. As young as she was, if she'd been left to her own devices, she would have made something of herself.

Though her apartment and financial power might be paltry by Leo's standards, she'd pulled herself up from the gutter to have something resembling a life, with food on her table, clothes in her closet, and her bills all paid.

The doorbell rang. He pulled away from Faith, but she clung to him. It was a strange turn of events. Leo gently took her hands off his shoulders, linked one of his hands with hers, and took her to face the firing squad.

The first person to arrive was his mother. He'd had no doubt it would be her, though she was coming all the way from Vegas. Gina Raspallo was absolutely punctual in everything, as if she had an internal mechanism that forced her body to be at the proper place at the proper time without deviation. Leo's father had died of a heart attack three years before, and his mother had become more punctual in the intervening time.

"Leo! Oh my baby! I missed you. You never come to see me," Gina said, bending and dropping the diminutive Yorkie that scrambled to get out of her arms. She pulled Leo into a bear hug.

Max scrambled into the entry way at the sound of the yapping. The golden retriever found the Yorkie fascinating in every way, like a chew toy, though he had never hurt the other dog. The Yorkie began to hop up and down at the sight of Max, his short legs barely making it an inch in the air before he landed again.

"And this must be your girl!" Gina released Leo and turned her attention to Faith, who had stepped behind her son.

Faith squeaked when his mother hugged her. "Let me see that ring!" She squealed in delight at the engagement ring. "Doesn't our Leo have the best taste ever? I'm Gina, but you can call me Ma."

"Ma . . . " Leo said. "Don't push her so much. You've known her thirty seconds."

"Well, she's gonna be family isn't she?" His mother pierced him with the glare he'd been waiting for. The *how dare you get yourself engaged without letting me meet her first* glare.

She stepped back and appraised Faith, causing the redhead to shrink back. "Well, she's not Italian, but at least she's Catholic. I'll take it. And I expect lots of grandchildren! She's young enough, at least. I was worried you'd pick somebody older. You know it's really better for a woman if they have the babies young. Now, what do you need me to do for dinner?"

Leave it to his ma to say the most inappropriate things about the childbearing years. He was surprised she hadn't mentioned Faith's great birthing hips.

"Ma, I told you. I've got people. We don't need you to help with dinner tonight. You just got here for God's sake. Relax. Go for a swim or something." He'd had the temperature and pH of the pool tested just that morning.

"But it's Christmas Eve. I don't know why we don't come here a few days before and cook all together in the kitchen like we used to. All the Brooklyn family gets to bring covered dishes, and I'm stuck doing nothing. I want to cook something for my boy. Now!"

It was pointless arguing. Once Gina got an idea into her head, woe to the man or woman who tried to stop her. Leo led her to the second kitchen, keeping a tight hold on Faith's hand.

Most of the time, he used the smaller family-style kitchen, but with his family here, everything had been upgraded to the large kitchen and even larger dining room. The doorbell rang again, and he left Gina with the kitchen staff to go greet the new guests. His mother was their problem now.

Faith fought to keep control of herself. If she had a meltdown now, she wasn't sure what Leo would do.

Meeting his mother had been bracing to say the least, but when the woman had mentioned grandchildren, Faith felt the world drift away into some strange oblivion she couldn't seem to hold onto anymore.

Grandchildren.

She'd been afraid to look into Leo's eyes after that. But he had to know this couldn't work now. He'd promised he wouldn't require sexual intimacy from her. In a big family that expected big families, this would never work. How would he keep them at bay if they were chomping at the bit for mini-Leos?

Did Leo want that? Did he want a marriage and a big family? It hadn't occurred to her to ask. All she'd wanted was to stay alive and not be violated or locked in a dungeon. The finer logistics hadn't crossed her mind amidst the other mental noise. How long would he accept this lie before he wanted something real with someone?

He'd said he wouldn't force her, but he must imagine someday she would willingly give in to him, especially in light of how she'd begun to relish their pretend kisses too much. He must know. What would he say when he found out she might not be able to have children? Would that be the end of everything?

And if she could have children, would she be forced to have them to keep up appearances with his demanding family?

The alternative was a "breakup." But then what would happen? If he didn't get rid of her, she'd be in the dungeon every Christmas for as long as he let her live. She couldn't get the image of spiders and rats crawling over her out of her mind. Her apartment had the occasional rat problem. She'd woken more than once to find a disgusting rodent crawling over her. The memory made her shudder and hold onto Leo's hand tighter as they made their way through the house, away from his mother but toward new dangers. Faith would rather have his babies—if she could—in a love-less pretend marriage, than spend any time in a dungeon with creepy crawlies.

When they reached the entryway, Demetri had already let the new guests in. This time, it was a larger swell of people. A few children—around eight or nine years old—already running around screaming and playing tag, a couple of women with Brooklyn accents, about forty-two necklaces layered on top of each other, too-painted faces, and big hair. Several men clung to the walls like malevolent gargoyles.

The men had hard, criminal faces. It was impossible for Faith to understand how their women went along with all this, pretending to be oblivious. It was impossible to be oblivious. Those faces said death and broken bones. Those faces said *you have forty-eight hours to get me my money or you're losing your kneecaps.*

It made Faith move closer to Leo, hoping he could and would protect her from them. Then the introductions started. The kids waved and went back to playing. The women, Dona and Rachele, appraised her as if they didn't quite buy Faith and Leo as a love match. "She's a bit young for your usual taste, isn't she?" One of them had asked. These two women could end her life with their skepticism.

The men sized her up too, but in a different way, a hungry way. Leo's hand stayed on her lower back, holding her steady as she tried not to faint from nerves. The men didn't try to make physical contact. They merely nodded from several feet away as they assessed her, no doubt visualizing her and Leo in intimate activities—or her in intimate activities with each of them. She blushed and watched the playing dogs to distract herself. She didn't catch the men's names when they were introduced.

The next few hours continued like this. More children. More women. Covered dishes. More men with that bone-chilling statue demeanor. His grandmother, Alba, and his grandfather, Carmine: called Grammie and Papi. Some cousins, Nicholas and Joseph. Other family members whose relationship to Leo escaped her: Mariella, Dante, Angelica, Fabrizio, Michael, Bernie, Noelle, Nico, Sofia, Aldo, Gabriel, Tony, Lalia.

She'd never remember them all. Maybe not even if they wore name tags. And she was the main event. Everyone wanted to know things about her. Every family member appraised her, trying to determine if she was a suitable mate for their son, brother, uncle, cousin, nephew.

Angelo and his boyfriend showed up late. There was a mild flurry of discomfort from several in the family, but they couldn't be bothered with Angelo's alternative lifestyle. Faith was fresh meat. Angelo smirked and led his boy toy off to their designated bedroom. The rest of the family followed suit, bringing in their luggage and settling in, then dispersing throughout the house. At least with them all in different areas, Faith had begun to feel less claustrophobic, but there was still dinner to think about, and all the other meals and moments they might all share together during the next week. A part of Faith would have preferred the dungeon if it wasn't too dank, and if he'd allow her to move freely down there.

The doorbell rang again, and Leo answered it. "Vinny! You big *goomba,* come here!" Leo hugged the man, beating him on the back in the way men did to show affection. He turned back to her with a smile that made his whole face light up. "Faith, this is my best friend, Vinny." A woman stepped out from behind the new arrival, a predatory look in her eyes. She reached out to touch Leo's arm and hugged him too long and too close. When she released him, he took a step back and said, "And this is Vinny's cousin, Caprice. Guys, I want you to meet my fiancée, Faith."

Each time Leo said it, it sounded believable. He said it with such smooth practice, no one would think to question the farce. Caprice's eyes darted to meet Faith's. She didn't bother to mask her contempt and jealousy. Caprice leaned closer to Leo and left a lingering kiss on his cheek, practically on his neck. Her breasts, which were almost falling out of her dress, pressed provocatively against him.

Faith was relieved when Leo looked more annoyed than turned on. It wasn't that she was jealous of the other woman, more that if someone came in and swept Leo off his feet, what would it mean for Faith and her safety? At this point she'd beg to have the man's babies if it would keep her above ground. It was at that moment, Faith realized how potentially precarious her situation could be. She had to win the family over. Especially his mother. Gina was the linchpin to everything.

"I need to go handle some . . . business, if you'll all excuse me," Leo said. Wherever he was going, he wasn't taking Faith with him.

No. No. No. Don't leave me alone with these people. Especially not this woman. Caprice looked like she'd just as soon eat Faith alive than have a pleasant conversation with her. But all Faith could manage was an agreeable nod, too afraid to embarrass him or herself in front of his friends and family.

When he kissed her, she gave more of herself this time, melting against him, opening her mouth to him. She felt the change in his body, the surprise at her reaction, but he masked it for their audience. When he pulled away and went down the hallway, she chanced a look at Caprice to find the other woman glaring darts into her.

"I-I have to g-go do something, too," Faith said, needing to get away and go somewhere where she could be alone, away from the endless cacophony.

Leo fought to keep control of himself as he made his way to the industrial kitchen. He'd hoped Vinny wouldn't bring his cousin. Caprice was an old lover. She'd never stop being hung up on him, despite how brief their relationship had been. Leo was always uncomfortable when she was around. She was the most manipulative, conniving, and aggressive female he'd ever encountered.

She was the kind of raging psychotic that a smart man didn't fall asleep beside. The odds he'd wake up with his balls in a jar were not slim. Leo didn't like leaving Faith alone with the viper, but he also didn't want her around for what he wanted to say and who he wanted to say it to.

Traveling down the hallway, he found himself distracted by the kiss. It only made him want Faith, more. If she kept kissing him like that, he'd enslave her the moment his family was out the door. What could have gotten into her? He'd think it was the presence of a rival, except he was quite sure Faith wanted to remain in her wing unmolested, not duel for his affections.

When he reached the kitchen, his mother was making sauce for the spaghetti, her small dog yapping around her feet for attention. Good luck when there was cooking involved.

"I managed to get in here before they started the gravy. Taste this, Leo," she said, holding her hand under the wooden spoon.

Leo dutifully opened his mouth to taste the sauce.

"Is it too much olive oil?"

"You know it's perfect, Ma."

She beamed. "Yes. I know. I just like to hear it."

He didn't beat around the bush. "Vinny brought Caprice. He didn't mention he was bringing her. I could kill him." Leo didn't get to see his friend much since he'd moved to Vegas. He hadn't considered that he should make it clear he didn't want Caprice there. Besides, she was Vinny's cousin. It was hard to see how that conversation could go well.

Gina's face turned sour. "At least you're not marrying her. You could spring a million engagements on me and I'd forgive you, as long as it wasn't Caprice."

"She never recovered after I wounded her pride and ended it two years ago," Leo said. "I think landing me again is still on her agenda."

His mother frowned. "Over my dead body."

"I thought you'd feel that way. Try to make friends with Faith. I don't want her to feel like she doesn't have an ally here. This is a bit overwhelming for her. We both know how Caprice can be, and I can't run interference all the time." It hadn't occurred to Leo how out of her element Faith would be, even if their engagement were real. With no family and few friends, she wasn't used to so many people. Add to that all the days she'd been isolated in his house, and flinging forty people at her at once was sounding less than brilliant.

"Leave it to me. That bitch doesn't have a prayer. She's way too aggressive for you. When I saw the way Faith clung to you, I knew she was the right one. You always were drawn to the softer types. Not the tough-talking Brooklyn girls like Caprice."

"Thanks, Ma. I knew you'd understand." He kissed her on the cheek and went back to get Faith, promising himself he wouldn't leave her alone to deal with his family again.

As soon as Faith excused herself from Vinny and Caprice, she made her way to the smaller kitchen. It sat tucked away to one side of the house, far from everyone else. She poured a glass of tea from the refrigerator; the cool liquid was soothing as it went down.

She tried to breathe and stared out the window at the setting sun and the herb garden.

It was too many people. Her fears had gone from Leo killing her or hurting her for messing up, to the blind terror of being surrounded by so many people— most of them criminals. A throat cleared behind her and she jumped and dropped the glass in the sink, causing it to shatter.

Faith spun around, at first thinking it was Leo, but the man's eyes were dead, and he didn't have a scar. Angelo. It was impossible to explain how Angelo could look more frightening when he was so perfect, and Leo could seem safer with the wicked scar slicing down his cheek. She gripped one of the larger glass shards, ignoring the pain as the jagged edge bit into her palm. She'd give Angelo a scar to match his brother's if he forced her hand.

His arms were crossed over his chest as he leaned against the door frame. "Tell me why you aren't being an obedient whore for my brother. If it's lack of instruction, I know guys in prison who could teach you a thing or two about sucking cock." His voice was lethal, and she was reminded of how scary Angelo could be. In the time she'd been with Leo, she'd been scared and uncertain, which had caused her to forget how much her situation had improved. Now the reminder was large and looming in front of her.

He unfolded his arms and pushed off the door frame, stalking her like prey.

"I asked you a question. What pathetic, sniveling thing did you do to soften my brother toward you? I know him. I know you aren't satisfying his needs. So why are you still alive? You were meant as a gift, not a burden. Maybe I should take you back with me and find someone who'll put better use to your charms. I'm sure one of my guys would like to take you home. I can't believe I spared you. I should have shot you in that dumpster."

"Leo!" she shouted. But as soon as the word exited her mouth, Angelo backhanded her. She stumbled and lashed out at him with the glass, missing his face and slicing his arm instead.

He gripped her wrist, bending it back to force the makeshift weapon from her hand. It fell to the floor, shattering into more pieces.

"You stupid cunt," he growled. "You'll pay for that." He pressed her against the sink, his hand wrapped around her throat, squeezing while she gagged and choked and struggled for breath, convinced these were her last moments. She scratched and clawed at Angelo's hands, trying to get him off her.

"Breaking my Christmas present?"

The pressure released from her throat, and she could breathe again. She'd never been so relieved to hear Leo's voice. He stood in the middle of the kitchen, watching his brother, his face unperturbed by a single recognizable expression.

Angelo grabbed her by the back of the neck and threw her on the ground in front of Leo. "*That* is where a slave belongs—at her Master's feet. You stupid whore."

Faith flinched and crawled closer to Leo. She couldn't make any sudden moves with Angelo in this state. She was unsure Leo would come to her aid. He hadn't ripped his brother off her, or yelled at him, or made any big display of gallantry. Surely he didn't care one way or the other what happened to her. Why would he? Angelo was right in a way, she was his brother's burden, and rescuing her from every little threat added to the annoyance. Drawing more attention to herself now by standing and riling Angelo further was a recipe for death.

"Why aren't you using her?"

"Is she mine?" Leo asked, rhetorically.

"Of course," Angelo conceded.

"Then she's not your concern. What I do or don't do with her or when isn't your business. Did you think I'd start training her before the new year? With the family coming in?"

"I hadn't thought of it," he said. "I was pissed she wasn't giving you what she was meant to give you. She's acting all entitled, like she's special."

"And whose fault is that? You're the one who told our mother we were engaged. It's because of you that we're acting out this drama."

Angelo sighed. "You know how Ma gets when she's around Davide. I wanted her focus somewhere else for a change. She's gotta give her harping a rest."

"Then all this . . . with Faith . . . is your fault. Don't interfere. I'll train her when I'm good and damn ready."

As their words flowed over her, Faith wondered if he'd been lying to her before or if he was lying to his brother now. Did he intend to violate and beat her and treat her like a slave once everyone was gone and he had more uninterrupted time?

Her blood ran cold at the idea that she'd only have a few days of relative safety before he started in on her. Maybe she should have chosen the dungeon to get used to it. Why pretend something so pretty on the surface: family and holidays and love and a wedding, when it masked cruelty and pain that would surface the moment they were alone in the house again with just the servants?

"Fine," Angelo growled. "But I didn't give her to you to be queen of the manor."

"Leave us," Leo snapped. For the first time, violence edged his voice.

When Angelo stormed off, Leo's arms came around her. She couldn't stop shaking as he pulled her up to stand. His hand touched her face where his brother had hit her, and she winced. Then he forced her clenched fist to unfold to find the dripping blood. Her palm throbbed from the pressure she'd kept on it. She'd barely noticed the sensation while Angelo had been so near. Her first thought had been survival.

Leo pressed his hands gently against her throat where Angelo had tried to choke her. "Does that hurt?"

"Yes," she croaked.

"Can you breathe all right?"

"Yes."

"Swallow for me."

She forced her throat to work. Eating would be difficult.

"Good. Let's get you cleaned up and taken care of."

Leo was about to explode. How *dare* Angelo touch what was his? He'd been so close to beating the shit out of his brother, but it would cause more problems for Faith in the long run. Better to diffuse the situation. There were too many hot tempers and too much violence in his family.

If Angelo thought Leo would take the side of a woman—especially a woman he'd just met—over his own flesh and blood, things could get ugly and stay that way for a long time. All he wanted was peace between his family members.

Faith clung to him as he led her through the house, avoiding the areas people had congregated. He took her back to her room and sat her on the bed. She was quieter than usual, her gaze downcast as tears slid down her cheeks.

He didn't know if it was the humiliation and fear or the physical pain that made her cry, but her broken sobs simultaneously awakened his protective urges and his urge to dominate her.

It took all his self control not to force her to her knees and empty himself inside her mouth. But he wouldn't be able to live with himself if he abused her like that when he was the only sense of safety she had. Still, the fantasy spiraled through his mind.

Leo left her alone on the bed and went to the bathroom for the first aid kit, then he searched through the drawers and closets for her makeup bag. He ran a washcloth under cool water, then brought everything back and sat next to her. She tensed. So she was back to being afraid of him—not just his brother.

"Turn your face toward the light so I can see where he hit you."

It might not bruise, but it was obvious she'd been hit. He wished he didn't know so much about covering the marks of abuse, but he'd helped his sister cover marks more times than he could count.

In his family's line of work where so much violence was commonplace, it was hard for some to separate the brutality they delivered to others from their own family—those they were supposed to love, protect, and care for.

Leo had left far worse marks than this on women, but never their face, and never out of anger. He was controlled. Was controlled violence any better? It was something he didn't like to think about. If it was consensual, wasn't it less evil? The Church didn't make such distinctions, and Faith certainly hadn't asked for Angelo's hand to come sailing across her cheek.

He wondered if the violence he'd been raised in was the root of his sadism. The adults had tried to keep him protected when he was young, but he'd seen evidence of things, things that something in his psyche must have taken apart and put back together like a sordid Rubik's cube, reshaping and refashioning it until all the pieces were in order again.

Leo wiped her tears, but they kept coming in a steady stream. "I need you to stop crying."

"I-I'm sorry. I'm trying."

He brushed the hair out of her face with his fingers. "I know you are. But I need you to try harder." He kept his voice soft so he wouldn't spook her. "I won't leave you alone with any of them again. Especially not after what happened in the kitchen."

While she tried to gain control of herself, Leo tended to her hand. The piece of glass that had cut her had been large enough not to leave any pieces embedded. It was a clean cut and not too deep. He cleaned her hand with an antiseptic and then dried it with sterile gauze. The bleeding had slowed to a trickle, so he pressed the gauze against her hand for a few more minutes.

"I'm going to use a liquid bandage instead of this. It won't be as noticeable and won't draw attention."

Faith nodded and watched as he brushed the liquid bandage over the cut. The moment he'd finished, she jerked her hand away and hissed.

Leo, grabbed her wrist and blew on the cut. "Shhh. It stings at first. It'll be fine in a second. You can handle it."

After a minute or so, she settled down. He went to the intercom box beside her bed and pressed the button. Demetri answered.

"Miss Jacobson?"

"It's me, Demetri. Let us know when dinner is ready. We'll be here."

"Of course, sir."

What he loved the most about Demetri was that he didn't ask questions. Of all the household staff, he was the one person who hadn't questioned what Leo would do with Faith once he got her there. He either didn't care, or recognized more than most that it wasn't his place to ask anything at all. His job was to see to it that the house ran smoothly and manage those who cooked and cleaned for the master of the house.

Leo locked the bedroom door. It would be better if no one disturbed them. And while he thought most of the adults would avoid a closed door, with so many kids in the house, there was no telling where they would bust in playing hide-and-seek or being nosy and exploring.

"Lie back on the bed."

Faith's eyes widened and her lip started to tremble. "P-please, you said you wouldn't . . . "

His brows drew together in confusion. Then he realized . . . the locked door. "I'm not going to touch you in any inappropriate way. I don't want kids coming in here and asking what's going on and taking the story back to the adults."

She looked wary, but seeing she didn't have any options, and probably not wanting to anger him, she scooted her body up the bed and lay against the pillows.

Leo went to the bathroom to run cool water on the washcloth again. He draped it over her face when he returned. "Relax." He sat on the bed beside her and held her hand, stroking her skin with his thumb.

"I'll keep you safe. I won't let anyone here hurt you. I won't leave you alone again." He stopped short of apologizing. An apology was weakness, and it was something he'd never been good at. At least not in the standard way. His apologies came through action. In time, she would understand that.

Eight

The washcloth was soothing and cool against Faith's heated flesh. It blocked out the world and gave her a place to hide. And in that place she was able to calm down.

Leo's thumb skimming over the back of her hand made her feel strangely safe. In spite of the kinds of things she knew he enjoyed doing to a woman, and in spite of his family, when he touched her like this, she couldn't help feeling like everything would be okay.

His voice penetrated the bubble she'd put around herself. "Do you think you can sit up now and let me fix your face?"

He released her when she pulled her hand out of his and pushed herself against the headboard. Reluctantly she pulled the washcloth away. Leo patted her face dry with another piece of gauze. He must have bought stock in a first aid kit manufacturer. Both his home and Angelo's were like a triage unit.

He didn't speak as he laid out the items of her makeup bag. She had several concealers and foundations, but she didn't think he'd know what any of them were for—or why one would have a yellow concealer and a greenish-tinged concealer to begin with. Her experience with men—at least straight men —suggested the contents of a woman's makeup bag was an arcane mystery impossible for anyone without female genitalia to unravel.

She was about to ask if she could try to cover it herself when he began opening jars and tubes and canisters, whipped out a small makeup brush, and went to work. He'd done this before.

Had he hit other women in the face like Angelo had? Was that why he hadn't reacted in the kitchen? Was this so commonplace and okay to him that covering his tracks had become second nature?

He'd said he would keep her safe, but he'd meant from others. Would he hit her like this if she made him angry? How else could he be so self-assured about which makeup to use and how? It took everything inside her not to start crying again, but she kept control. If her endless blubbering messed up his work, she might have to find out why he was such an expert at this.

After a few minutes, he closed the tubes and canisters and handed her a compact. "What do you think?"

Faith took the small mirror and turned her face this way and that. The evidence was gone. She nodded, not trusting her voice as a single renegade tear started its way down her face.

He quickly brushed it away with his thumb before the wet trail could undo his work. "Look at me."

His voice was stern and brooked no argument. Faith's eyes rose to his. She felt a flood of warmth at the unexpected kindness in his expression.

"No one is going to touch you. No one is going to hurt you. I will not leave your side again. I didn't anticipate Angelo's behavior, but I should have known he'd suspect you and I weren't carrying on the relationship he intended." Leo pulled her into his arms.

Everything inside her broke into a million pieces; God help her, but a tiny part of her was falling for him. She wanted so desperately for the ruse they were playing on his family to be real, for the story to be true. She wanted to be someone he loved; she wanted this tenderness to be honest.

Leo nudged her off him and reached back to undo the clasp of the gold St. Christopher medal he wore under his shirt. He put the jewelry around her neck. "My ma's favorite saint. It'll give you an in with her."

The medal was warm from his skin, like something magic and alive. It felt like a talisman that could protect her from anything and everything.

The intercom buzzed. "Mr. Raspallo?"

"Yes, Demetri?"

"Dinner is ready."

"Thank you. We'll be right down."

Faith took a deep, shuddering breath as he helped her to her feet. Whether it was wise or not, she *did* trust him to keep her safe from his brother and anyone else who might pose a threat. When he offered his hand, she took it and followed him downstairs to where the family gathered.

The dining room was large and filled with voices speaking part English and part Italian. If she had to name it, she'd call it Italish. True to his word, a buffet table was set up filled with seafood and pastas and sauces. Another table overflowed with cookies and cakes and fruits and nuts. And of course there was wine. Bottles and bottles of it along with alternatives for the kids.

"It looks like *agita* tonight," Uncle Bernie said, patting his overlarge stomach as he looked at the buffet table with something close to lust.

Faith clung closer to Leo, too overwhelmed by so many people crammed into one room.

"Who brought the *zuppa di pesce*? It looks amazing," one of the men asked.

"Gemma did," answered another voice.

"It's a new recipe. I hope it's okay," a voice answered from the back of the room.

"Gemma, I didn't know you'd arrived," Leo said, turning toward the dark-haired beauty. His voice had gone softer, kinder—as if he were trying to settle a spooked horse or a stray dog that had been abused and kept in a cage.

The room grew chilly as the woman looked away. A few guests closest to her stiffened as well. It was as if a behavioral contagion had been let loose on the room.

"This is my fiancée, Faith. Faith, this is my sister, Gemma," Leo said, as if nothing was wrong. His tone, his posture and body language . . . none of it revealed what might be going through his mind or whether he noticed the change in the atmosphere.

"Hi," Gemma said shortly, not making eye contact either with her brother or with Faith.

Faith didn't have time to puzzle over the coldness of the sister because an older man was giving her the once over. Not in a lecherous way—more sizing her up like she was a prize heifer at the state fair.

"The babies will be good drinkers," he said after a beat. Then he looked to Leo. "You had to go Irish on us? I didn't mind when you were just dating them, but marrying one? For God's sake . . . "

"Uncle Sal," Leo said. It sounded like a warning, but there was no bite behind it. Nothing like the encounter with Angelo earlier. "She's Catholic. Let that be enough."

The old man shrugged. "We'll see. I just hope those babies have your strong Italian looks."

Faith was sure she winced visibly at that and equally sure Leo's uncle believed it was about her heritage. No one could suspect the real source of her angst. Would she truly be expected to be Leo's baby factory? He'd promised he'd never make her do any of that, but what would he tell his family when no babies came? Would they pity her or be angry she'd taken something away from them which they felt entitled to? When no children came, would they then hold her racial background against her?

"At least she'll *have* babies," Gina said. "You'll need to get started on that soon, Leo. At forty-one, you aren't getting any younger. Thank God, you didn't join the priesthood, or there would be no one to carry on the family name." She pinned Angelo with a glare and crossed herself. Whether this was to put a point on her thanks, a prayer against her other son's homosexual nature, or guilt for disparaging the priesthood, Faith couldn't be sure. Maybe it was a melting pot of all three.

Faith tried to hide her shock at the revelation. Leo's priestly ambitions hadn't been on the questionnaire. She knew he was religious. She'd asked one of the household servants where he'd gone one Sunday, and the answer had been "Mass, of course", as if it were ludicrous for her to ask what the man might be doing on a Sunday morning. But the priesthood? Never would she have guessed he'd once had such saintly ambitions. It made her feel safer—even if she knew that was ridiculous.

A man's goodness or badness could not be measured by whether or not he was a member of the clergy. Scandal after scandal in the news had proven that. Nevertheless—like many people—she couldn't resist the desire to trust those who were closely entwined with the Church.

Angelo and Davide sat at the far end of the table trying not to look like black sheep and sinners. No, they would never have grandchildren for Gina. And Leo's mom would hate Faith when she realized Leo may as well have followed his original plan.

What else didn't she know about him? As she glanced around the table, she wondered if everyone knew the family business or if the women were kept out of it. Did all the men know or only some of them? Not every man at the table looked like a thug, but some fit the stereotype to a T. Were they all involved in crime, or had some opted out like Leo? What was with the iciness between Leo and his sister, and why had Leo almost become a priest? More importantly, what had motivated him to abandon his calling?

Faith wondered if Sal was the boss, or if Angelo was. Angelo had seemed pretty powerful to her when he'd kept her at his house, as if he were the one who gave all the orders for how the mob universe should run. But something about the power that emanated off Sal told her different. But then, what about Leo's grandfather, Carmine? He was old, certainly, but he could still be the boss. He clung to the back of the room like a fading cologne, observing everything in silence. Maybe he was the one to be afraid of.

Before she could avert her gaze, he smiled at her— a smile with too many layers to untangle that sent a chill running down her spine.

Leo spent most of dinner talking to Fabrizio. From the bits of conversation Faith could pick out, his cousin wanted to open a sandwich shop near Carroll Gardens. He needed start-up help, which Leo was happy to offer.

Most of Faith's attention was taken up by Leo's grandmother, Alba. Her Sicilian accent was still strong, even after so many years in America. While most of the family had an accent straight out of Brooklyn, Alba was a first-generation immigrant, and proud of it, since every other sentence started with: "In the old country . . . "

The matriarch of the family was a touchy-feely sort who couldn't speak a word to someone without putting a hand on their arm. But Faith didn't mind. It was unusual but comforting, a sharp contrast to Alba's cold, silent husband.

The ugly lie of the fake engagement squirmed through Faith's insides. Maybe the elderly woman would mercifully pass before she ever had to suspect the truth. She could die with the unshattered hope that babies were still on the way to carry on Leo's line. Faith felt a twinge of guilt for fantasizing about the woman's demise.

Inwardly, she scolded herself. This man was keeping her from freedom. A less secure freedom, sure, but still. Shouldn't she be able to meet a man in the normal way and fall in love? Shouldn't she have a mate? And if they wanted children . . . if she could have them . . . children she'd *chosen* to have? And if she didn't want them, shouldn't she have the peace of mind to know she never had to bear them? Shouldn't she be able to come and go freely and have a job if she wanted and hobbies and places she went and people she saw?

It was becoming increasingly difficult to maintain anger or fear toward a man surrounded by his family with all its boisterous and colorful conversation and good Italian food.

She startled when Leo laid a hand on her arm. He was so warm and solid and safe. He shouldn't be safe. Sure, he hadn't harmed her. And after that first night he'd been careful not to scare her and to keep his distance.

Whatever sexual needs or desires he might have, she knew he'd taken her primarily to keep her safe, and then *that* started to make her feel guilty. And selfish. After all, she wasn't the only one whose options had been cut off. What about his right to choose an appropriate wife? Someone who was wired like him, who liked the same sexual things he liked? What about his right to have children? What about him not having to keep someone locked away like a household pet to keep them from the barrel of Angelo's gun?

All fair questions.

Leo leaned in, his lips and warm breath brushing her ear. "Are you all right?"

"Fine," she whispered.

He squeezed her arm. "Good."

He turned back to his cousin while Gina engaged Faith's attention to discuss . . . what else? Weddings and babies. It was pointless for Leo to have bothered to learn anything on the questionnaire. The family's biggest concern about her past was her Irish heritage, which they were working to overlook. The only other thing that mattered was being a good wife to Leo and breeding good quality Italian-looking stock. They'd overlook the lack of pure Italian blood if she could give them enough tiny dark-haired babies to admire and coo over. They were nice enough people. A normal family like everybody else's—if you turned a blind eye to the crime, but it was still unnerving how fixated they were on this one subject.

In Catholic wedding vows, women promised to accept children as they came from God. And yet, this obsession with procreation went above and beyond standard Church doctrine.

By the time everyone moved on to dessert, Faith was ready to hit the panic button.

"Leo?" she said, low enough that she didn't draw too many curious stares.

"Yes, sweetheart?" he said with practiced precision. She could almost believe the ruse. Something inside her twinged and ached at that moniker, wishing it was real instead of an act for his family.

"Can I go to my room for a few minutes?"

"What's wrong?"

"N-nothing. I'm overwhelmed. T-too many people here."

Concern passed over his face, then flitted away. "Be back soon. We still have to go to Mass."

Of course. Christmas Eve. Midnight Mass. She hadn't been to church in so long that she dared not participate in the Eucharist, lest some angry lightning bolt strike her down.

Leo watched Faith's slight body disappear through the doorway. He pierced Angelo with a glare when his brother's predatory gaze went after her. In Angelo's mind, Faith was always going to be a loose end. Leo could almost see the thoughts tumbling through his brother's head. What if she talked? Even inside Leo's house, there was family here, and not all of them knew what was what.

The women, particularly. They may suspect something wasn't quite right, but they were wise enough to never ask questions, to always carefully skirt around topics that might prove their worst fears. So the family ran some casinos in Nevada? It was honest work. It was legal. No reason to suspect anything. Or so they kept telling themselves.

And if any of them were uncomfortable by the quick migration half the family had taken across the country five years ago, they told themselves a comforting story that made everything feel better again. After all, weren't their lives better? Weren't they stronger financially? Didn't the kids now have a brighter future out west? If Grammie and Papi could cross the Atlantic, surely they could cross the country. It's who their family was . . . the brave ones who traveled to new opportunity when they found themselves stifled in their homeland.

Angelo settled back into his dessert after another short glare at Leo. Leo raised an eyebrow as if to say: "You gave her to me, what are you so pissed off about?" Being twins, the two of them could have carried an entire telepathic conversation without much trouble, but Angelo's gaze went back to his coffee, and Leo allowed Fabrizio to pull him back into talk of the sandwich shop.

Angelo's internal morality had come into the world broken, and the examples he'd received from the men in the family hadn't served to straighten him out. He'd always been too observant. That, combined with his willingness to cross lines, made him ideal for grooming into his current position of leadership over the Brooklyn crew. Meanwhile, Uncle Sal oversaw both Vegas and Brooklyn and reported back to Papi, who had stopped taking an active role years ago but still liked to remain informed.

Once upon a time, Leo had been offered a chance to climb the ranks. Sal liked him, trusted him. Would things be different now if Leo had chosen that path instead? Could he have managed to keep any integrity or sense of identity that wasn't covered in blood? He feared had he chosen that life, it would have unlocked the kernel of evil inside him, allowing it to bloom into something truly gruesome.

Fabrizio continued to go on about the sandwich shop while Leo half listened, his attention now turned to his sister, Gemma: the reason he knew about covering bruises. She shot him a disgusted look and went back to her cannoli, coffee, and conversation, pretending he wasn't there at all. If there was an easy way to be with the whole family where Leo wasn't involved, she would have taken it in a heartbeat.

He couldn't blame her, but he'd done what he'd had to do. Her husband had been beating her and nobody had stood up to protect her. It wasn't their business. It was between Gemma and Emilio. But she was his kid sister and he couldn't follow the unspoken rules.

Emilio's body now rested in pieces in some garbage bags in the bottom of a harbor three states over. Leo's handiwork. If the body were to be discovered, there was unlikely to be enough evidence left for an ID. It had happened more than a decade ago, after all.

Leo had been a week outside taking his final vows and being inducted into the order when he'd found Gemma, standing on the doorstep of his small apartment, trembling in the middle of a harsh winter snow, with mascara trails going down her cheeks and those angry bruises and fractured jaw. He'd taken her in and cared for her like a broken bird. He'd given her sanctuary from Emilio.

Six days later, the man was gone. No one suspected Leo, despite the scar Emilio had given him. Leo had explained it as a freak gardening accident, and the family accepted it. Maybe they accepted the story so readily because it was what they'd been trained to do: accept ridiculous lies to keep their delusions safe, to believe their men were good.

Or maybe it was the fact that he'd been practically a man of the cloth, and no one had seen the darker edges inside him that he kept carefully under wraps. The priesthood had been meant to divert his urges. The fantasies that twisted and gnarled inside him to own a woman, to dominate and subjugate her, to watch a whip make a bright red line across her flesh and the strange sense of serenity the idea brought him as it took him over the edge to orgasm. He'd been disgusted with himself. The priesthood would lock all that up in a cage and keep him from doing damage to anyone or to his own soul.

But Emilio changed that plan. Leo had caught him alone, knocked him out, and taken him to an abandoned warehouse where he'd spent the next forty-eight hours torturing him. Leo had taken the once powerful bully and turned him into a quivering lump of terror who could barely speak his own name. He'd finally killed him and taken apart the body piece by piece with a kind of glee that had scared him.

Once the evidence was gone, he'd locked himself away in his apartment. He couldn't finish taking his vows. He was no longer a potential monster who hadn't yet attacked. However he might justify it, he was tainted beyond the repair of the priesthood. And nothing could have convinced him otherwise. It had taken years for him to go back inside a church. He'd gone to medical school, intent on making amends, healing instead of harming. And along the way, he'd found healthier outlets for his sadism.

Most of the family still didn't believe Leo had done it, but Gemma had seen the look in his eyes that night when she'd come to him. She knew, and no matter what Emilio had done to her or the terror he'd kept her in, she'd never forgive her brother for taking her husband from her and their small boy. He didn't much blame her. If she'd seen the damage Leo had done to the man before he'd allowed him the sweet mercy of death, she wouldn't be able to be in a room with her brother at all.

The women started to clear the table, taking Leo's plate right out from under him.

"Ma, we've got people for that," he protested, knowing as he said it that it was wasted breath. Gina would do what she would do, and God help the poor fool who tried to stand between her and washing the dishes.

"What am I supposed to do until Mass? Huh? Watch the television? Teach Max to roll over? You won't let your poor old ma do anything for you without complaint, will you? It's not enough that you haven't given me grandchildren yet, you can't let me take care of you, either."

Leo wisely shut his mouth and let the women do what they were going to do. There were perhaps some Italian families where everybody was a chauvinist, where the men kicked off their shoes and watched sports while the women unhappily slaved away before and after dinner. But if you knew a family, you knew this was as much the women as it was the men. Should an enlightened male make his way into the family, he'd quickly be shooed away and shown his place in front of the television.

Leo suspected the women didn't just cook and clean and wash dishes. They gossiped about the men. While the men in the family had their secret crime meetings and cues and signals, the women were just as bad. What they did or didn't know about anything, no one could be entirely sure because they couldn't get close enough to the kitchen to ever find out. The women had untapped potential. Who knew how brutal the mob could be if it had been run by women instead.

Nine

Faith had gone straight to her room, Max following behind her. It was night, but with the outdoor floodlights she could see giant puffs of snow drifting down in a steady pattern.

While she'd been at dinner, one of the servants had started a fire in the fireplace. Moments like this obscured reality as if she were visiting royalty instead of a prisoner.

But she was trapped inside a Christmas card. What could be wrong with that? What kind of idiot complained or felt sad about that? She was still waiting for the other shoe to drop, for Leo to come blazing in to claim what was his, to make her pay with her body for all the kindnesses he'd bestowed. After all, she was his property, his ill-conceived early Christmas gift from his psychotic brother.

Max laid his head on her lap, and she absently stroked the soft, gold fur. He'd become her shadow these past few weeks, as if checking to make sure she was okay and then reporting back to his master with a daily status update. It had taken awhile for the cat to accept the dog's presence, but now Squish was an expert at ignoring him. She'd briefly hissed when he'd entered the room before snuggling back into Faith's pillow. In another week, he'd be beneath her notice entirely.

Half an hour or more passed like this when the doorknob jiggled. Before she could ask who it was, Leo stepped inside. He returned the key to his pocket and shut the door behind him. Since the last time she'd tried to lock him out, he'd taken to carrying the key with him. It was a reminder that she couldn't keep him away from her. This house and everything in it was his.

"Are you okay?" He must not have believed her excuse about all the people.

Faith shrugged and turned her gaze back to the window. "It hurts. This lie. Pretending I'm your fiancée while I'm really your prisoner. They think I have this great life and everything is normal, but I'm like a captive animal. I don't know if I can stand a week of this."

She chanced a look at him in time to catch his wince, and immediately felt guilty.

"I told you, you can have whatever you want here. I can't let you go. I can't risk that you'd go to the police about Angelo."

"He's a monster," she said, barely above a whisper. "I can't understand why you'd protect somebody like that."

"He's family. I won't choose a stranger over family, so drop it. We're leaving for Mass in an hour; be ready."

He left and locked the door behind him. Leo was right. He owed her nothing, but it still hurt. And yet, if she was only a stranger and family meant everything, why had he protected her from Angelo in the kitchen? Why had he given her this room? Why did he care about her comfort at all?

The drive to the church was silent—at least in Leo's car. Faith's body angled away from him in the passenger seat. They hadn't spoken since their conversation in her bedroom, and now she was somewhere far away, staring out the window at the snow. He imagined she was contemplating the possibility and opportunity for escape. After all, it was her first time outside the house since he'd taken her.

A pang of guilt stabbed him. She was right. She was a captive animal kept in a cage, presumably for her own safety. But Angelo was the criminal, and she was the innocent—no matter how much Leo might wish to ignore the truth.

Gina sat in the back, squeezed between Uncle Sal and Aunt Lily. There was a loud sigh from the backseat. It had to be Sal, because nobody else in the family could sigh in such a heavy and all-encompassing way.

"Lily wasn't Italian," he said finally, as if he'd been brooding about Faith's Irish blood since dinner. And probably he had. His quick dismissal of the Irish Problem betrayed how the thought dominated his mind. At least he was now acknowledging his own hypocrisy, given how his wife had been as fair as a Nordic princess. Maybe not Irish, but not Italian either. He'd suffered his own share of ribbing when he'd brought her home—if the family stories were to be believed.

Leo caught Lily's reflection in the mirror as she made an annoyed look and flipped her blonde hair. "I'm *still* not Italian, Salvatore." It had been a long time since her hair had naturally been that color, but she'd maintained it in the fight against the encroaching gray army with the help of a salon professional.

"Yes, dear," he said, humoring her. The truth was, once they'd had kids, and they had come out of the womb all shiny black eyes and hair and olive complexion, her ancestry had been forgiven on the spot. Though, one of their grandchildren was fair like Lily. Surrounded by everyone else's dark looks, Angelica looked as if she'd been kidnapped. But if the family noticed, they didn't mind. After all, looking like Lily was far from a criminal act.

His Ma started to go on about weddings and babies and how long before she could have grandchildren. She made it a point to note that she didn't care if they came out polka-dotted. All she wanted was babies to cuddle and coo over.

Leo winced and glanced over at Faith, who had gone stiff. He'd promised her she wouldn't have to have children for him. And he meant it. He wasn't about to violate her to keep up family appearances, and a turkey baster was too crude even for him. Either way, forcing her to incubate his progeny would be almost as bad as rape. In some ways perhaps worse. They'd invent a story of infertility.

This whole thing was spiraling too far out of control, far beyond the scope of his original intentions.

Locking Faith in the dungeon each year for the holidays would have been less trouble. But then he came back to himself. As long as Faith was in his home, no matter where she was, he couldn't have a normal life. These were things he hadn't paused to consider when his concern had been keeping his brother from killing someone Leo could save.

Angelo had given him an obligation, not a gift. A package of guilt and frustration. All he wanted was to take Faith and fulfill his every twisted fantasy with her, but his brother had gotten all the sociopathic genes. Leo didn't have the heart to follow through with an unwilling victim.

He parked the car on the far side of the church and growled in annoyance as he observed the bundled people rushing for the door. The Christmas Eve late-night Mass was always crowded. Although it was midnight and most people were tucked in their beds dreaming of sugarplums and fairies, for the faithful of St. Stephen's, Christmas Eve was the longest night of the year. Even the New Year didn't inspire staying up so late. It was countdown, kisses, champagne, and then passing out.

He came around to let Faith out of the car as a doting fiancé should. She blushed and looked away when he took her hand and helped her out, catching her as she stumbled in the three inches of snow. Did she feel the spark between them? It would be safest for her if she didn't. If she gave any indication she wanted him, her protected bubble would burst. He wouldn't be able to make any promises about what he would or wouldn't do with her then.

Faith sat in the pew toward the back of the church, sandwiched between Leo's mother and Leo. She felt Gina's shrewd eyes on the two of them, and God knew what the woman was thinking. She was probably fantasizing about baby outfits. The thought made Faith recoil. On the other side of her, Leo's hand squeezed hers. She was so fragile sitting next to him, with her tiny hand trapped in his larger one.

They were in the last row of the benches the family had taken. Angelo and Davide sat two rows up, practically cuddling. Angelo had looked back and shot her an evil look once or twice during the service, but each time, his attempt at menace was interrupted by standing or kneeling or reading or singing.

When it was time for the Eucharist, Faith didn't move. Leo's mouth brushed next to her ear. "Are you not going up? It'll look bad to the family."

"I can't," she whispered, "I haven't been to confession in a long time."

"I can't imagine how you could have offended God." The sincerity of his statement caught her off guard.

"I wouldn't feel right about it," she said, hoping that would be the end of the discussion. She didn't know what she'd do if he tried to make her partake.

He nodded and disentangled his hand from hers to make his way to the line with the rest of the family. Caprice waited for him in the aisle with a man-eating look on her face. She looped her arm through his, guiding him toward the line and flashing a smug look back at Faith.

Something tightened in her gut. Faith was only concerned about Caprice for what it could mean for her safety. Right? Surely she wasn't worried Caprice might steal him away based on some misguided attraction. Wanting Leo would be suicide. He'd already made plain the nature of his desires. The thought of what he might be into chilled her blood.

Caprice's inappropriate flirtation was cut short when they reached Leo's mom. Gina looked back at Faith and then whispered something to Leo.

Faith didn't give two hoots what his family thought about it. She may be a lapsed Catholic, but she wasn't about to go receive the body and blood without having her sins purged. It wasn't worth the risk to her soul. Let them think what they wanted. This farce had gone too long anyway.

Watching the mobsters participate in the ritual, she wondered how many of them had recently killed or beaten someone or committed some other crime. She wondered if they'd gone to confession and if so, what they possibly could have told the priest to absolve themselves for their crimes.

Faith glanced to her right and noticed Uncle Sal hadn't moved from his spot. His hard look met hers for the briefest guilty moment, then he looked away quickly. The rest of the family was in line going to the front. Even Angelo and Davide, who were sinning on a regular basis according to the Church. She very much doubted they'd been to confession, either.

When Leo and his mother returned, Gina sat beside Faith and patted her hand. "It's all right, dear," she said.

Faith looked to Leo who shook his head. Whatever lie he'd fed his mother to appease her, Faith didn't want to know about.

The snow had stopped falling at some point during the service. When they got outside, the clouds had drifted away to leave a cold, crisp night with stars that looked like brilliant pieces of glittering ice. It was barely Christmas morning, and instead of being alone in her apartment with her cat feeling sorry for herself, she was surrounded by people she suddenly wished were her family, even if there were a few killers in the mix. It was a family. And for all their faults and crimes, they loved each other.

The kids ran ahead and began making snowballs. One of the snowballs—thrown by a nephew—narrowly missed Leo, only to clip Faith on the ear. Everyone stopped and stared, waiting for her reaction.

She dropped her bag in the snow and formed a ball of her own to throw back, hitting Dante in the shoulder. The fight was on in earnest. Faith was surprised to see how spry Gina and Uncle Sal could be when balls of frozen water were involved. Sal's grim darkness melted in the face of play, and even Angelo was less severe and threatening. For a moment she could pretend these were normal people who just really liked spaghetti.

She eased back from the fight and watched Leo. His eyes lit with glee as he threw and dodged snowballs. He was one of the few who hadn't been hit. He was so beautiful, and decent in his way. Why couldn't this be real? Why couldn't he love her like a normal man? Self-pity gripped her, and a tear slid down her cheek, freezing halfway down.

"Is he hurting you?"

Faith spun to find Gemma lurking beside the hood of a nearby Oldsmobile like a harbinger of doom. "I'm sorry . . . What?" His sister had misinterpreted the self-pity for something more sinister.

"You heard me. My brother is not the saint he pretends to be. And I think you know it. If you want my advice, get out now. Don't trust him. All he knows how to do is lie and hurt people."

"I . . . um . . . " What did one say to a proclamation like that? It wasn't as if Faith didn't know the score. It was possible she knew more than half the women in the family, given the activity she'd caught Angelo in on the night they'd met. But Gemma wasn't one of the naïve lambs, nor was she content to keep to the family code of silence.

Leo's sister looked Faith over. Once she'd seen whatever she was looking for, she said, "He killed my husband. And I suspect he wasn't quick about it."

"Why would he . . . ?"

Before Gemma could answer, Leo ambled over. Another nephew, Michael, got him in the back of the head with a snowball when he turned from the group. "Cheap shot!" he called over his shoulder.

"Whatever," Michael said. "There are no rules with snowballs."

Leo's attention turned to Faith and his sister. "Gemma," he said, nodding. But his face was tight, his eyes cold and narrowed. If Faith had any doubt before, it was gone. He'd killed Gemma's husband. She took an involuntary step back and Leo's sharp gaze shifted from his sister to Faith. In a fluid blur of energy, he took her arm and pulled her back against him in a parody of an embrace.

"Don't do anything stupid," he whispered against her ear.

Faith froze.

Leo returned his focus to his sister. "What interesting gossip have I missed?" His grip tightened on Faith with each syllable out of his mouth, though it appeared to be an unconscious action on his part.

"That's on a need-to-know basis. Like every fucking thing else in this twisted family," Gemma retorted.

"Don't test me," Leo said. "What did you say to her?"

By now, family members had dropped their clumps of snow and drifted closer to hear the commotion, except for the few adults who were herding the children away into their cars—sensing things were about to turn very mature. The other parishioners had left during the snowball fight, and the priest had retired to the rectory. It was just adult family members now. And Faith.

"I don't think you want to open that can right now," Gemma said, "Not in front of the whole family."

"I'm sure I don't know what you mean," Leo said. The warning in his tone was unmistakable.

"Let's put it this way. You're the only member of the family I'm a hundred percent sure is a murderer."

There was a thud as a body hit the ground.

"Grammie!" Leo shouted.

"It's okay," Sal said when he reached Alba. "She just fainted."

Gina crossed herself. "It can't be true. My Leo's such a good boy. He would never hurt a fly."

"Fuck," Leo muttered. "He broke Gemma's jaw and one of her ribs. She was a mess the night she came to my house. And it wasn't the first time. He would have killed her eventually, and none of you did a goddamn thing about it!"

"Language!" Uncle Sal said.

"Fuck language. Emilio deserved to die. Nobody touches any of my family. Being married in won't keep you safe from me if you hurt someone I love. I don't care if it's not my business." He let go of Faith and stalked toward the car.

Gemma stood in the middle of the snow like an abandoned angel with her mouth gaping open, unable to believe the truth had been spoken.

Everybody else went to their own cars. Maybe they were too jaded and used to pretending bad things didn't happen to behave any differently. They'd all probably reboot like a bunch of computers and forget all this unpleasantness in the morning. Suddenly the night felt colder, so cold that it could suck the soul out of each of them, leaving only frozen corpses behind.

"Seriously!?!" Gemma shrieked, her breath making large white puffs in the air as she spoke. "He kills my husband, and you're all getting in your cars like it's nothing?"

Leo stopped and turned back to the group. "Emilio was a vicious bastard."

"If Leo hadn't done it, I would have," Sal admitted.

"You'll never know what it cost me to kill him," Leo said, his voice cracking. "Never. I thought joining the priesthood would fix what's inside me, but after Emilio I couldn't."

"What did you have that needed to be fixed before killing my husband? What could you possibly have done in your perfect little life to give you a big enough complex to take holy orders? Because I know you didn't have some big dream to become a priest." Gemma turned to Faith. "Is this the family you want to marry into? Do you even know who the Raspallo family is?"

"Yes," Faith whispered. "I know."

Gina crossed herself again.

"You TOLD her?" Sal bellowed.

Leo turned at his uncle's gruff voice. "Of course not. But it's not like rumors don't fly around about us. It's the 21st century. It's not as if she knows any incriminating details. No more than any of the other women in this family. And my future wife is my business." He glared daggers at Faith, as if this were her fault. Or maybe he was daring her to challenge the white lie he'd told to paint over the cracks and make things okay again.

What was she supposed to do? Pretend she hadn't heard what Gemma said? Act too stupid to pick up on the innuendo? It was too insulting to pretend to be that idiotic surrounded by a bunch of men that looked like they'd stepped out of *Goodfellas*.

"Well, hell, why don't we take an ad out in the paper, if everybody's gonna know everybody's business? It wasn't like this when I was young," Sal said.

If looks could kill, Faith would be swimming with the fishes. Wisely, she chose not to verbalize the cliché. It wouldn't endear her to Uncle Sal, who had only just made peace with her heritage.

The ride back to the house was tense. Lily stared out the window while Gina quietly cried. Both women were trying, in their own way, to insulate themselves from the almost visible, demonic rage curling off Uncle Sal in the backseat.

"You'd better not become a liability to us," Sal said.

Faith didn't turn around. If she'd thought she wouldn't die at the hands of a member of this family, she'd been kidding herself. What difference did it make if it was Angelo, Uncle Sal, Leo, or some random hired gun? She'd be dead no matter what. Yet something stupid inside her wanted to cling to the slim hope Leo had extended, that he was up to the task of saving her, that there was something in him that was good and decent and not like the others. Some noble instinct that had moved him in the direction of the Church and prayer instead of crime and death.

"Sal!" Gina hissed. "Of course she's not going to be a liability. She's Leo's fiancée. She's family. How can you say such a thing?"

"We don't know her from Adam. Leo, you better keep your girl in line."

"If you've got a problem, you take it up with Gemma. She's the one who opened her big mouth," Leo said. "And you will leave Faith out of this. I wasn't kidding back there. Faith is *my* concern."

"Are you threatening me, boy?"

Faith clenched and unclenched her hands in her lap. She wanted to scream. She wanted to blurt out the truth. Nothing would have felt better than to say: "No need to worry. I watched Angelo mow some poor guy down in an alley. Leo and I aren't really together. I'm his prisoner to protect you assholes." But she was too afraid of what Leo might do to her if she lost control and spoke her mind. And the situation was too dangerous with Sal at the moment. This wasn't a family that made idle threats.

It was bad enough that she'd said what she'd said, admitted she wasn't some naïve flower like she was supposed to. But Gemma had all but thrown the truth in her face. Even if she hadn't known anything, it would be ridiculous to think she wouldn't now. She'd rather they consider her a possible liability than a possible idiot.

Ten

This had to be the most fucked-up Christmas Leo had ever had. It took all his self-control not to blame Faith. The other women in the family probably knew more than they let on. They weren't stupid. But they did their talking in private, away from the men. Never in public. It was the separation and division that was necessary for everyone to remain sane. Denial and pretending. And now it was shattered forever.

But then, why be mad at Faith? It was Gemma who'd been the one to crack. He'd been kidding himself since Emilio. He'd comforted himself with the idea that his sister wouldn't suspect the truth. Emilio had been into some bad shit. That created a lot of enemies. The proximity of the time of his death to her worst beating could have easily been a coincidence. It was the lie he'd repeated to himself over and over. But the tension between them over the years had proven with little doubt that she knew. And tonight he couldn't deny it any longer.

Once they got back to the house, Leo dragged Faith to her room. "Lock this door," he growled.

"Wait . . ."

"WHAT?"

She shrank back at the evidence of his temper—the temper he'd inherited from Uncle Sal. Like Sal, he'd learned to keep a lid on it most of the time, to allow bits of steam to come off the surface. Sal's outlet was crime. Leo's was sadomasochism, but they were both treating the same disease. And lately Leo hadn't been able to use the release valve.

He took a deep breath and said more quietly, "What?"

"Are you mad at me? Gemma was the one who . . . "

"I know. I'm not mad at you. I need to smooth this out with my family. Keep your door locked. I want you safe."

Now wasn't the time for trembling and a quivering lip from her. Even with his family in the house, his deepest urge was to take her downstairs and fuck morals. Fuck her consent. Fuck all of it. All he wanted was to bend her bare ass over the spanking horse and light into her until she was as bright red as a Christmas ornament, then take her from behind until he was too tired to care about any of this. He wanted to stay locked down there with her in their own world until after the New Year when the house would once again be quiet and peaceful.

Faith wrapped her arms around herself as if trying to still her trembling and nodded. "O-okay. I'm s-sorry."

"It's not your fault." He shut the door behind him, and let out a breath when he heard the lock click into place. At least she was smart enough to listen to him and not defiant enough to challenge him. Right now he couldn't handle either stupidity or willfulness.

The other women were sent off to their rooms to much protesting, like recalcitrant children. And the children were treated the same. The men retired to a large den Leo had created for privacy and quiet underground next to the wine cellar. They would never know that on the other side of the cellar was a locked steel door that led into a dungeon where he allowed his own brand of darkness to run free.

The den was a cave of a room compared to the rest of the house. If any place could calm the nerves of these men, it was this place.

He poured and passed drinks and cigars around. According to the clock on the mantle, it was past two in the morning. The kids would be up by eight screaming to open presents.

"Ange, might I have a word with you in private?" Leo said, piercing his brother with a glare.

Eyebrows rose around the room, but no one said anything. Although they were twins, Leo's request for a word in private with Sal's *capo* under the circumstances created a sense of greater intrigue.

Angelo handed his glass to Davide and strode out of the room ahead of Leo. Leo rolled his eyes at his brother's posturing, but now was a stupid time to fight for the alpha title, even in his own home. Angelo had a lot to prove already in the minds of the other men, given his orientation. Leo would give his brother this one freebie.

He waited until they reached a far, private corner of the wine cellar to speak. With that much space and a closed den door they could be assured of some level of privacy while keeping an eye on the one exit so that nobody came out to eavesdrop, not that anybody would. Nobody in his family was that suicidal.

"What the hell is wrong with you?" Leo asked.

"ME!? What does this have to do with me?"

"Oh let's see . . . giving her to me for one thing. You could have killed her and never told me about it. Involving me was unfair. You shouldn't have made her my responsibility. You shouldn't have told me about her at all! Letting me think that I could save her . . . that if I didn't it would be my fault she was dead . . . what is *wrong* with you? Do you hate me that much?" He looked down to find his hands shaking with anger, his fists clenching as everything inside him screamed to wrap those hands around his brother's throat.

"*Marone!* Are you kidding me? You've always gotta be breaking my balls. Mother *fuck.*" Angelo took a slow breath to gain control of himself. "You're my blood. My brother. But you're so fucking uptight all the time. I wanted to give you what you wanted but didn't have the balls to take yourself. And STILL don't have the balls to take, it appears. She is your *slave.* Use her. She owes you her life. You should be collecting some form of payment. It's such a waste giving you anything, you *fucking* Puritan. I don't know why the hell I bothered."

"I wish you hadn't," Leo said. In his brother's mind, this was still an appropriate Christmas gift. It was the recipient of the gift that was the problem. Not the gift itself. Angelo didn't appear to grasp that giving someone a human being for Christmas wasn't just immoral, it was gauche.

"Don't worry, this is the last time I try to help you in any way. Go ahead and long for what you want but can't bring yourself to man up and take while it's right under your nose in your goddamn house."

"Why did you have to tell Ma we were engaged? The family is mostly over the gay thing."

"Ma's not over it. This whole week would have been all about me and Davide and how I need to settle down with a girl and give her grandchildren to carry on the family name. You know it would have. It's time you picked up some of that slack and nagging."

"So now Faith is supposed to be the family brood mare because you prefer men? Even if I could use her like you suggest, you think I could ever be so cruel as to force her to bear children on top of everything else we've done to her?"

Angelo shrugged. "I've given up trying to figure out how your mind works."

"Same."

"Are we done here?"

"We couldn't be more done," Leo said. Had he expected an apology from his brother or any remorse or sign of guilt or responsibility for the way the holiday had been ruined? Of course not. Nothing was ever Angelo's fault. There was always someone else to blame, or kill if blaming alone turned out not to be satisfying enough.

Leo slammed the den door behind him when they returned. He took a deep breath. He had to put this fire out before it got out of control.

"My brother thinks he's too good for us. He's always thought so," Angelo said. "May as well rub our noses in it with this fine house, better than anything any of us have, because he can justify it with the IRS. All bought with his *honest* money that he flaunts at us every Christmas."

On top of everything, Angelo had to bring the money up again. Well, why not? It was overdue. "I don't think that. All I've said is that there are alternatives. Either own what you do, or don't do it, but stop fucking whining about it and making excuses. But that's not the point of this meeting, and you know it. Faith is not a threat. She doesn't know anything more than what anybody can find with an Internet search."

"And we know that how?" Leo's Uncle Bernie asked. Uncle Sal had already voiced his issues.

"I'm too old for this shit," Carmine interjected.

"Papi . . . " Leo said.

"What? It's the truth. We need to move to the front business and forget the back business. It's not like it used to be."

"Right. Because there's a ton of dough in carpet installation," Vinny said. "How would we feed our families?" It was one of many businesses, and at least on paper, it was successful. The Raspallo front businesses ran more to casinos in Vegas and construction work in New York. It was hard to prove bids were rigged. And a little illegal gambling alongside the legal stuff was easier to paper over, especially given that most mob families had largely abandoned Vegas, so the heat was elsewhere.

"You work in Vegas at the casino now. You wouldn't be doing installation," Leo's grandfather retorted, still remarkably sharp for nearing ninety.

"I just want to do the sandwich shop," Fabrizio said.

"Oh, so you're out of the business, now," Angelo said. "Maybe *you're* the liability."

"Hey!" Leo said. "Leave him alone. Even if he ran a sandwich shop, you know he's not going to sing. No more than I would. Aren't we all self-employed in our own ways? Can't we respect each other's choices without acting like everybody who does something different has gone Judas?"

"I didn't say I was out of the business," Fabrizio said. "I'm saying if we all went straight . . . " Fabrizio must have rethought the extra connotation of that word and changed midstream. " . . . Honest . . . if we all went honest, I'd do the sandwich business. I'm just saying I'm not into carpet installation, all right?"

"Nobody is seriously considering doing carpet installation," Angelo said, as if the idea turned his stomach.

"Papi is."

Carmine cleared his throat from across the room. "When I formed this family, I mirrored what the *Ndrangheta* in Calabria does . . . keeping it all in the family or married in. It's easier to keep the *omerta* and harder for the feds to work their way in."

Leo's gaze shifted to Davide. Davide wasn't married in, but then he'd been in already. Papi had started the family with a few friends who weren't related, and Davide was the grandson of one of those friends. Same with Vinny. But ever since then they'd been strict about who they allowed to join. A blood relation of one of the original members, or married to one of their women. There was no other way in, and Papi wasn't wrong. It had made their organization harder to penetrate and kept most of them out of the system. And when they did go away, it was always for something relatively small.

Carmine took a sip of his drink and continued. "I wanted a tight ship, not all this fighting. It was the idea that eventually we'd get out when there were better opportunities, but even with what we do, we're no more corrupt than most of the corporations of the world. Aren't we doing the same things? Bribing the government to operate how we like? They call it lobbying. But we're all using the same playbook. You think there isn't crime and death in most large corporations? What about the pharmaceutical companies? You're in medicine, Leo, tell me that's not corrupt as hell. Tell me thousands or hundreds of thousands of people aren't dying each year because of drugs rushed through the FDA that aren't safe. Your Grammie almost died from one of them last spring."

"I can't argue with you, Papi," Leo said.

"Damn right, you can't. Their hands are stained with blood, yet it's respectable, but what we do isn't? And don't get me started on the government. The government is mafia. Big corporations are mafia. They all screw the little guy, intimidate, threaten, and harm. They're all out for money and power. The only difference is public tolerance. I want us to go honest to get out from under the law, but what does going honest mean? Everyone with power and money is mafioso. Every single person."

"Even Leo?" Angelo piped up.

"Leo's a part of this family whether or not he chooses to be involved with everything we do. I can't speak to the honesty of his business. I'm sure there are exceptions."

"Of course. He's the golden child. We all take huge risks for this family, and Leo gets a free pass. He forgets those stock scams that financed his honest business."

"That's enough, Angelo," Papi said.

Angelo sank into a chair with his cigar and brandy and pouted like he was twelve.

It could be argued that Papi was an old man talking nonsense, or that in his old age he sought justification for his life of crime, but there was an eerie level of truth in his words.

"Things used to be so much better," Sal said. "This all used to mean something. And now we've got this shit with Faith. How much can we trust her? Women aren't like us. They'll talk sooner if they feel threatened or scared. They can't keep the *omerta* like we will."

Unlike other families, the women had been strictly forbidden from doing anything illegal. No drugs, no shady dealings. They weren't even allowed to smoke pot. It might be sexist, but it was true. Women talked easier. They betrayed easier. They had a lower threshold for pain, and most of them couldn't be trusted to keep the code of silence. It was work for the men and only the men.

"Nobody is hurting the girl," Papi said. "I'm still boss of this family. If anyone lays a finger on her, they'll be dealing with me. Leo loves this girl. They're getting married. So what if she knows we're mafia? If you think your women don't suspect this family is mixed up in crime or that most of us have killed someone at one point or another, you've all got your heads up your collective asses. You know they know, or at least suspect to the point that actually knowing would make little difference. But they've got plausible deniability. That's what's important. And we keep it that way. Understand?"

Leo let out a breath at Papi's pronouncement of protection over Faith.

"Fine," Uncle Sal said.

"Whatever," Angelo said. As if Angelo had intended to kill her. He had to keep up appearances. If Uncle Sal caught wind of how Faith had come to be here, it would be his head on a pike.

Everyone else nodded.

The mood in the room lightened and Davide said, "Hey, I was in Greenwich Village the other day and I saw a T-shirt that said *New York City, Family owned and operated since 1920.*"

Several of the guys chuckled; even Papi cracked a grin at that. Despite his grandfather's talk and hopes, Leo knew the family wouldn't ever go honest, but he also knew the old man was proud of the way Leo had made his money. Carmine lifted a glass to his grandson and Leo nodded in return.

Faith had been lying in bed tossing and turning for close to an hour when there was a knock on the door.

"Leo?" she said as she approached, wrapping a robe around her. She was a split second from opening it when she heard a drunk voice on the other end.

"You stupid cunt," Angelo slurred from the other side. "I ought to kill you. Do you know the trouble you've caused for this family? You aren't doing your job. Why aren't you doing what all good sluts do? My brother owns you, bitch. He *owns* you. You owe him gratitude and blow jobs and anal and whatever fucked-up shit he's into for stepping in to save you."

Faith backed away, stumbling over the foot of the bed in her attempt to get to the intercom.

A groggy Demetri answered when she pressed the button. "Yes, Miss Jacobson?"

"Angelo is outside my door, drunk," she whispered.

Demetri became alert, and the touch of annoyance evaporated from his voice. "It'll be taken care of."

A few minutes later there was arguing on the other side of the door and then silence and then another knock. This time, Faith didn't make a move, having learned that lesson—almost the hard way.

"Faith, let me in. I don't have my key on me."

She released the breath she'd been holding and let Leo in.

"Get your cat and come with me."

"W-where are we going?" Although it was ludicrous, by this point she worried he'd lock her in the dungeon and tell the family they had a fight and broke up. Angelo was right about the trouble her presence was causing.

"You're sleeping in my room." He must have seen the fear that passed over her face, because he continued with, "I need you where I can keep you from my brother. He's not going to start banging on *my* door and being an ass in the middle of the night."

Faith tied the robe around her and bent to pick up Squish, who'd been rubbing against her legs and purring, oblivious to the surrounding drama.

Her heart pounded in her chest as she took Leo's warm hand. In spite of everything that had happened tonight and the heightened danger and seeing Leo's anger and Gemma's warnings about her brother's dishonesty, Faith couldn't help the way she felt safe with him. Her hand in his had become a welcome comfort.

Even so, sleeping in his room reminded her of when he'd first brought her home. Would he try something now? She was surprised to find her attitude to that possibility had shifted when she wasn't paying attention. Being the object of his protection, and the displays of public affection he'd shown her for the sake of the family, had done a funny thing to her heart. Now the idea of sleeping with him didn't seem quite so terrifying or horrible.

But it didn't mean she was stupid.

When they reached his room, she dropped the cat on the floor, who went right up to the love seat Max was curled on and hissed. The dog jolted from a dead sleep at the sight of her and leapt off the furniture at her demand. She stretched in the spot he'd made warm for her and then flicked her claws a couple of times before snuggling into the soft fabric. Max did the dog equivalent of a shrug and slunk to the chair, curling his large body into the smaller space that would have been better suited for the cat, had Squish been willing to settle for second best of anything.

Leo locked the bedroom door and shook his head at the animals. "I think Max doesn't realize he ever got bigger than a puppy and can actually defend himself."

Faith stood frozen on her side of the bed. Would he make her sleep naked again?

"Get in bed."

"I . . . um . . . " She blushed.

"Take off the robe and get in bed. It's after three. I don't do well on little sleep."

Leo peeled his robe off, revealing nothing underneath. Faith quickly averted her gaze from his erection. It seemed a permanent fixture of his physique.

"I can sleep on the couch," she said.

"You are sleeping in the bed. Get in. You can wear your pajamas. I already told you I'm not going to fuck you, but you aren't going to be in my house sleeping on a damn couch."

Had he lost interest? What a stupid question. Her gaze flitted briefly back to his hard on. Of course he hadn't lost interest. And why should she care anyway? Didn't she want to be safe from him? Wasn't having her own space in this house the kindest thing he'd done for her? Maybe it was the adrenaline of fighting with his brother and no real outlet to release any of that pent up energy.

She took off the robe and slid into bed, tense and waiting for . . . anything.

But the bed was large, and it wasn't difficult for him to sprawl comfortably on his side without touching her. She held her body rigid for several minutes before allowing herself to relax. He wasn't going to touch her. She quickly buried the unexpected disappointment that accompanied that realization.

"Leo?"

He sighed. "Yes, Faith?"

"Do they want to kill me?"

"Nobody is killing anybody. Go to sleep."

A few more minutes of silence passed. Then, "Leo?"

"Yes, Faith?"

"T-the stuff you do in the dungeon . . . is that why you were going to become a priest?" It was the only thing Faith could think of that Leo might have been trying to suppress.

"Yes. Go to sleep."

She had more questions, but they were things she'd never ask him. Things about Emilio to convince herself that the death Leo had meted out wasn't only deserved but had come from protective urges and nothing else. A kind of self-defense by proxy. She could cope with self-defense. Uncontrolled violence for its own sake, she couldn't.

Gemma's voice drifted into her mind. *And I suspect he wasn't quick about it.* What made her suspect that? Had he tortured Emilio? Was that another flavor of whatever was inside him that he needed the priesthood to erase?

How long had he harbored the desire to hurt Gemma's husband before he'd snapped? How long before he snapped with Faith in other ways?

Eleven

orning was heralded by kids running down the hallways banging on doors and shouting for everyone to get up. The cacophony resembled a frat house filled with unruly college boys. Faith glanced at the wall clock to find it was seven-thirty. A tiny strip of sunlight slipped between the heavy curtains at the far end of the room. The cat was already lying in the beam.

Squish twisted her head and yawned at Faith, then went back to sleep.

Leo rolled over and pressed a pillow over his head. "Goddamn kids. And my mother wants me to have a house full of them. If she likes them so much, they can live with her."

Faith sat up against the headboard and stared at the glittering diamond on her hand. Even in low light, it was dazzling. "This isn't going to work."

"What isn't?" His voice was muffled underneath the pillow.

"This. All of it. We can't maintain this lie forever. Half your family wants me dead so I'm not a threat. The other half wants me to have babies. This is a mess. I wish Angelo had shot me and been done with it."

But it wasn't just that. It was the carrots that were being dangled in front of her that weren't real. An attractive, successful fiancé. A beautiful home. Family. Even as screwed up as Christmas Eve had been, a real family holiday with everything she'd dreamed of. The food, the laughter, the warmth. All the things she'd always wished she could have, presented to her with all the reality of fool's gold. "Just give me back to Angelo and let him finish it."

Leo got out of bed without a word and threw on his robe. On his way out the door, he said, "Don't leave this room."

Ten minutes later, he returned with a grumpy, yet fully dressed, Angelo. Leo locked the door and came to stand next to the bed. Faith's eyes widened at the sight of the gun with the silencer in Angelo's hand. Despite his tiredness, his eyes lit with a malevolent gleam.

Leo's voice cut through her mental hysteria as he looked at the gun. "Assassin's special? Nice."

"I still carry it from the old days before I got promoted," Angelo said.

"Faith has decided she doesn't want to live anymore. She's right, this lie won't work. So go ahead, Ange. Clean up your mess." He crossed his arms and took a step out of his brother's way.

"I should have killed the bitch to begin with. See, baby? This is the price of not giving my brother what he wants."

"We don't need the commentary," Leo said. "Do it and get out."

"W-what?" Faith pinched herself, sure she had to be having a nightmare. This couldn't be real. It wasn't until this moment that she realized she'd actually trusted Leo a little.

Angelo raised the gun. Leo didn't stop him. Her instincts engaged, bypassing the denial still going strong in the forefront of her mind. She rolled out of the bed. But both Leo and Angelo were in the way of the door and she wouldn't be able to unlock it and open it in time. She backed away, her hands held out in front of her.

"No. Leo, please. Please." The panic started to bubble up.

The brothers moved almost as one unit toward her. If not for Leo's scar, Faith wouldn't know which was which right now. Leo stood the closest, with Angelo a few feet behind and to the side of him. The gun raised again, aimed to kill—not wound.

Having nowhere to go, she dropped to her knees. "Please don't let him do this. I don't want to die. Please. Please. Please."

A moment later, the gun went off, and even with the silencer, it was the loudest sound in the world. The bullet lodged in the wall, a couple of inches above her head.

She fought not to hyperventilate as she looked up for Leo's reaction. Maybe he was bluffing. Maybe he would be angry at Angelo—if for no other reason than for the bullet hole in his wall. But his face remained stoic, cold. It was as if a switch had flipped inside him.

There was nobody home. She was locked in a room with identical sociopaths.

Even so, she scooted closer, pressing her face against his leg, as if getting close enough to her former protector would prevent a bullet from going through her. "Please, don't do this, Leo. I'm sorry. Please. I'll do whatever you want. Please. Please."

Had Angelo meant to miss? The slightest miscalculation would have killed her. Or maybe it was the slightest miscalculation that had left her breathing. It was impossible to determine the true scenario.

"Faith, I'm going to say this once," Leo said. "I have sacrificed everything for you. Any hope of the kind of life I would want for myself. All so you can live, because I can't take more blood on my hands. I've chosen not to violate you. Everything I've done has been unselfish and for your safety and interest. I'm sorry that your life as you knew it has been taken from you. I'm sorry you're in this situation, but the words you speak have consequences. Do not *ever* imply you want to die or wish Angelo had killed you again, unless you are truly ready for death, because you might bluff, but we don't. Do you understand?"

"Y-yes." Finally, she could breathe again. Assuming Angelo didn't lose his temper and shoot her anyway, she'd be allowed to live this time.

"Good."

Angelo didn't disguise his disgust. "You better please him, little girl. You were intended as a gift."

When he was gone, Leo helped her stand.

"L-Leo?"

"Yes, Faith?"

"Are you going to make me . . . I mean are we going to . . . " *Are you going to rape me? Are you going to beat me? Are you going to chain me in your dungeon? Are you going to hurt me?* But she couldn't bring herself to say any of those awful things, so instead, she looked at him helplessly, praying he could read her mind. After all, he'd told her not to say things she didn't mean or there would be consequences, and she'd said she'd do whatever he wanted to live. And she knew exactly what he wanted.

Her first night here, when she'd begged for his mercy, he'd been affected by her tears. This morning it was as if he were farther away, harder to reach and reason with. How long until nothing could sway him to show her mercy? How long until his sexual frustration peaked? Living here with him wasn't safe. It was only temporary safety. When the safety ended and he took what he'd been aching to have, would she wish for death and mean it? How would she know?

It wasn't until Angelo had pointed a gun at her for the second time that she realized nothing had changed. She still wasn't brave enough to die. But she wasn't sure if she was brave enough to survive, either. Not with Leo's compassion becoming harder to earn. It was as if being around Angelo and the rest of his family for an extended period had begun to unlock his criminal side.

"Go get cleaned up. I'm sure the women are already making breakfast," he said, ignoring her question.

Leo grabbed his clothes and went down the hall to shower, careful to lock the bedroom door behind him. Angelo waited in the hallway with his arms crossed over his chest.

"You're too soft. I wish you'd let me shoot her," he whispered.

"If she had wanted to die, I would have. If she's going to live in this house unmolested, she needs to show me the smallest respect by not tossing half-hearted suicidal words around. I don't think she understood how ungrateful it was. Now she understands."

Angelo followed down the hall. "So, now that you've got part of your balls back, are you going to take what's yours?"

"I haven't decided yet."

"I've caught the way she looks at you," Angelo said. "She might not know it yet, but she wants you. This could work."

"She's vanilla."

"So?"

"So, she might want me, but she wants me in a Disney princess sort of way with soft candlelight and missionary position and love and candy. She doesn't want me in a 'chained down in the dungeon while I lay pretty welts down across her ass' way. If she were kinky, I'd take her and turn her body against her no matter what she said she wanted. I'm not sure I'm up to that challenge with someone who isn't wired like me."

When Leo reached the bathroom, Angelo put a hand on his arm. "I'm sorry. Okay? You're right, I should have killed her that night. You've done so much for me, supporting me and Davide when nobody else would. I wanted to give something back. When it went south, I didn't want to admit I'd hurt instead of helped you. I'll stay out of it. You don't need more shit from me."

"Thanks, that means a lot, Ange."

They hugged and beat each other on the backs, then kissed on the cheek.

"And we make up on Christmas morning," Angelo said, chuckling.

"It's a Rockwell moment."

Leo ran the shower hotter than normal, fighting with himself over what he was going to do with the woman in his bedroom. Why couldn't she be a freak like him? Physically, she was just his type. She was smart. She wasn't a psychotic like Caprice.

He considered utilizing the submissive tendencies she *did* have. The ones that made her want to placate and appease and get along. It wouldn't make her any more receptive to anything in the dungeon, but maybe he could compromise. A quieter, gentler dominance. One that wouldn't look kinky to the untrained eye but that might still be enough if he held full control and she gave him her obedience.

She was his no matter what she was or wasn't into. Whatever he actually did or didn't do with her didn't change the fact that he *could* do anything. That point had been made clear. He could have her destroyed at the point of Angelo's gun at any time. And now she knew it.

When Leo reached the kitchen, he was surprised to find Faith already eating breakfast. Angelo kept a respectful distance.

Most of the family, in fact, was somewhat back to normal. Uncle Sal appeared to be assessing her in a wolfish way, as if determining if her head should go on his office wall, but Leo hadn't expected Sal to back down overnight.

Gemma sat in the corner, whispering with Caprice. Great. The psycho and the sister who didn't know what was good for her, both huddling together in conspiracy. At least they couldn't be conspiring on getting him and Caprice together, unless Gemma wanted to punish him and realized Caprice was punishment. But as self-involved as his sister was, he didn't expect her to have picked up on that subtext.

At the kitchen table, Gina was trying to fatten Faith up with second helpings.

"She's not eating for two," Leo said, approaching the table.

"Not yet," Gina said giving him a conspiratorial wink.

Faith looked up, fear still in her eyes. She'd managed makeup to minimize the evidence of crying, but that stark look was still there. He hoped the family thought she was rattled from the previous night's drama, rather than the truth that she was actually afraid of Leo now.

He stepped behind her and wrapped his arms around her, kissing the side of her neck. He lingered until her breathing went back to normal and her muscles unclenched themselves, then he sat in the chair beside her, and his mother's attention went to loading up his plate.

"Admit it, Ma. You want us all fat."

"Hush. It's Christmas. One week out of the year isn't going to take away your good looks."

Leo took the moment of his mother's distraction to steal a kiss from Faith. She gasped against his mouth when he turned her to him. He wanted to gauge the truth of what Angelo had said.

For all his faults, Angelo could read people. It was part of what made him such a good *capo*. He knew if someone could be trusted, if someone was fucking him over. He'd known immediately that Faith wasn't having sex with his brother like he'd intended, something Leo didn't want to know how he'd guessed.

In spite of her fear and the events of the morning, she melted into him like butter on a hot griddle. *Interesting.* He allowed his fingers to trail through her hair and used his other hand to touch the side of her neck. Her pulse was racing. Fear or something more?

Her face was flushed, her eyes glazed. She looked away quickly, back to her plate. That wasn't fear, and she wasn't a professional actress. Angelo was right. No matter how conflicted or terrified she was, she wanted him.

But it didn't matter. She didn't want *him*. She wanted the version of him his family saw, the cleaned up, respectable version. The holiday edition. She didn't want his darkness. *That,* she cowered from. He couldn't be with a woman who would cringe in fear from such a pervasive part of him. As attractive and nearly perfect as he found her, that single missing ingredient made the entire cake fall.

Leo glanced down to find Angelica crawling near his feet with Christmas paper in her mouth. "Someone has been unwrapping presents without us." It had escaped most of the adults' notice that the kids had disappeared from the kitchen.

"Angelica is a baby. She can't open presents by herself," Alba said.

Leo laughed. "I know that, Grammie, but if she's got wrapping paper, someone had to give it to her."

The adults migrated to the large family room with the Christmas tree and the mountain of presents. Michael and Nico had taken it upon themselves to divvy up the loot, creating a careful pile for each person, while the other kids tore into presents.

"So much for me playing Santa this year," Leo's cousin Dino grumbled.

The kids had made a pile for Leo and Faith next to a black leather couch along the back wall. He watched Faith's eyes widen at the large pile of presents with her name on them. Most were from him, but several were from other family members who'd heard through the grapevine, a.k.a. Gina, that he had a lady friend.

"Leo, can I talk to you for a minute in private?" Caprice said.

He rolled his eyes. He wanted to watch Faith open her presents. Though he also didn't want to contemplate why he cared so much to see her reactions to everything. "What about?"

"That would be the private part," she said coyly. Her nipples were erect through her thick sweater.

Unbelievable. She was making a play for him with Faith standing right there. He wanted to kill Vinny for bringing her to the family holiday. While he thought of Vinny as family, that sentiment didn't extend to his cousin.

"Faith, don't open anything until I get back."

"Okay."

He could see the uncertainty in her eyes and could practically read the thoughts right out of her head. Suddenly, the protective instincts that had caused him to rescue her in the first place came flooding back. He squeezed her hand and caught her gaze. "I'll be right back."

She nodded and sat on the couch, staring at the pile in front of her.

Leo followed Caprice down the twisting hallways until they were clear on the other end of the house. She opened a door into an empty bedroom and slithered inside, her intention not subtle. She crooked a finger at him, and he followed. He may as well not berate her out in the hallway.

The door had barely shut and already she was pulling her bright Christmas-red sweater over her head. She hadn't bothered with a bra, but then Leo had suspected as much.

For the briefest moment, he allowed her to press her body against him, allowed her to press her small hand into the front of his pants as she strained to find his cock. Her hot, searching mouth trailed kisses over his throat.

"Please," she whimpered. "You know Faith will never be enough for you. She's too young for you. She's too sweet and innocent. Not like us. Tiny woodland creatures probably follow her wherever she goes. You don't love her."

Leo took a step out of her reach. "How do you know that?"

"I pay attention. She doesn't light you up like I once did. You think such a sweet, virginal type will ever be what you need?" She dropped to her knees at his feet and looked up, all demure temptation. "Please, Sir, take me to the dungeon. You have to let it out, Leo. Let it out with me."

"I'm getting married, Caprice." But his resolve was melting, and she knew it. Whether she knew the marriage was a sham or not he couldn't guess. It wouldn't make a difference to Caprice. She would hunt what she wanted, when she wanted, with no regard for the sanctity of anyone else's sexual unions but her own.

"I don't care. And I'll give you what you need after you're married if you want. Please, let me please you."

"It doesn't work with us. You're too deceitful. None of this is real."

She rolled her eyes. "What difference does it make? No, you don't own me. I'm not submissive. But I like the things you do to me, and you like doing them. So let's do them. I'm not asking to be your soul mate. I'm just asking you to use me. You use me. I'll use you. We'll both scratch our itches, and then I'll go away. I promise."

"That won't be how it happens." It had taken an act of God to detach her the last time. Though, she'd been living in New York back then.

"When was the last time you let it out?"

"Months."

She smiled. "That's what I thought. I can always tell when you aren't getting your needs met."

"I'll take you to the dungeon on one condition."

Her eyes sparked. "Name it."

"As soon as we are done, you will leave this house. You will not stay for the rest of the holidays."

"But I came with Vinny," she pouted, already trying to sway him with her useless ploys.

"I'll call you a cab and I'll put you up in a nice hotel until Vinny can come get you and take you back to Vegas." He wasn't going to have her in the house with Faith if they were going to do this.

He let out a hiss when she laid her cheek against his crotch. It really had been too long. He'd been living like a priest.

"And . . . will you come visit me there?"

What harm would it do? He wasn't in a real relationship with Faith. God knew how long it would be before he got any of his itches scratched again. Then Caprice would be back in Vegas, too far away to be drama.

"On the understanding that this is a short-term fling. We will not have a relationship. I will not be dumping Faith. And you will quietly go away when I tell you to."

"Done," she said, her eyes lighting with victory.

"Oh, and one more thing. You will address me as Master and you will not try to control anything. If you seek control or try any bullshit with me, you are out on your ass and I'll never touch you again." The last part wounded her pride, but she swallowed hard and nodded. No, she wasn't submissive. But if she could pretend, then so could he.

"Yes, Master, whatever you want."

Leo wasn't stupid enough to think she meant it. Oh, she'd do things his way for the next week, but afterward she would make her play for more. At which point he'd put her ass on a plane and send her back to the other side of the country.

"Put your sweater on and let's go."

Caprice got her sweater back on three times faster than she'd gotten it off. Then Leo took her hand and poked his head out the door to check the hallway. It was clear, so he led her to the back stairs that went to the dungeon and locked the door behind them.

The dungeon was the equivalent of two stories down, with stone walls and ceiling that would filter out the loudest screams. Even so, he was gagging her. He didn't want to hear her smart mouth. He only wanted to see her tears and hear muted, desperate mewls.

Between everything else and the vanilla nightmare he was living out upstairs, he needed this, no matter how much angst he knew it would cause or how much he couldn't stand this woman. She was a willing victim, so he'd take it.

"Undress. Don't seduce me. We don't have time for that. And no eye contact. You look me in the eyes once, and I'll stop."

She quickly shifted her gaze to the ground and whispered, "Yes, Master."

Impotent rage burned beneath the surface, but her determination to win the game she was playing and get her own needs met silenced any protest she may have made as she quickly disrobed.

Leo followed suit. The whole thing was so . . . perfunctory. There was no passion here, no feelings. It was as cold and sterile as his operating table. It was a quick wank in the shower while random images floated through his mind. Masturbatory.

When her clothing was on the floor, Leo grabbed her wrist none too gently and pushed her down on the spanking horse.

"Hey! Ow!" she protested.

"Shut your mouth."

She did, and he tied her down. Caprice was ready to protest again when he took the ball gag from the toy box.

"What did I say about trying to control things?" he said, before she could open her mouth again.

"But . . . I . . . " For the first time in all the time he'd known her, she had a moment of true fear and indecision. Indecision looked strange on Caprice.

"Don't you trust me?" he asked. "Why would you want to play with me if you didn't trust me?"

"I trust you, I just . . . " She looked up into his eyes then, the pleading visible.

"What did I say about eye contact? Right now, your body belongs to me. You agreed to this. Whether we do this or not, when we leave this room you are leaving my house. Don't you want to feel like you won a round?"

She looked down quickly—back to the old Caprice —and said, "Yes, Master." Playing on her sense of competition was too easy. For all her conniving and borderline insanity, she was easy to read and manipulate. She was unable to step back from a situation and judge cost versus benefit once she'd settled on a course of action. Perhaps he'd beat some sense into her today.

"Good girl. I imagine you never hear that phrase. Must be such a novelty, and perhaps demeaning, all things considered." He pushed the black rubber ball past her lips and snapped the gag into place before she could utter the comeback that had surely begun to weave itself together in her mind.

With the family upstairs opening gifts and wondering where the hell he was, all he wanted was to get his fix, to get his sadistic urges out on a live and somewhat willing human being. He went straight for the cane. It was maximum impact for limited time allotment.

One by one, he laid the welts across her ass and thighs in sharp, practiced strokes. The anger in those welts mirrored his own. His anger at the situation he was in, at Caprice's machinations, and at his own carnal weakness in falling for her scheme. But oh, he would make her pay for it. She had to know that.

She screamed around the gag so loudly that he was glad for the obstruction. As soundproofed as the dungeon was, you could never be too careful with your mother and a pack of small children upstairs. "Why did it sound like you were murdering someone?" wasn't the question he wanted to entertain on Christmas morning.

There was something vulgar in this display on such a holy day. They'd been out of Mass for a short eight hours and he had one woman tied down, beating her, while the woman he was marrying sat upstairs, abandoned to his criminal family.

He stepped back to admire his work and ran his hands over the hot, red marks. Leo pressed a finger inside her, unsurprised to find her wet and needy. Even with no warm-up or love and kittens, she could rise to the occasion, and so, it would appear, could he, if his hard-on were any indication.

It didn't matter who was under his cane or whip. The effect on his body was the same every time—a fact which disturbed him.

Leo went back to the toy box and retrieved a vibrator with leather straps attached. He pushed the toy inside her, making sure the external nub pressed firmly against her clit, then he secured the straps around her thighs and waist and flipped the switch that brought it to life.

He didn't bother with a tease. Instead, he went for the highest setting, intent on overwhelming her into a fast orgasm and then torturing her with the added unwanted stimulation until he had gotten his.

As her orgasm crested, he unsnapped the gag and pulled it from her mouth, replacing the rubber ball quickly with his cock, muffling the sound of her orgasm against his throbbing erection. No way in hell would he risk impregnating her.

"Suck like your life depends on it."

She did. It was one thing she excelled at.

Leo gripped her shoulders, digging his nails into her skin as she fellated him. He bit his lip to stifle his own moan as he came. Caprice didn't try to get out of swallowing: she accepted him wholly and completely, almost convincing him of her submissive act.

Perhaps he'd given up on her too soon. But, this wasn't his life now. And one trip to the dungeon wouldn't change her entire faulty personality.

He put his clothes back on and smoothed his hair before turning off the toy and releasing her from her bonds. "Get dressed," he growled.

She practically slid off the spanking horse like an invertebrate without any bones to hold her together and crawled to her pile of clothing. Her gaze shifted to the large leaner mirror against the wall. She lingered, running her fingertips over the red welts, a small smile curving her lips before she reached for her clothes.

"I'm going upstairs to call you a cab and pay for a hotel. Go to your room and pack your things, then wait in the lobby for your ride."

She nodded, not making eye contact as she struggled to make her legs work so she could use the stairs.

Leo checked his watch. Their entire encounter from the moment she'd pulled him down the hallway into the spare bedroom had lasted exactly twenty-five minutes. Not bad time.

Twelve

The family finished opening presents, then they turned to watch Faith. Gina's Yorkie tilted his head to the side. Faith looked down at her hands. Leo had asked her to wait. So she waited.

"Where's Leo?" Gina asked as if just noticing the host had gone missing.

The kids had been in such a hurry, ripping through paper and tossing clothing into a pile to cope with later, then going straight for the toys and electronics. The good stuff. It was hard to keep track of the location of all the adults in that bedlam.

"Caprice wanted to talk to him." Even as Faith said it, she felt like the biggest fool in the world. She looked like a philanderer's stupid girlfriend, too oblivious to know what her man was doing. From the looks of pity around the room, including ones who'd wanted her dead the night before, she knew they were thinking the same thing.

But Leo wasn't her man, and he had every right to sleep with whoever he wanted. Still, the idea of it being

Caprice scared her. Caprice would move in and then where would Faith go? Caprice would insist on Faith's removal from the property. It wasn't losing a nice house and being without a job now, it was losing her life—something she'd been reminded she still hoped to keep.

Would Leo sacrifice her life on the altar of his libido? He'd already been about to let Angelo kill her that morning. And he'd made a point of how much he'd sacrificed, so it was fresh on his mind.

Gina's mouth turned down in disapproval. Leo's mother disliked Caprice as much as Faith did, if that were possible. The woman's eyes held a wisdom and knowledge that were probably the natural side effect of being a member of the Raspallo family for far too long.

Leo returned disheveled—confirming Faith's suspicions. It wasn't that his shirt was untucked or his hair unkempt. His hair looked fine, and his clothing was the way it was supposed to be, save for a few barely noticeable crinkles in the fabric. It was something in his facial expression and manner that made him seem disheveled and wild. He'd either just had sex or buried a body. Since it was Caprice, Faith hoped for the latter.

"What's going on with Caprice?" Gina said, suspicion in her eyes.

"Really, Ma? You know how I feel about her."

"How *do* you feel about my cousin?" Vinny asked, rising from his chair near the kids.

All adult eyes turned to him. The kids were too busy with their iPods and smart phones and fighting over whose video game equipment was getting hooked into the TV in this room and who would have to relocate, to care about the grown-up conversation happening feet away. When you had a new video game console, adult conversations were algebraic equations.

"I feel like we aren't right for each other. Also, in case you forget, I am *engaged*." Leo made a sweeping motion toward Faith to underscore his point, which made her feel more on display and humiliated by what was obvious to everyone. "Caprice has decided to leave. I've called her a cab and set her up in a hotel so she has some place to stay."

"Why would she decide that? Why would she want to be by herself for the holidays!?" Vinny asked, his eyes narrowing.

"Don't make a fuss. She's embarrassed and doesn't want to stay. She didn't expect me to be serious about Faith."

"She can't be alone on Christmas day," Gina said, twisting her hands in her lap.

A few minutes later, Caprice rolled her large suitcase past the family room. The whole family, minus the kids, got up and followed her into the hallway, all protesting loudly about her leaving.

Faith was sure the majority of them hated Caprice, and yet everyone was trying to wrap up food for her, insisting she just stay or at least stay to open her presents, but Caprice refused.

"I'm going, and there's nothing any of you can say to stop me," Caprice said, her face flaming.

Gina seemed relieved, though she continued to protest the departure. By this point Caprice's gifts had been put into bags, and she'd been loaded down with Tupperware filled with Christmas Eve leftovers—

enough food to last her a week if she got caught out in a snowstorm.

Faith felt oddly uncomfortable with Caprice leaving. Maybe nothing had happened between her and Leo. If it had, why would she be leaving like this?

When the cab arrived and took Caprice away, Faith and Leo drifted back into the family room to open their abandoned presents.

When he'd been gone with Caprice, she'd stared at the pile with her name on it, unable to believe anybody had gotten her anything or that Leo had gotten her so many things. She'd reminded herself he was keeping up appearances and doing what the family would expect him to do if he were engaged.

Gifts from other members of the family included an imported Italian leather journal, a nice fountain pen with her full name engraved in a classy script: *Miss Faith Jacobson*, sweaters, a few wool scarves, and boots. Someone had spoken with Leo to get her sizes. Aside from midnight Mass the previous night, she hadn't been allowed out of the house. She wasn't sure any of that would change, but she thanked everyone and tried to look happy.

Then came the Leo gifts. There was some jewelry in Tiffany blue boxes, wrapped with white satin ribbons, as well as a couple of sexy—though still classy—dresses. Where did he expect her to wear these? Was he going to take her out? Was this for show? She looked up with a question in her eyes, but he turned away and went back to opening his things.

"Hey, Angelo, this is nice, thank you," Leo said, holding up a clearly expensive black leather jacket.

"It fell off a truck," his brother retorted, the sarcasm thick in his voice.

Uncle Sal punched Angelo in the arm.

"Owww. What?"

Uncle Sal shook his head.

When Faith got through all her gifts, she turned to Leo and kissed him. It was awkward at first because she'd never initiated anything intimate with him before, even as part of the ruse.

After an initial shocked tension, Leo relaxed under her kiss, his fingers threading through her hair. She couldn't tell if he was acting or if he wanted her, but soon the family started making kissy and *oooooh* noises. Mostly the kids who had been distracted from their video game. All human beings under the age of fourteen had a special mental alarm that went off whenever someone was making out in their vicinity.

Faith broke the kiss and looked down, unable to bring herself to look into his eyes to see what might be there. Desire. Pity. Indifference.

"I got you one other thing."

"You already got me too much," she whispered, too aware of all the eyes on them.

"Just wait a second."

He left the room and returned a few minutes later with a big, wrapped box that had large holes in it and was making sounds. First thumps, as whatever it was ran and slammed itself into the side, then scratching noises, and plaintive, irritated mewls. Somebody wasn't happy about their accommodations.

That made two of them.

"You got me a *kitten*?"

He grinned. "Damn, the surprise is spoiled. Open it. You don't know what color or what kind, yet."

Faith wasn't sure what it was about the kitten that undid her when nothing else did. The rest could be part of keeping the lie going, but getting her another pet was personal and considerate, a gift no one in the family would expect. It was him making an effort to co-exist with her or maybe something deeper.

She tore through the wrapping and lifted the lid to find a white Persian ball of fluff staring up at her with too-innocent blue eyes. The kitten squeaked.

"Oh my gosh. It's so cute!"

"So you like her?"

"I love her! Thank you!"

Leo looked taken aback by the sheer joy, and it occurred to her, he'd never seen her truly happy before now.

Later that evening, as Leo savored his coffee and cannoli, his mind flashed to the dungeon. He'd wanted to take more time, make more welts. He'd wanted to make his willing victim stay displayed for him while he sipped a glass of wine and admired the marks he'd left. He wanted to enjoy it at his leisure, with the gag firmly in her mouth so she wouldn't speak and destroy the moment. He wanted to pretend it was Faith. Why couldn't he have Caprice's masochism and Faith's sweet spirit combined into one woman?

By now it was clear Faith was submissive, but she wasn't kinky. Caprice was kinky, but she wasn't submissive. The universe was playing a cruel joke on him.

After dinner, the family retired to the game room, where there was a larger flat screen, as well as a poker table and a pool table, and a couple of free-standing arcade games: Pac Man and Donkey Kong—the only two Leo had ever gotten into. Yes, he was that old school.

The kids fought over the TV and who got to hook up their video game equipment, which game they would play, and who got to play. One faction: the girls, claimed that the boys had gotten to hook up their game system in the family room that morning, and so it was their turn. The boys claimed this was a bigger screen and they had a racing game that would look awesome on such a large screen and the girls had a stupid game that would play fine on any stupid screen.

Leo stepped in the middle. "How about we watch a Christmas movie, something you all can enjoy?" He wasn't keen on hearing either group yell at the screen all evening.

"No, that's lame," Michael said. "Can we go swim? We brought our suits."

Leo smiled and shook his head. "Of course you did. Go, then." In truth, he was happy to have some of the noise dispersed to another part of the house and the kids out of his hair for a while.

Vinny, Uncle Sal, Uncle Bernie, and a couple of the other men sat around the poker table divvying up chips. The women were still in the kitchen, cleaning.

Leo had asked Faith to join him so she wouldn't be left with the women. After the Caprice incident and the drama the night before with Gemma, he didn't want to leave Faith to the wolves who would poke around in her head for as many dirty details as they could.

He joined her on the sofa, and she snuggled against him for a long time, not speaking. He wanted to take her somewhere private and find out what she suspected or knew about what had happened that afternoon leading to Caprice's departure, but he waited until it was time for bed.

His mother gave him a conflicted look as he led Faith to his room. He suspected she knew something had happened with Caprice. If she'd known the details, it would have sent her into a Christmas Day heart attack. It was bad enough she thought something normal and vanilla had happened.

In her head, her son sleeping in the same room with Faith might keep his interest off Caprice, but at the price of living in sin. Such a conundrum. Leo was glad he didn't have to live in his mother's mental cottage.

He shut the door and locked it. Faith was beside the bed with the kitten who they'd decided to leave in the box with the top off when they weren't playing with her until she was fully litter trained. The box was far too tall for the little cotton ball to climb out of, though she made quite an angry and repeated effort.

"Did you decide what you're going to call her?" Leo asked as he stripped down.

Faith looked away from him when he got down to his boxers and turned her attention back to the box. "Snowball. I know, stupid name."

"It's not stupid. She's too warm for a snowball, but she looks the part."

His nudity made her uncomfortable, but it was his room and his bed and he didn't wear clothes to bed. And Faith shouldn't either. It was unnatural. She should be grateful he wasn't pushing the issue. After his family was gone, she could go back to her room and feel safe behind her own locked door.

"Get your pajamas on and let's go to bed," he said.

She looked relieved that he wasn't going to insist on her nudity and scurried into the bathroom to change. Even with his liaison with Caprice, he was aroused again, so he couldn't blame her for the fear. So sweet and defenseless. She always looked as if she'd stepped out of a professional soft-focus portrait.

Caprice was probably right about the woodland creatures. He had a red-haired Snow White in his castle. But weren't redheads supposed to be more fiery? More opinionated and strong-willed? He'd waited endlessly for that part of her personality to assert itself, but if it existed at all, it came out in small, ineffective protests. He didn't mind her reserved nature, but it meant he had to be more careful with her. He was never confused on where Caprice was mentally, but Faith held back more of herself. Too much.

She came out of the bathroom in pajamas with images of various chocolate candies on them and slid into bed. He turned out the light and joined her. Squish kneaded the pillow between them and curled against the soft fabric. Max knew better than to get on the master's bed. The dog briefly raised his head from the chair he'd squeezed himself into, his tongue hanging out happily, as if he knew what was coming for the entitled kitty.

Leo picked the cat up and set her down on the floor. Squish gave him a dirty reply halfway between a growl and a meow, then went to the kitten's box to lay next to it. Snowball settled with the close presence of the other cat.

It was quiet for a blissful five minutes, until Faith's previously silent tears got loud enough for Leo to notice.

He turned on the lamp. "Why are you crying?"

"I'm scared."

"Of?"

Faith's body was curled away from him, shaking. Even if he hadn't heard her, the strength of her crying was becoming enough to vibrate the bed.

She sat up. "I know we aren't in a real relationship, and it's not my business what you do with Caprice, but this is my *life* at stake. Did something happen with her?"

"It did."

"What if it gets serious? What happens then? Will you let me go? Will Angelo kill me?"

How could he convince her he and Caprice would never be serious? That train had long ago left the station. He pulled her against him and held her, stroking her hair.

"Shhhh. Stop your crying. I won't let Angelo kill you."

"But this morning . . . "

"This morning I needed you to understand I don't appreciate ingratitude after I saved your life. If you wanted to die, then yes, I would have let Angelo kill you. What would be the point of keeping you alive against your will and shrinking my options in the process? But if you want to live, I'll never kill you or let anyone else hurt you. Are we on the same page?"

"Yes," she whispered, but it didn't sound like she was convinced. A moment later, he knew why. "I just . . . you're going to resent me or take what you want, anyway. This isn't realistic. It can't go on forever like this. You have to know that." She huddled in on herself after she'd forced the words out as if he might hurt her for saying them.

"Are you jealous of Caprice?" It might be easier to deal with this from another angle. She'd sent him multiple mixed signals about her desires since the previous day when the family had arrived.

"I don't know. I know you don't want me, but this lie . . . it hurts."

He lifted her chin. "Faith, look at me."

Reluctantly, her gaze met his.

"I want you. But I'm not a rapist, and I'm not going to terrorize you with my kinks when they would alarm and upset you. Between Caprice and you, I'd rather have you any day. If only you were wired like me."

"I can't do those things you want . . . in the dungeon . . . but I could do the more normal stuff. I *am* attracted, and with you mostly leaving me alone these past few weeks, I feel safer with you than I did when I first came here."

Leo shook his head. "I'd rather be celibate than in a vanilla relationship. I was preparing for a life of celibacy anyway before Emilio." He didn't voice that perhaps *this* was his penance. He'd wanted the priesthood to hide and subdue the things inside him that made him feel different. At the same time, he wasn't going to live vanilla. It would be like Angelo settling down with a woman and having babies.

"I don't do normal," he said. "You're either in it all the way with me, or not at all."

"Aren't we in it right now? Is the way you're holding me in your bed platonic?"

If Caprice had said it, it would have been with an air of sarcasm. He would have wanted to smack the smart look off her face. But Faith was just being honest.

"When my family leaves, you'll go back to your room in the east wing. I admit it's dangerous getting this close, but we'll both get over it and readjust when the holiday is behind us."

The next thing she said was so quiet, he had to strain to hear it. "W-what if I gave consent?"

His breath stopped and his grip on her tightened. She couldn't mean that. She didn't trust that Caprice wasn't a danger to her. She only wanted to keep him from going to the hotel.

He took a slow breath, not trusting his voice. "If you gave consent for what?"

"T-the things you like."

"I think you should think about the consequences of that very long and hard. If you give me your consent, you'll be treated as my slave, and I won't allow you to take it back. You make that choice and you don't get any more free choices in this house." Her body tensed against his. Good. She needed to know she couldn't tease him with this. He wouldn't let her play with his emotions by trying to give him something only to take it back every time she became scared of it.

"W-would you be mean to me? I mean . . . would you be a lot different than you are now? Would I still be safe with you?"

He pressed a kiss to her forehead. "You'll always be safe with me. I would expect you to obey me at all times. If you disobeyed, you would be punished. The dungeon is both for punishment and for play. I play rough, but I'm not mean."

"I . . . um . . . "

Leo placed a finger against her lips. "Not tonight, Faith. You can tell me your choice after the family leaves. You need more than one day to think about it. Trust me."

She lay against her pillow, the relief of being spared such a drastic decision for another week palpable. When she was settled in, Leo got up and began to get dressed. Now that he was thinking about it, he'd never get to sleep with a willing slut waiting for him at a hotel.

"Where are you going?"

He gave her a stern look as he put on his belt. If she was contemplating giving herself fully to him, surely she knew that prying into his personal life wouldn't be acceptable.

"You're going to see her, aren't you?"

A tear slid down her cheek, and part of him wanted to punish her for it, though she hadn't yet signed away her free will. Even without malice and intent, tears could manipulate, and he wouldn't be controlled by her emotional outbursts, no matter how sincere they might be.

Leo didn't give her the satisfaction of an answer. Instead he grabbed his wallet and keys off the night table and flicked off the light. "Go to sleep. I'm locking this door behind me. I'll let myself in when I get back."

He was a bastard for doing this, but Faith would never consent to his desires. She didn't have it in her. She was merely bargaining for her life. Caprice was his last chance for a while to get his needs met from someone he wasn't in danger of developing an emotional attachment to or damaging beyond repair.

Leo went through the kitchen to the wine cellar door, then down below to the den and grabbed his large, black medical bag from the secret compartment behind the bookcase. He unlocked the door to the dungeon to load the bag with the things he would need. Ropes—the scratchier and more unpleasant against the skin, the better—a gag, blindfold, various whipping implements, various clamps, a couple of dildos but no vibrators this time.

He was angry with Caprice, with himself, with Faith, with Angelo, with the whole fucking world. Some of it was nobody's fault, but for each troubled thought and motivation spiraling through his mind, Leo needed to assign a villain. He didn't plan on letting Caprice have an orgasm tonight. All he wanted was for her to feel raw and used to appease him.

She was such a masochist that it would be fine with her. Whatever he wanted to do, she just wanted him to touch her. If it weren't for her personality, she'd be the perfect woman. But Leo couldn't trust her. He'd always be paranoid about her motivations. Relationships were all one big chess game to her, and he wasn't going to be a pawn on her board.

Standing outside in the snow, bundled in a black coat, holding a bag filled with torture devices, he felt like Mr. Hyde going to set about the dirty business of feeding the darker impulse so the mild-mannered Jekyll could continue to go about life in peace during the day.

"You know it's a bad idea."

Leo jumped at the sound of his brother's voice, and Angelo stepped around the corner he'd been lurking behind. He dropped his cigarette into the snow and it hissed as the frozen water put it out, sending a spiral of smoke up from the ground.

"Damnit, Ange. I know it's a bad idea." He didn't pretend confusion. They knew each other well enough to dispense with the ritual of denial.

"Isn't Faith in your room?" Angelo pointed up at the window.

"She is."

His brother shook his head. "I practically gift wrapped your new toy and you won't even play with her. It's enough to give a brother a complex."

"It's not right," Leo said.

"And using Caprice is?"

When Angelo became the moral one, you knew the earth had tilted fully off its axis and only flaming apocalypse could follow.

"There are degrees," Leo said. "Caprice knows this isn't going anywhere. She's not a victim. She's never been a victim for one day in her life. Faith is different.

She's at my mercy, and that wasn't her choice. I can't stand the thought of hurting her."

"I'm pretty sure *this* hurts her. I've seen the way she looks at you," Angelo said. "She's ripe for picking." He was determined to play matchmaker and see that his gift was put to good use. His new strategy was temptation. Leo was surprised his brother hadn't followed him and Faith around with mistletoe.

"You know what I mean. I mean *damage* her. We aren't in a relationship. We're two people stuck together by circumstance. That's all."

"Keep telling yourself that."

Angelo pulled out another cigarette and leaned against the building. He flicked the silver lighter, and his face glowed as he took a drag to catch the flame. When he was finished being dramatic, he said, "Maybe you're afraid to be happy. I never noticed it before, but I think you aren't satisfied in life unless you feel guilty about something. My brother the saint. Tell me, does the weight of the world ever get heavy?"

"Fuck off."

Angelo's laughter followed him through the snow to his car.

Thirteen

Leo had called five hotels before he'd found one to put Caprice up in. The last thing he'd expected was for The Plaza to have an opening on Christmas day or to have a room available for an entire week block. Sometimes life was funny. He'd set her up in a deluxe courtyard room on the ninth floor. It was the least he could do, isolating her during the holidays as he was. But he didn't want her around Faith.

He hadn't bothered calling, and it was coming close to midnight, but Caprice would let him in if she knew what was good for her. He'd caught the floor when he'd made the reservation, but now the room number escaped him. He took a breath and approached the registration desk, trying not to look sinister.

"Could you tell me Caprice Clementi's room number please?"

"I'm sorry, sir, but we can't give out the room numbers of our guests. I could telephone her for you if you'd like?"

Leo looked like he was there to whack her, so he couldn't blame the hotel staff for their concern. And he *did* intend to whack her, just not in the way they probably thought. He set down his bag and pulled his wallet out, placing his driver's license and credit card on the marble. "Leo Raspallo. I paid for the room."

Panic entered the man's eyes at the name, then his attention turned to tapping keys at a speed that would impress any secretary. He checked the name on the license and the card number against what was in the computer and cleared his throat. "I apologize, Mr. Raspallo. I didn't know. She's in room 912. Would you like a key card?"

"I would."

Why knock if he was paying for her accommodations? He was here to take what he wanted from her anyway, why pretend with pleasantries and knocks on doors that he wasn't fully entitled to her body until she got on a plane?

The man scanned the card and slid it across the counter with a weak smile. Leo returned a smile of his own, collected his bag, and got on the elevator.

Inside 912, Leo hung his coat in the entryway. A lush master bathroom was on the left. And then further in, toward the back, was the bedroom. He was surprised when he reached the foot of the bed to find Caprice going at it with a strange man—no doubt an old friend she felt justified in catching up with.

"I'm sorry, Caprice. Did you feel it was appropriate to *hook up* in a room I'm paying for?"

She scrambled off the man she'd been straddling and struggled to cover herself with the bedsheets. The man looked uncertain.

"Hello," Leo said, addressing the stranger. "I'm Leo Raspallo. Get out, while I'm feeling generous."

There were moments having that name came in handy. Though his hands were mostly clean of the family business, Leo never hesitated using his name to make an impression.

The man's eyes widened. "I-I'm sorry. I-I didn't know she was yours."

"Hey!" Caprice snapped. "I'm not furniture."

"Oh, you are if I say you are." Leo appraised her like a piece of meat he was considering from the butcher. He turned back to the man who was trying to get to his clothing without flashing everyone in the room. "What's your name?"

"I ... uh ... um ... John."

"Mm-hmm," Leo said, not buying that name for a minute. "Well, *John,* I think it would be better if you put your clothing on out in the hallway. Don't you agree?"

"But ... I ... uh ... "

Leo raised an eyebrow. *John* grabbed his clothes and fled from the room. When Leo was alone with Caprice, he said, "You're going to have to be punished for being such a rude, naughty slut, of course."

This would have had Faith huddling in a corner, but Caprice smirked. "Was that scene necessary?"

He shrugged. "I've got a lot of pent-up energy."

"I didn't know you'd come see me," she said, pouting.

"Like you said, Faith is never going to be enough."
She smiled.

"Same rules as before. Starting now, no eye contact, address me as Master, only. Do you understand?"

Caprice looked down at the pattern on the bedspread. A shuddering breath left her when she said, "Yes, Master."

"Did you manage an orgasm with him?" Leo asked.

"No, Master."

"I'm not surprised. You won't be having one with me, either." His pronouncement excited her more. Perhaps she saw a challenge in it—or a game. She'd find out soon enough he was serious. The only person coming tonight would be him. Or there would be dire consequences.

This time, he took it slow. There were no guests to get back to, and for better or worse, Faith knew where he was. He spent half an hour tying Caprice up. He wanted her immobile and unable to squirm away, while still being accessible and open.

"Ow! These ropes are too tight, and they're scratching me."

Leo stepped back to observe his work, ignoring her whining.

"Leo!"

He extracted a collapsible, stainless steel cane from his bag, then with a flick of his wrist, extended it to its full size. He whacked her on the ass, and she let out a squeal.

"What did I say my name was?"

"Master," she gasped. That tinge of fear was back in her eyes, and remembering herself, she quickly averted her gaze to the floor as the tears started to flow.

Leo went to the minibar and poured himself a drink, then sat in an overstuffed chair, his eyes drinking in his captive.

"Why are you with her?" Caprice asked after a few minutes.

"What kind of question is that? She's my fiancée."

"But she's not like us. I just don't understand what you see in her. Are you trying to be a martyr? I can give you what you want. If you break off the engagement, I'll do anything. I swear. We shouldn't have broken up."

He downed the rest of his drink and placed the glass on the side table, his eyes narrowing. "You'll manipulate and connive and cheat and get whatever you want while pretending to be my slave. You'll play the good girl when I'm watching and do whatever the hell you want when I'm not. I put you up here as my guest, and I walk in to find you screwing another man under the sheets my credit card paid for. We might not be in a relationship, but that's tacky by anyone's standards."

She turned away.

"Well, am I wrong?"

"You want too much," she said, barely above a whisper.

"Yes, and that was the conclusion we came to the last time we had this conversation when we were breaking up. You gave me an ultimatum, and I told you to leave. The fact that you felt you could give me an ultimatum is 90 percent of the problem. I don't want to play a game with you!"

"Then why are you here playing one? Is the vanilla suburban wife game going to be any more appealing to you? Missionary position, lights off. Is that better than this? I can't give you everything, Leo, but I can give you something."

Two women in his bed in the same night, both promising him half of the whole he craved. It wasn't enough. From either of them. He rose slowly, alcohol and predation running through his veins and bent to grab the back of her neck.

His face moved in close to hers. He practically growled when he spoke. "I'm not playing into your manipulation again, Caprice. We are not getting back together. If you can't handle that, I will pack up my things and leave now. I want to hear you say it, say you understand me and you accept the terms of what we're doing here."

She glared up at him. "What *are* we doing here, Leo?"

He released her and picked up the cane again. With one hand, he covered her mouth, and with the other, he raised the implement. A blur of silver sliced through the air and connected with her flesh. She let out a muffled howl against his hand. When she'd composed herself again, he released her.

"You can't follow the simplest rules. I said while I'm here you will call me *Master*. If that's too complic-ated for you and too much for you to remember, I'll leave."

Panic filled her eyes. "No, wait. I'll be good. I'm sorry, Master. I'll do what you want. I promise."

"Say you understand and accept my terms. I have to know that you understand you won't gain a relationship out of this. If that's what you think your goal is, lose the delusion."

"I understand, Master." Her head dropped to the bed and a single tear slid down her cheek.

Leo had a moment's hesitation where everything paused and went quiet. Inside the stillness of that moment, he knew the truth. She loved him. Or what passed as love in her world, anyway. She felt for him as much as she was capable of feeling for another human being, and he didn't return that affection. It was wrong to keep going here, to play with her. No matter what she said, deep down he knew she believed if she pleased him enough, he might keep her and send Faith away. She didn't know how to be honest, and that was a deal breaker for him.

And yet, here she was all tied up, begging him to use her. Faced with a long stretch of celibacy and no outlets for his sadism in sight, Caprice was too much temptation. She was a last meal on death row.

But like before, being here with her was weak satisfaction, like masturbation that results in a bad orgasm, where you go through the motions only to find the resulting pleasure is such a dim shadow as to have been a complete waste of time.

That was how Leo felt standing in the deluxe courtyard room on the ninth floor of The Plaza hotel. Having driven half an hour from his estate to get to the edge of the city and then another forty-five minutes fighting traffic, and here was a willing woman tied down, waiting for him to use her in whatever way appealed to him.

But when he looked at her, in his mind's eye, he saw Faith there, pushing past her fears to submit. It would mean more because it was a sacrifice for her. As much as Caprice wanted to do anything to be with him, once she had him, her tune would change. Her resolve would melt like snow to reveal the dead grass underneath. Her willingness to do anything would drift away and he'd be left with yet another sham.

Caprice, he would never own. She wasn't the kind of thing a man could own. Faith, on the other hand, was his. Even with his resistance to hurting her, she belonged to him and would never be able to walk out the door and out of his life. If he wanted to tie her down and whip her, he could do it. He could do any depraved thing to her that his mind could dream up. The only barrier was his conscience. If he didn't do this with Caprice, if he didn't take the edge off the hunger, he would end up losing control with Faith. Then he'd be the monster he'd always suspected he was.

Caprice didn't resist when he took the gag from his bag and pushed the rubber ball into her mouth. The truth was, even being who she was, her words could still touch him. Without them, she was a mere thing, a masturbatory sleeve, a blow up doll, a punching bag. Without a voice she had no life or form to stop him or create uneasy guilt. The guilt would come later. With or without consent, it always did, and yet, he couldn't stop himself from gorging on the hedonistic delight of a woman's naked and bound body taking pain for his gratification.

Faith thought she was safe with him? She was a fool. If he couldn't keep the beast in check, she'd find out how much of a fool she was soon enough. Wanting to be with him? She had no idea what she was asking. Neither woman did.

With the gag in place, it was safe to take his time to wring out every ounce of agony he could take from the woman who had stupidly put herself in his hands. Although it was lightweight, the steel cane was more harsh than the rattan. It would be dishonest to say he'd chosen the steel only because it was collapsible and fit easily into the bag.

The welts and bruises he'd left on her that morning were more visible than before, so he moved on to an unmarked area on her thighs. She screamed around the gag, as if she was dying with every stroke, the tears streaming down her face.

When he'd marked all of her he could safely mark, he collapsed the cane and returned it to the bag. He watched the relief fill her and then drain back out again when he pulled a whip from the bag.

"It'll hurt more if you're tense."

She whimpered behind the rubber obstruction. The display was pitiful enough for him to show some mercy. What was more, it wasn't a calculated act meant to control him. It was real begging. After the cane, when she was still overloaded from the soreness of earlier in the day, her distress was genuine.

Leo unsnapped the leather from the gag and pulled it from her mouth. "Tell me, what did John have to say about the welts and bruises on your ass? Do you think he realized it was me who put them there?"

"I didn't let him see them. I was on top so it wouldn't hurt and he wouldn't notice."

"Ashamed?" Shame didn't fit on Caprice. He'd always envied her that.

"He wouldn't understand."

"I see. So it appears I'm not the only one dipping a toe into the vanilla pool."

Even in pain, she rolled her eyes, breaking the spell of the few moments he'd had with her before. "Andy is an old friend. We went to school together. We ran into each other in a bar. We were lonely. It just happened."

Leo put the gag back in her mouth and started on her back. When he drew blood, he moved on to a fresh area until she was marked to his satisfaction.

Half an hour later, he cursed himself as he surveyed the damage. She would heal. He hadn't done any permanent harm, but if she went into a nasty streak, she had evidence to show the police. There were witnesses placing him here. Just another example of how she held all the power and why he didn't want this.

If Leo wanted to break free of Caprice, it wouldn't be until after the holiday when she was home. He'd have to be more careful about leaving marks the rest of the week. As vindictive as she could be, she would use what had been consensual to put him behind bars. He didn't do well caged.

He untied the ropes and unsnapped the gag, placing everything carefully back in his bag. There would be time for other toys another day.

"Why are you stopping?"

"Stretch out on your stomach and don't question me. The rules are still in place."

"Yes, Master," she managed.

Leo removed a smaller bag from the larger one and unzipped it to reveal bandages and ointment. He went to the bathroom to wash his hands, then he smoothed the cream over each of her whip marks and welts and bruises. After the ointment he sprayed a soothing antiseptic spray, then applied bandages.

When he was finished, he undressed and got in the bed, pulling her against him and cradling her, much as he had Faith a few hours before.

"You don't want to be with me, Caprice. You like the idea of me. The reality is never quite as good."

"That's not true," she said, her words muffled against his chest.

"Yes, it is."

Fourteen

Faith wore a glitzy black evening gown and some of the jewelry Leo had given her for Christmas. When she'd first unwrapped the dress, she couldn't figure out when or where she would wear such a thing, but as it turned out, Leo's New Year's Eve party was more of an affair than Christmas.

The party was black tie optional, and some took the *optional* seriously. Mariella, Leo's seven-year-old niece, had decided to wear her princess Halloween costume, including tiara. Leo's Aunt Mimi sported something almost as creative: a red dress that had feathers coming out of it, along with a matching feather boa and headpiece. She had glittery red shoes, long gloves, and a cigarette popping out of an old-fashioned cigarette holder. Quite possibly a Halloween costume, too.

"I hope you don't think you're smoking that in the house," Leo said, appearing from nowhere in a classic tuxedo.

"No respect for elders anymore," Mimi lamented. "Relax, Leonardo, it's part of my look."

Leo's grandmother had opted for more casual attire: gray pajamas with puppies on them—in complete defiance of the occasion. "I'm dropping right into bed after this," Grammie had announced loudly after her fourth glass of champagne, which was technically supposed to be for the New Year, not the hours leading up to it. But Leo had been prepared with plenty of alcohol. He'd said Grammie's tolerance was legendary.

On one table were glass champagne flutes with bottles of champagne, and on another were plastic champagne flutes with bottles of sparkling white grape juice for the kids. A large cheese tray occupied a table in the middle.

Most of the kids wore party hats and played with noisemakers. Angelo, Davide, and Uncle Sal sat in a corner in black suits with their hair slicked back like they were on mafia business.

It was half an hour until midnight. Netting with red, black, and silver balloons was strung below the high ceiling of the dining room. Hanging close to the ceiling was a long, clear, plastic bag with red confetti inside. There were two pull cords against the wall, one that would release the balloons and another that would release the confetti.

The large flat screen from the game room had been rolled in so they could watch the ball drop in the city. Though it wasn't far from here, the experience of standing in Times Square was for tourists and those who enjoyed adventures in bladder control. Faith was glad the family had chosen to stay inside Leo's warm fortress instead.

He interacted with his family, laughing and talking while he kept her close, a hand on the small her back as if reassuring himself she was still there. In public, he'd been the perfect fiancé, holding her hand, kissing her at all the appropriate moments, and looking at her as if her existence alone made the rest of his world real and solid. But behind the door of his bedroom he kept his distance, not making conversation, rolling over immediately to go to sleep—when he came to bed at all. If he still wanted her, he was doing a great job of hiding it.

Several nights he hadn't come to bed until way into the night after she'd already fallen asleep. She knew where he was during those times. Faith didn't want to speculate about what happened in the hotel between Leo and the other woman. Probably a lot of it was stuff she'd just as soon not do, but the threat of Caprice loomed ever larger in her mind, her stomach now tied in knots by the fear that the other woman wouldn't go back to Vegas, and the larger fear that being Leo's mistress wasn't her end game.

If Caprice didn't get on that plane, it was only a matter of time for Faith. Though Angelo had started to be nicer to her, she didn't hold any illusions. Being with Leo kept her breathing.

A few minutes before midnight, Demetri and the rest of the staff made sure a plastic or glass flute filled with the appropriate beverage was in everybody's hands.

At midnight, Demetri pulled the cords and the balloons and confetti came down. Leo and a few others were smart enough to raise their glass to their lips at exactly midnight to take a sip before pieces of foil drifted into their champagne flutes. Faith had to drink around a shiny bit of red.

Leo took her drink after she'd had a sip and put it on the table along with his, then he pulled her into a kiss she believed with every ounce of her being. It was filled with passion and longing and tenderness. It was the promise of new beginnings. It was penance. It was everything a kiss could ever convey wrapped into one brief moment of mouths pressed together. She wondered if Leo's kiss spoke any truth, or if he was that accomplished of an actor. Was he thinking of Caprice as he pulled Faith closer? Was that the reason for his intensity?

She wondered if her own desperation and fear were being broadcast. Did he read as many words and meanings into her kiss as she had his? He pulled away and stared at her until she couldn't take the intensity of his gaze any longer.

"Well, that's it for this old woman. I am going to bed, and I am sleeping in. Leo, don't you rush me out the door tomorrow. I'll leave after I've had some good sleep and some good food. And maybe some hair of the dog." Alba winked and wobbled on her feet.

"I wouldn't dream of it, Grammie," Leo said, enlisting Demetri to help her to her room. Papi was still up and ready to play a game of cards with some of the men.

When Leo and Faith reached their own room, Faith went to the bathroom to change, still not able to disrobe in front of him, not when he represented so much of a threat. As attracted as she was, even with him leaving to see Caprice most nights, she couldn't bring herself to do anything that might look like an invitation.

What she'd offered on Christmas night still hung over her. The choice Leo would ask about once the family was gone the next day. And she still didn't know her answer. Some fucked-up part of her brain wished Caprice could settle for mistress. He could do his scary kinky stuff with her, and he could be sweet and safe with Faith. But whether Leo would go for such an unconventional option, she knew Caprice could never be trusted. She wouldn't stop until she had everything, even if the price was Faith's life.

Faith came out of the bathroom in her pajamas and hung the black dress in the closet, wondering if she'd be here to wear it next year.

She glanced down at the cardboard box beside the bed. Squish may have bullied Max, but she loved the new kitten, insisting after the first night on sleeping inside the box snuggled with Snowball. The two were already settled in for the night, contentedly purring.

Leo was in bed, writing furiously in a black leather journal.

"New Year's resolutions?" she asked, feeling stupid for saying anything at all. She was a child next to him. It felt as if everything he did and thought was more sophisticated than she would ever understand. There was something wise and worldly about him. He knew things she couldn't fathom, and he was probably writing them all down in the mysterious black book for future generations to marvel at.

"Something like that. Go to sleep."

She was surprised when he turned the lamp off and lay down. What did that mean? If it was Caprice's last night here, wouldn't he want to be with her? Maybe she wasn't leaving. Faith had to know—whether she would believe the answer was another question entirely.

"Leo?"

"Yes, Faith?"

"Is she leaving tomorrow?"

"Yes, she's leaving. Don't worry your pretty head about her. She's getting on the plane with Vinny."

"Okay."

Faith held her breath at the airport as Caprice handed over her boarding pass. She sent one last pleading look to Leo, begging to stay, but he returned a stern expression and shook his head. It wasn't until Caprice walked through the gates and the plane took off that Faith relaxed.

It was quiet when they got back to the house, even with a dog, two cats, and a full staff of servants. There were no kids running around screaming, no Gina trying to plan a wedding, no Gemma shooting glares at Leo and complaining, no Caprice scheming to get him into bed. No Angelo or Davide or Uncle Sal or Papi.

Demetri took her coat and hung it in the hall closet while she stood there, not sure what she should do now or where she should go. She'd forgotten how uncomfortable things could be with Leo and no set routine. During the holidays there had been nothing but distraction. And in those moments she'd seen him as more than her captor.

In fact, he'd become her rescuer more than anything. Her protector, constantly keeping her safe, from Angelo, from Caprice, from Gemma. Even from his mom, though the threats from Gina were all well-intentioned.

No matter Leo's sexuality, he could be kind and caring. He'd taken care of his family, been a good host, given her a kitten. But now the *choice* hung over her. She'd be lying if she said she didn't want him.

The feel of his lips pressed against hers and his hand wrapped in hers had been imprinted forever. In brief moments when her guard was down, she'd fallen for him a degree at a time, imagining this was her life and not merely a play for an audience who didn't realize they were watching one.

She'd expected Leo to demand her answer as soon as they crossed the threshold, as if it were some imaginary line that defined the rest of her life, but he went to the back of the house, toward his office, shattering the importance of the moment. Faith went to the game room and plopped down on one of the sofas in front of the television, trying to decide what to do. She'd assumed he would insist on her answer. Now that Caprice was no longer here to service his needs, she'd thought there would be pressure to do something, but he'd acted as if she didn't exist at all.

Maybe he didn't want her anymore. He'd seen what he could have with a woman who could handle him and now he wasn't interested in a woman little more than a child. Faith angrily scrubbed away an escaping tear. Why should she care one way or the other? None of this had been her choice. It wasn't as if she'd pursued him. He'd brought her home in the same way he'd brought the kitten home. Like some pet, some animal who didn't get a choice in where they were going to live, or the conditions they would live in, or the kindness or meanness of their master.

The images on the screen flickered past her, a series of flashing lights with no content her mind could grab onto. Likewise the spoken words were mere noise. She turned off the TV and went after Leo.

She found him in his office, a room she'd been forbidden to enter. He sat at his desk, writing in that damned black book again. He didn't look up.

"Yes, Faith?"

"Y-you said I could tell you my answer after everybody left."

He closed the book and spun in his chair to face her, one leg propped on top of the other in a relaxed posture. If this meeting created any emotions, he didn't give them away.

"Well?" he prodded, after a few moments.

The answer is no. I'm sorry. I'm going to go back to my room in the east wing if that's okay. "Yes. I want to be with you."

"Don't you want to see the dungeon before you make that decision?"

Her eyes went to the floor, unable to stand the way he looked at her. Through her. "Okay."

She waited for him to give her some kind of instruction, tell her what to do with the rest of her life or just this moment. What to call him? Would she have to call him Master like he'd insisted that first night?

The idea was still weird to her, but at least it wasn't terrifying. Not like the other worse things he would insist upon.

The chair creaked when he got up. "Follow me."

He took her down several hallways she hadn't been down because they were forbidden. They were smaller and more ominous, warning visitors away with their lack of light. At the end of one of the hallways was a large metal door. Leo took a key from his pocket, unlocked the door, and pushed a switch on the wall.

A string of LED lights along the ceiling came on, lighting the path of the carpeted spiral stairs that went on and on into an endless abyss, maybe even into hell. And here was the devil standing beside her with a smooth smile and his hand extended like a gentleman toward the waiting doom.

"After you," he said.

If she went down these steps, would he ever let her back up them again? She chided herself for being so dramatic. They were getting married in June. Of course she'd come out again. Caprice had survived whatever they'd done together and kept coming back for more. Leo had killed the man who'd abused his sister. Whatever these feelings were, they couldn't be her worst fears. It didn't line up with the facts.

She was surprised the dungeon was posh. Like a cave one might escape to in order to read a book if there had been strong enough light.

"Look around. Nothing is off limits. I want you fully informed. No excuses."

Hesitantly, Faith explored the vast underground room. How it could be so big, so ominous, and so cozy all at once, she didn't know. There was standard living room furniture and a bed and a small kitchen and a bathroom. Then there were several pieces of black- and red-leather furniture that looked like high-fashion torture equipment. The actual dungeon part had concrete floors, while the apartment area was carpeted, though it was all one, unbroken space save for the bathroom.

Along one wall were several hooks that held mysterious metal objects, riding crops, whips, and paddles. Underneath this section was a tray of sorts that slid out from a slot in the wall and held long pieces of metal and wood. She trembled as she ran her fingers along the top of one of the metal rods. She didn't know what these rods were called, but she knew Leo hit people with them.

"Those are canes. Why don't you give one a nice slice through the air? You don't begin to truly under- stand it until you hear it."

Her hand shook as she picked up one of the imple- ments. The sound it made when it ripped through the air would have made her drop it and run if not for Leo's words interrupting her panic.

"With my medical knowledge, there are so many things I could do to you and bring you back from."

He was trying to scare her away. There was no other reason to say something so crazy when she was so close to giving him what he wanted.

Faith took a deep breath and placed the metal cane on the tray, but it slipped out of her hand and clattered on the concrete, bouncing several times, the tin sound ringing in her ears. She snatched it up and put it back, sliding the metal tray into the wall slot and taking a shaky breath to steady her nerves. Leo made no move to comfort her.

"Go ahead and check out the toy box. Everything I keep in there is made of materials I can clean. It's all been sterilized, so it's safe. Except the rope, but all the rope is new."

The giant black leather container was Pandora's box with all the evil of the world inside. Vibrators, dildos, handcuffs, ropes, anal plugs, containers of lubricant, and a few things she didn't recognize.

While the box was open, Faith imagined she heard screaming inside her head. Noise and warnings and anxiety swirled around her like invisible smoke. When she shut the box, they stopped. She turned to find Leo sitting on the red leather couch against the wall, his arms spread along the back, and she wondered for a second exactly how long she'd been staring into that box like some brainless zombie.

"Come here, sweetheart."

Making one foot move in front of the other felt like breaking out of a block of solid ice.

"No. Come on your knees."

She might have hesitated, except that crawling was so much less taxing than walking at the moment. She felt lightheaded. It required less force of will to travel across the floor on her hands and knees, no matter how demeaning it might be.

Maybe she could still get out of this. Would he allow her to make the choice to stop everything? If she stopped it, though, she might remain celibate the rest of her life, cloistered away in the glassed-in room with all the sunlight but no real warmth. How would she live, never being touched by this man? But how would she live down here letting him use all those things on her?

When she reached him, he stroked her hair and she leaned against his leg, trying not to cry. The last time she'd been this upset had been the night he'd brought her home. The difference now was that she knew what he would do, and it wouldn't be a one-time thing. This was something he *needed*.

"Why do you want this, Faith?" He continued to stroke her hair while he spoke in a soothing, low tone as if he were hypnotizing her. If only he had that power, everything would be easier.

"I-I want you, I-I want it to be real. I can't live a lie every year for your family, indefinitely. It would break me." There was a sad kind of pity on his face. When he caught her studying him, she looked back down. She couldn't look him in the eyes and still force herself to say the rest. "And you said you couldn't be vanilla. Y-you said you had to have the whole package."

"You watched me send Caprice away. Are you sure this isn't about your fears? I told you that she and I were never going to be an item. She's not what I want in my life."

"If not Caprice, it will be someone else. What then?"

"I would never put your life at risk."

"Can't you trust me and let me go? Don't you know me well enough to know I'll never say anything?"

"I may believe that, but Angelo won't."

She knew she might be digging a hole, but she had to say it. "I don't believe that's the reason you're keeping me."

He laughed. "What other reason could there be?"

Faith went quiet. There was no way she could put it into words, and if she succeeded she would only feel foolish when he laughed at her. Again. Maybe it was about Angelo and not being able to let an innocent bystander die. But he had to know that keeping her in a cage wasn't much better than a quick death.

"Go move your things back to your room, Faith. We aren't doing this."

"I-I'm sorry if I offended you."

"You haven't offended me, but we both know you don't want this."

"I want *you*." Even as she begged to be his, part of her hoped he would send her away and spare her.

"But not enough for this. I can see it written in your body language. This isn't for you. Go before I change my mind."

She hesitated.

"Go!"

Faith fled out of the dungeon. She didn't stop until she reached Leo's room. Whatever his reasoning, he didn't want her. She'd practically thrown herself at him, and he'd pushed her away. What the fuck kind of magic powers did Caprice have that made it possible for her to seduce Leo when Faith couldn't manage it? The other woman wasn't even that pretty.

Leo cursed at the empty room. *She said yes, you dumbass,* said the demon on one shoulder, who looked more like Angelo than Leo in his smooth Armani and scar-free face. *She's too scared for this, you did the right thing,* said Father Leo on the other shoulder.

In reality, he knew she wouldn't talk. She wasn't the type who wanted to be a hero or get involved with the police. Given all the time he'd spent with her, and the time Angelo had spent with her, he was certain he could convince his brother that she was safe to release into the wild.

But she was *his*. Even if he could never bring himself to break down and use her in the way he wanted, he'd grown used to thinking of her as his to protect and own. Even if he never whipped her or tied her up or fucked her, he owned her more than any woman who had ever been in this dungeon, and he couldn't bring himself to let that go. She was all promise and possibility—the only thing standing in his way was himself. And some day that barrier would crumble and he'd be free to have her.

Faith was his only chance to feed the urge that lived underneath every other urge. To own a human being was the driving need that underscored everything else. He couldn't bring himself to give that up, no matter how many weak rationalizations he had to make. He could never let her go.

It was like owning an exotic bird. The idea wasn't enough, a picture wasn't enough, visiting one at the zoo wasn't enough. It had to be there, in his home, in his possession.

Leo turned out the lights and locked up the dungeon, then he went back upstairs to his office and opened the black leather journal. He'd made lists of alternatives. There were kink clubs he could go to, people he could meet for casual flings. Ways he could do this that didn't involve Faith losing parts of herself she could never retrieve or him traveling further down a path of no return—sins that even a priest couldn't absolve him of.

A relationship with someone else was out of the question. No matter how obedient any potential sub was, letting her find out about Faith would be an extra complication he didn't need. What if Faith got fed up and tried to get help? He could trust Demetri and the rest of the staff. They'd been with the family for over a decade. He couldn't trust any random, kinky woman.

And subs were perceptive. Sometimes too perceptive. They spent all their time studying their dominant, learning to be receptive and available to his every need almost before he knew it himself. That kind of observation didn't create a fertile environment for lies. Whoever he brought into his home as more than a casual spank and fuck would figure out there was more to the Faith situation and his complicated tangle of feelings than whatever he would say. Then there would be jealousy and drama.

Whatever he did had to stay contained and emotionally distant with all the parameters laid out clearly in the beginning. It couldn't be another Caprice. He tried to push down the voice in his head that said he couldn't be happy with a woman who couldn't give him everything. And everything included her heart.

A month passed in frosted hell. Faith had been on the phone with Leo's mother more times than she could count, planning a wedding she didn't care about. More than once, Gina had remarked that she didn't seem very excited. Faith had told her she didn't like big events—all the people and expectation made her nervous. All she cared about was marrying Leo. This satisfied his mother.

She and Leo had been eating meals together in the smaller kitchen. Demetri and the other staff left them alone during these times, so either she cooked or Leo did, alternating between Italian and American cuisine.

Faith surprised him one night with cannolis for dessert. She'd noticed how much he'd liked them at Christmas and had gotten Gina's recipe one afternoon during a marathon wedding-planning conversation.

When she'd brought them to the table with his coffee, his face had lit up. His hand had inched across the table closer to hers before he'd abruptly pulled it back. After that, he'd stopped eating meals with her. When she tried to engage him, he claimed he had to work late and would grab something later.

It didn't matter what time of day she went to the kitchen, he wasn't there. Either Leo was fasting or Demetri was informing him of her movements in the house so he could avoid her. He'd felt something, and he was scared.

Scared he'd hurt her? Scared he'd love her?

Either he was scared or she made the world's worst cannolis.

Once a week, a different woman would show up at the door. The woman would be dressed in some slutty black leather number with what looked like a dog collar on, smiling demurely as she stepped into the house and lowered her gaze.

Faith wasn't sure where he was getting these women. Was there an escort service that supplied women who liked to beg and be hit? She tried to be okay with it. After all, it was obvious these women meant nothing to Leo. But he hadn't done this before Christmas. Whatever he'd done with Caprice had reawakened something he could no longer keep in a box on the back shelf.

It was early February, and the Christmas décor still hadn't been taken down. Faith was starting to wonder if Leo loved Christmas so much that everything stayed up year round. The doorbell sounded, and Faith hid behind the large tree in the entryway. It was Friday evening at 7:30. Like clockwork. It was the same time but a different woman every week.

Demetri answered the door to reveal an exotic Asian woman. The same woman who had been here the previous week. Was he getting attached? During Christmas with the Caprice debacle, if Caprice could have been trusted, Faith could have coped with being in a tame relationship with Leo while someone else handled his darker needs. Now, though, something had shifted. Even if some other woman *could* just be a toy, Faith no longer liked the idea of sharing.

Demetri took the woman's coat and stepped out of her way. "You know where to go, Miss Lin."

"Yes. Thank you."

Faith wasn't sure if Leo was already in the dungeon and she didn't want to risk their paths crossing, so she waited a while longer behind the tree.

"Miss Jacobson," Demetri said, coming to stand in front of her. "Where on Earth will you hide when I take down the tree?"

So it *did* come down at some point during the year.

"I'm sorry. Excuse me," Faith said, trying to brush past the butler. But he blocked her path.

"You know he doesn't care about these women. He wants you." The man had never been so overt about anything in all the time she'd been there. He'd been nothing but professional, but something must have been building and stewing. He'd probably calculated his odds on getting fired for this one were slim.

"Then why is he avoiding me? Why is he parading these women in front of me?"

Demetri smiled and shook his head. "I've known him since he was a boy. My guess would be that he doesn't trust himself around you. And for your second question . . . he has to be in control. He won't give up his territory for your convenience."

It was the most Demetri had ever said to her at one time. For weeks now, she'd thought the man was only capable of speaking in one-sentence bursts. She tried to brush past him again, but still he refused to move.

"It's none of my business, but do you mind if I ask you something?"

It didn't appear he was going to let her pass him otherwise. So it was either answer his riddles or knock down the tree and climb over the other way. "What?"

"It's clear to me that Mr. Raspallo isn't the only one harboring some feelings. Why aren't you the one with him instead of Miss Lin?"

Faith blushed and became intensely interested in a red-and-white glass ornament that looked like old-fashioned, wrapped candy. The silence stretched between them. Demetri's post at the Raspallo estate had made him infinitely capable of waiting.

"Y-you know what he's into?"

"I've seen the dungeon."

"I'm sure Leo thinks I'm a prude, but I'm not into all that. And it isn't like I pursued him. It's not as if I'm here by my own choice."

"Do you think he'd throw you down and pick the most painful implement he could find and go at you full force?"

"Maybe. I don't know what he'd do."

"He cares about you. He'd go slow. If you were willing to try it."

The conversation made her want to disappear. Leo's dungeon and his activities therein weren't spoken about. By not speaking about it, it could be part of a dim dream world and nothing more.

"But he said if I say yes, my consent isn't revocable. I can't change my mind later. So if it's too much, I can't ever get out. The only safety I have right now is saying no and hoping he honors that. If I say yes, I don't have any more choices ever."

Demetri laughed. "That's what he thinks. The truth is, from the moment you stepped into his life, he couldn't stand for any harm to come to you. That sadistic side of him you're so scared of isn't all he's about. He's a healer and protector. He would do anything to not damage you. If you couldn't handle it, he'd stop. He doesn't want to be played with. He needs someone who belongs to him completely, like you do. He's had too many woman who came here and then tried to control things, giving and taking consent like submission meant nothing to them. It's the reason Miss Lin is the only one so far who has made it to a second visit."

Faith didn't reply, but if what the butler was telling her was true, the Asian woman was the first true threat.

Demetri excused himself and left her alone with the tree. When he was far enough away, she slipped off to the dungeon. Maybe she *was* a masochist. If she didn't like pain, why did she keep going back there every Friday to listen in on what happened with Leo and the others? She wasn't a voyeur. She didn't get a burst of excitement from watching or hearing other people going at it. She just couldn't stand not knowing the status of things.

Despite how much she protested and denied, she knew if things went far enough, she wouldn't be able to prevent herself from begging Leo to do what he wanted with her to keep the other women away. She couldn't understand how any of this had happened, how he had transformed into someone she had real feelings for. All the time spent getting to know each other to trick his family, all the public affection and time spent with others and the meals they'd made together, had created a crescendo of need she could neither explain nor deny.

The past weeks of no interaction with him, and the women and what they did in the dungeon, had created an aching longing as well as a blind terror that she'd almost do anything to stop. Could any physical pain be worse than the pain she felt now? What if he fell in love with this woman? Even if he didn't get rid of Faith, how could she live like that? Trapped in this house, watching him with someone else, while she remained forever without anyone to fill the hole created by the lack of him?

Why couldn't he be normal? Why couldn't he crave equality and moonlit strolls on the beach?

Faith crept down the winding hallways in the darkness. She felt along the wall until she reached the end. The door was cracked as always, so she slipped down the stairs to the halfway point—close enough to hear what was happening, but far enough away that she could make a quick escape without being caught when they were finished.

In the dungeon, Leo's voice changed. It went deeper—as if the devil himself had taken possession of him. It was a change so visceral that she could feel it on the staircase where she hid.

He made the women call him Sir. The night he'd brought Faith home, he'd insisted on Master. Faith pondered this difference. Did he want them to call him Sir because he didn't consider them his property? Would calling him Sir have been easier? Would she have found it less weird? She wondered what Caprice had called him: Sir—or Master because of relationship history? Did one go from Sir to Master? Or from Master to Sir? Was this how everybody like Leo operated?

Faith wasn't a naïve idiot. She was vaguely aware of the world of kink, of spanking and bondage and whips and stuff like that. Only the more arcane implements and toys confused her. It wasn't that she didn't understand *what* it was. She didn't understand *why* it was. Why would any woman allow a man to do this to her? Why voluntarily put yourself at so much risk at the mercy of another? Why face pain with every sexual encounter? Was there something wrong with them? There had to be. It wasn't normal to need to be hurt or hurt someone to get off.

Over the weeks, Faith had grown familiar with the sounds of the different implements as they sliced through the air and made impact with flesh. The reactions differed depending on the woman. Some he gagged so that only muffled sounds of distress could be heard. And yet, when they left the dungeon later, they always displayed a peaceful look—as if everything in their world had been set right again. What did Leo do to these women? Faith got a strong sense of the physical things that happened from her perch on the stairs and her earlier tour of the dungeon. The part that was confusing was the end result. They looked . . . happy when they left. Satisfied. Secure. Confident. What the hell? It didn't match what she heard. The mewls, the whimpers, the screams and cries and begging for mercy.

Yes, there was sex, or something sexual that resulted in orgasms for both parties, but how could that make up for the rest?

There was something severely wrong with these women. And with Leo. Faith should be happy he'd turned his attention to them and away from her, but every time she heard him utter some endearment or sign of pleasure or satisfaction with the woman at his mercy, a piece of her broke apart. She didn't want him to do those things to her, but she couldn't stand for him to do them to someone else.

And this week it was worse, because Miss Lin wasn't new. She wasn't a one-off. What if she started coming here every week? Faith couldn't let that happen, but she didn't know how she could stop it.

"Faith."

She looked up, startled to find Leo on the stairs, a rattan cane in his hand. Her crying must have gotten louder than normal, loud enough for him to hear. Faith had been so wrapped in her thoughts that she hadn't noticed when things had gone quiet and Leo had climbed the stairs to investigate.

"Faith? What are you doing here?"

He was still a few steps down from her. Enough that she had space to get up, so she did. She ran up the rest of the stairs, down the hallways, through the entryway, and up another flight to the east wing. She locked the door behind her even though it was useless.

That other woman knew Faith had been there. What must she think? Was she going to be angry about it? Embarrassed?

A moment later, the key turned in the lock and Leo stepped into the room, sucking all the air out. Snowball and Squish hid under the bed. Whether they were responding to his energy or her fear, Faith couldn't be sure.

She eyed the cane firmly clasped in Leo's hand. This could be the moment he lost control. She dropped to her knees, her legs not able to support her in the face of what might come next. She held her arms defensively in front of her. "Please, I'm sorry . . . "

He looked down, as if only now noticing he still held the cane. He crossed the room and set the rattan on the fireplace mantle, then stood next to her while she stared at his shoes, hoping for the moment to end or for Leo to develop amnesia and forget he'd found her crying and pathetic, hiding while listening to everything he did.

"How many times have you been there when I've been downstairs with someone?" His voice had softened, but only by a fraction. There was still some-thing in his tone that demanded absolute obedience and honesty *or else.*

"A-all of them. E-every time a woman has come here."

"Why?"

"I-I don't know."

"That's bullshit," he bit out. "Tell me why you were listening."

She looked up at him, pleading in her eyes. "Leo, please, I'm sorry. I won't ever do it again."

"Answer me."

"I can't stand you with them," she blurted. "I can't watch this. Let me go. Let me leave this place."

"I can't."

"Can't or won't?" She chanced a look into his eyes. His expression was hard.

"Won't. Besides, what would you do now? Your job is long gone."

"I'll find another one. I'm very qualified for what I do. I'm young. And I have savings. I'll be fine."

"I'm sure you would be. But you aren't leaving here." Leo crossed to the intercom box. Faith struggled to stand and sat on the edge of the bed.

He watched her briefly, then pressed the white button. "Demetri?"

"Yes, sir?"

"Would you please go untie Miss Lin? I shouldn't leave her alone like that. Instruct her to stay in the dungeon and wait for my return."

"Right away, sir."

Leo turned back to Faith, his arms crossed over his chest. "Now. What are we going to do about this situation?"

"What situation?"

"The situation where I want you and you want me and neither one of us is happy."

"You still want me?" She sounded so needy. It was mortifying that he'd found her crying over him. And now to pathetically beg for reassurance that the man holding her hostage still wanted her. Maybe she had that Stockholm thing.

"I do."

Faith started pacing. He was everything she could ever want in a man except for one thing. Every guy had that *one thing*. But this wasn't a minor irritation like random scratching or belching at the table or refusing to throw out the socks with holes in them.

She rounded on him, fed up and frustrated and lost. "Why can't you be normal?!"

It was the wrong thing to say. He came toward her full of purpose and force like a freight train, backing her against the wall. He pinned her.

"Why can't *you* be kinky? You're submissive, now why can't you be a good little masochist?"

Her breath came out in pants as her bravery deflated, leaving her staring at the floor again because she couldn't take his intensity for longer than a few moments at a time.

She cried out when his hand came up in her peripheral vision, but he only brushed her hair out of her face and wiped away the few stray tears on her cheeks.

"Mei down there is submissive and a masochist. Do you know how hard it's been for me to find a genuine sub and masochist? Someone who doesn't play at being one or the other? Should I not be happy?"

"No, the man keeping me prisoner shouldn't be happy! Let me go and live happily ever after with her. Tell Angelo I'm not a threat and release me. Please. I'm dying here. Please."

He stared at her a long time before he spoke again. "Part of me thought I could train Caprice to be submissive. When she was here, we had a few moments where I thought maybe I hadn't tried hard enough to break through her walls. But deep down I knew I could never trust her. She'd be a danger to you so I sent her away. Mei isn't a danger to you."

"Maybe not to my life, but she is a danger."

"How long have you been here with me?"

"A couple of months," she said, puzzled by the question. It had to be rhetorical because surely neither of them could have forgotten that night or when it had occurred, so close to the holidays.

"In that time have I harmed you?"

The first night he'd spanked her and briefly touched her, but if she was honest with herself, it was mild compared to what he could have done. And she couldn't bring herself to classify it as *harm*. "No."

"Have I forced myself on you?"

"No."

"Have I tied you up or locked you in the dungeon?"

"No, but you threatened to," she said, remembering his intensity as he'd gotten her on board with the fake engagement. She glanced at the glittering rock on her hand and another tear slid down her cheek. Gina was supposed to call again tomorrow. She had new ideas for color schemes and themes, no doubt trying to get Faith excited about her wedding. Gina was going to see through this sham long before June arrived.

"But did I actually do it?"

"No."

"Then do you trust me?"

If she didn't know where his line of questioning was leading, she could say yes without reservation, because he had kept her safe and taken good care of her, and being a doctor, she knew if she got sick or hurt he could heal her. But a *yes* was all the invitation he needed to shoo Mei Lin out of the dungeon and replace her with Faith.

"Please let me go," she whispered.

"Never." He practically spat the word at her, his eyes blazing.

"But why? I frustrate you. Sooner or later, we both know you'll take what you want from me."

Leo backed away from her, giving her room to breathe. "You're the only one I've ever really owned. I need the other things I do down there, but they can't replace the one thing I can't get in any moral way. I know it's wrong to keep you, but I can't help myself. You're like a priceless piece of art kept in a glass case. I can't do anything with it but look at it, but I know it's mine. And sometimes that's enough."

Faith wondered if that was why Leo had put her in this room. With all the large windows, it *was* like a glass case. And she was the fragile figurine he kept inside.

"But it's not enough. You don't just want to look at me."

His gaze swept over her in such a predatory way, it was as if he'd stripped her bare. "Come here."

She took a few tentative steps toward him until she was within easy reach. He took her into his arms and pulled her against him. His fingers threaded through her hair and his lips met hers, hungry, exploring, his tongue pushing past the barrier of her lips. She couldn't help the involuntary whimper he drew from her.

It was the first time he'd kissed her, the first time he'd touched her at all since the holidays. And in private. Not for an audience. That made it the only real kiss they'd ever shared.

"You're mine whether I use you or not. You get that, right?"

His words were harsh and cold, but there was so much warm intensity in his tone that all she could manage was a breathless *yes*.

"I'm showing you mercy by not taking you down-stairs. Remember that."

There were electric butterflies in her stomach: arousal as well as fear over what she was about to say next. "If you want to show me mercy, send Mei Lin away." She shut her eyes, her breath suspended while the words floated on the air like snowflakes.

"Will you take her place?"

She looked away. "I'm scared."

"I know you are." His tone did nothing to disguise how much her fear excited him.

"You sent me away the last time I offered because you said I didn't want this, what changed?" It would have been easier if he hadn't rejected her, if he'd forced her to keep to her word after she'd given it. Asking her to say yes again, after sitting on the stairs, listening to what sounded like torture, was too much. It wasn't reasonable to ask this of her. And yet, she couldn't stop herself from making the offer because whatever he might do to her down there would hurt less than the bond he would otherwise form with someone else, shutting her out a piece at a time.

"The last time I thought it was about you being afraid for your safety if I became interested in someone else. Now I know it's more. You have feelings for me separate from the situation you find yourself in." He stroked the side of her face, causing her to look up into his eyes. "Tell me you'll take her place, and I'll condition you to love everything that scares you."

Leo descended the stairs into the dungeon to find Mei Lin sitting on the red leather couch against the wall, her feet pulled up with her. She hadn't bothered to get dressed, but had put down a towel from the bathroom to sit on.

She looked up when he entered the room, and he felt a moment's guilt for what he was about to do. Mei Lin was the whole package, and if not for Faith, he might have tried to see what could develop. But taking his ownership of Faith to the next level had become an all-consuming obsession.

Her consent upstairs had been given with a large amount of fear, but an equal amount of dignified determination. He was almost tempted to call it off again, but he needed this. How could he know what she could and couldn't handle if he didn't give her the chance?

"I'm not going to see you again, am I?" Mei asked. Hearing Faith's crying on the stairs was all she'd needed to start putting pieces together. "We keep missing each other. I'm with someone or you are. Perhaps in another life?"

"Another life, definitely."

Leo extended a hand to help her off the couch then pulled her into an embrace. "I don't want to be your rebound, Mei," he whispered in her ear.

"I know."

She'd split from her master of six years over the holidays—a man she'd truly loved. Leo had heard about it through the grapevine when he'd been on the prowl for a play partner. This wasn't their time. As a Catholic, he didn't believe in reincarnation, but if Mei Lin was right, his agreement for another lifetime was sincere.

He released her and took a step back. "Turn around. I want to look at the marks I left one more time before you go."

Mei Lin turned silently, her silken hair falling in a black cascade down her back. She bent to retrieve the shiny silver hair sticks she'd left on the couch on her arrival. He enjoyed the view until she righted herself and pulled her hair into a bun, securing the soft wisps into place.

Leo eased closer, running his fingers over the whip marks across her back and the welts on her ass. "Such lovely skin," he murmured against her shoulder. "None of us deserve to mar it like this."

She laughed. "You're such a gallant gentleman when a woman is free. Those wouldn't be your words if you were my Master."

"No. They wouldn't be." Because in that case, she'd be his to do with as he wished. It was the same as how you might dog-ear the pages of your own books, but never a book that didn't belong to you.

He trailed kisses along the marks he'd left and then stepped back to enjoy the vision in front of him one last time. "I'll leave you to get dressed. You can show yourself out."

"Yes, Sir," she said. Her voice stopped him when he reached the stairs. "Leo?"

He turned. "Yes, Mei?"

"Be careful with her."

He nodded and went upstairs to have another talk with the possession he'd finally fully acquired.

He knocked softly on the door when he reached Faith's room.

"Come in." Her voice sounded terrified from the other side of the wood, as if he would unleash some uncontrollable animal on her before the ink was dry on their agreement.

He pushed the door open to find her at the desk, a solemn expression on her face. It didn't escape him that she'd moved as far from the bed as humanly possible, as if to dissuade him.

"We need to discuss some business," he said.

"Business?"

"A few details. Meet me in my office in twenty minutes." He wanted to give Mei time to clear out so the two women wouldn't have an awkward meeting in one of the hallways.

She nodded like she understood the stakes, and Leo left and shut the door behind him, a small smile of triumph curving his lips.

As recently as the family's departure, Faith had thought she just wanted to live and stay safe. But as the other women began to arrive, the pain and fear had crept up on her—the fear that he would turn that look of pleasure and approval on another woman, and Faith would become like lonely furniture forgotten in a corner of the room.

But now that she'd attained his undivided attention, the idea of being forgotten furniture felt so much safer.

She watched the clock above the fireplace as it moved far too fast to the moment she would see Leo again. She dreaded whatever *business* he had to discuss with her. But as long as he was talking, he wasn't hitting.

When she couldn't wait any longer without being late, she got up and made her way to the office. An imaginary, disembodied voice echoed off the walls: "Dead woman walking."

She stood in the doorway to the office, her arms wrapped around her.

Leo glanced up from his desk and put his pen down, closing the black book she'd seen him writing in before. He motioned for her to come to him.

He rubbed her arms when she got closer. "You look white as a ghost. Are you cold? Do you need a sweater?"

"No."

"No, *Master*," he corrected.

"No, Master," she whispered, her gaze cast down.

"We're just going to talk."

She nodded and sat in the offered chair on the other side of his desk. She clasped her hands in her lap, staring down at the ring on her finger. "A-are we really getting married?" It was still too impossible and bizarre to be true.

"Yes. I told you already, it's either that or stay in the dungeon during Christmas every year. Is that what you want?"

"No, Master."

"Then yes, we're getting married."

"But you don't love me." She couldn't say she didn't love him because she wasn't sure anymore. If all this were real and normal and without all the layers of strangeness on top of it, she would have accepted a proposal from Leo without hesitation. But this wasn't her fantasy, this was the real Leo, and she knew the engagement wasn't real to him, even if the end result would be legal.

"Marrying for love is a new idea. For centuries men and women married for many reasons that had nothing to do with their feelings. Grammie and Papi had an arranged marriage, and they love each other now. Feelings grow over time. We are attracted, and that's more than what most had. Do you think I would keep you here if I didn't at least want you?"

She wondered if he would take a mistress, but she didn't ask. It was inappropriate to badger him as a normal fiancée might. She had no right to demand anything, least of all fidelity. Faith wasn't sure if he experienced love in a way she'd recognize, anyway.

"Are you on birth control?"

Her head snapped up. It was one of the last things she expected to hear and brought back the fears that he'd try to make her have babies to promote the sham marriage. After all, hadn't she given him her consent . . . for anything?

"You know I'm not," she said.

"I have no way of knowing that. The shot lasts three months. You could have taken that right before you met my brother. You could have a contraceptive implant, or an IUD, both of which can last several years."

"No. I'm not on any form of birth control." In all the anxiety about pain and scary kink, Faith had forgotten the normal things couples in sexual relationships obsessed about: diseases and pregnancy. With him being a medical professional, she was sure Leo had been careful with the former, but the latter remained a small risk. "A-are you going to make me have babies? Before you said that you wouldn't."

"Do you want babies?"

The truth might upset him, or he might use it against her. "There's about a 90 percent chance I can't have them. That's what my doctor said. I've always had issues with my cycle, and I had an illness. The odds aren't good for me."

"If you could have them, would you want them?"

She shrugged. "A-are you angry?"

"Why would I be angry?"

"I could be infertile . . . and your mom . . . "

"I told you I wouldn't force you to have children if you didn't want them. Do you think my word is worthless?"

"No, Master," she said quickly, grateful he wasn't angry.

"Decide if you want them. You'd be surprised how often a 10 percent chance turns into a pregnancy. If you don't want them, we'll use birth control. I won't force you to have my children."

"What about your mother? She'll hate me." Gina had been so nice. Most of them had, in fact. Having family was still a new and novel concept. She hated the thought of dashing all their hopes and dreams for more children in the family and being resented for it.

"It's not her business. We'll say we can't have them."

"And then they'll wish you'd married someone who could have babies."

He shook his head. "I don't think they would, but if it became an issue, I would tell them the doctor told us it was me. I won't make you bear their contempt."

It was another thing to add to the list of things that made Leo feel safe and honorable. None of it matched the change that came over him in the dungeon.

"You can return to your room now. That's all I wanted to talk about."

Faith got up to leave, confused that nothing scary had happened, and that he was keeping her in the east wing for now. He intercepted her at the door, wrapping her in his arms. His lips pressed against her forehead.

"You *will* survive me, I promise," he whispered.

Fifteen

A week passed and Leo still hadn't taken Faith to the dungeon, though he had resumed meals with her in the kitchen. One afternoon, he'd given her a few books on BDSM and asked her to read them so she would know more of what to expect. That night at dinner she'd been more pale than the night she'd offered herself to him in Mei Lin's place.

When he asked if she had any questions about anything, she'd shaken her head and looked at her plate, her hand shaking as she brought the fork to her lips.

Leo had spent much of the week digging through old medical texts on psychology. He had little respect for the field—considering it a pseudoscience at best. And yet everything he did with women in his dungeon, and everything between himself and Faith . . . it was all psychology.

He'd skimmed past the parts about Stockholm Syndrome. He didn't want to believe Faith's feelings could be merely a survival mechanism. The look in her eyes when he'd kissed her, the way she responded to him . . . that had to be real.

Hadn't the scientific community determined we were all just chemicals swimming around—that behavior was a mechanical reaction to stimuli and nothing more? Nothing mystical or magic, mere cause and effect. If they were right . . . would any love or feeling be real? Would Stockholm Syndrome be any *less* real, if that was what she had? Did a personal judgment on the value of one set of chemical reactions over another make one empirically better or more real than the rest? Leo believed humans were more than stimulus-response machines, but the men who'd written the psychology books in his den didn't.

Leo shook the textbook thoughts from his head as he watched his timid slave. He could drag this on for another six weeks without touching her once, and she'd still have that terrified look on her face—maybe more intense.

He poured wine as they sat down for their Friday meal together. "I'm taking you to the dungeon after dinner."

The tension that had been coiled in her for the past week pulled tight, jerking her head up like a puppet on a string. Her eyes widened as if she wanted to beg him to go back to Mei Lin or any other woman and leave her in peace.

"What did I tell you before I sent you off to bed last Friday?" He had no doubt she remembered everything he'd said or done since that moment. She'd watched and listened to him as if her life depended on memorizing every nuance of every interaction between them.

"Y-you said I'd survive you, Master."

"And you will. I'll take you into my world slowly. I'll make you crave it." Since she'd given her consent, Leo had been filled with anticipation over the idea of turning someone with no kink inclinations into his willing slave who learned to beg for each lash of the whip or strike of the cane. After a week of delving more deeply into Skinner and Breland's work on conditioning, he was convinced he could create in Faith everything he needed. She already had the most important component—an inborn submissive tendency. With that one trait, he could work miracles.

In their early weeks together, he'd assumed her reactions to him were all fear-based, but as time went on and she'd begun to trust him, her behaviors hadn't changed. Her shy deference, the way she couldn't meet his eyes—not due to some duplicity as would have been the case with Caprice, but rather, something in him made her shrink back in recognition of his dominance.

He watched as she picked over her meal.

"Are you all right?"

"Fine, Master," she whispered as she tried to get through the baked ziti.

He was toying with her. Leo wondered if his sadism had kicked up a notch. Was he now only satisfied if there was more fear and resistance? What separated him from a serial rapist or a serial killer if he was willing to let this line of consent blur? She'd said she would do these things, but she was clearly so terrified, she might pass out at any moment. Could any attraction or feeling she'd developed for him make this okay in her mind? Or his?

He went to the side pantry to get a roll of aluminum foil. He wrapped his dinner and put it in the fridge then took hers away as well. She was too nervous to eat; she was picking over it. It was better to move them forward now, to let her see that he could ease her into his world and there was nothing to fear.

"The human body is a funny thing. It can be programmed like a computer," he said. "I can reprogram you so that you like the things I like. I don't want to torture you." He wasn't one hundred percent sure on that last part. But if he said it out loud enough times, maybe it would become true.

"Come here, sweetheart."

She took his hand and he pulled her into his arms and held her. It was the first time he'd touched her since the previous week when he'd kissed her in her bedroom and sent Mei Lin away. He'd been afraid if he started touching her again he wouldn't stop. And his touch involved whips and belts and canes and clamps.

He held her for several minutes, rubbing her back as she trembled in his arms. He was moments from canceling everything, but that would solve nothing. The only solution that didn't involve her tied up in his dungeon was setting her free, and no matter how much guilt he felt, or how much he believed she was no longer a threat to his family, he couldn't let her go. He had to possess her.

When she'd settled in his arms, he picked up a cloth napkin from the table and pressed the soft fabric against her face to catch the tears.

"Please don't cry, Faith. These aren't the kind of tears I want from you."

"I'm sorry, Master."

"Shhh."

Faith's appetite had fled the moment he'd said he was taking her to the dungeon. She was glad he hadn't forced her to eat dinner because she was sure she wouldn't be able to keep it down. For the past week she'd been on edge, her appetite shrinking each day. If Leo had noticed, he hadn't said anything. Each day she woke wondering if today was the day. She wasn't like those other women. She couldn't do this.

The reality of what was coming should have made her hate him. It should have wiped away any residual attraction or fuzzy emotion. If it could have, she might have begged to be released from her promise. Even if it meant she'd never have love or companionship, it would protect her from the things downstairs.

But she still felt for him, and watching him take other women would only kill her by degrees. When he'd pulled her into his arms, he was the safest person in the world. She'd almost forgotten he was the cause of her angst.

When he opened that metal door, she thought her legs would buckle, but Leo prodded her down the winding stairway into hell.

He didn't speak at first, instead going to the wall where all the whips and crops and paddles hung. Her legs stopped supporting her and she crumpled into a ball on the floor, her knees tucked under her body as if she were practicing for a school tornado drill. Her instincts screamed that she needed to protect as much of herself as she could from him.

"Faith, come here."

His voice had taken on that change, that edge she'd always heard while eavesdropping. Was the nicer version of him there anymore? It was as if the upstairs Leo had receded to allow the beast in the shadows full reign while down below.

She crawled to him, not sure she could force herself to stand. When she reached him, he bent and pulled her to stand beside him.

"Now," his voice curled around her and squeezed, "which of these things is scariest to you? I want you to rate them from least to most scary."

She searched his face. What game was he playing? Sure, tell the sadist which items would upset you the most so he doesn't have to do any work to figure it out.

He sighed. "Faith, what happened to the trust we built?"

Her gaze went back to the lined-up canes.

She gripped the tray to stay upright while he went to get the black leather book. He opened it to a fresh page and uncapped a pen.

"Well? We don't have all night."

Faith ran her fingertips over the smooth canes. "This one is the worst," she said, touching the metal cane. "Followed by this one and the rest like it." She pointed to the rattan.

The pen scratched against the paper in a quick scrawl that probably only he could read.

She took a breath and looked up at the wall. "I-I don't know what these are."

"Those are clamps. Those are called butterfly clamps and the others are alligator." he said.

"What are they for?" She thought she knew, but she hoped she was wrong.

"Nipples. But I have other kinds for labia."

Not wrong.

"Do they hurt?"

He raised a brow at her. Stupid question.

"Of course they hurt, but the alligator aren't bad. They hurt more when they are being removed than when they go on."

"Why?"

"Blood rushing back to where it was denied. You go numb so it doesn't hurt as much, but when the clamps come off, sensation rushes back all at once."

"Why do you like this?" She couldn't blend the Leo who was into causing pain with the Leo who had protected her more than once from Angelo. Or the Leo who'd shown her mercy and given her a private room, or who had chosen to create a sham engagement and marry her so she wouldn't have to be kept tied up in the dungeon during the holidays. All of those things were so extremely kind, and this was so extremely evil. His contradiction was more frightening than if he could keep to one persona consistently.

He shrugged. "I've experienced every object in this dungeon. When I first decided to explore this lifestyle, I hired a dominatrix to teach me. I asked her to use everything on me because it was my responsibility to be intimately familiar with each item. She taught me how to moderate my strength and how to deliver the amount of sensation I wanted to deliver and nothing more or less. There is nothing here you will endure that I haven't been through myself."

Leo raised his sweater and turned around. Faith couldn't help running her fingers over the thin, faint scars that criss-crossed his back. They were old and almost faded now.

"Are you going to mark me like this?" she asked, working to keep her voice steady.

"I haven't decided."

"I'm not as strong as you. I can't take what you can take. Please . . . "

He pulled the sweater down and turned to face her, his hand resting on her cheek. "Whatever happens or doesn't happen, when it happens you will be able to take it, whatever it is. I'm not going to throw you down and scar you. I'm not an animal."

She looked back at the tray of canes. "What made your scars?"

"A bull whip."

"W-which one is that?"

Leo pointed to a large, single-tailed whip on the wall.

"I want to change my list. Make that one the worst one, and then the canes underneath it."

He chuckled but scribbled in his book. "Noted."

"What kind of whip is this?" she asked, pointing to a smaller whip that had several strips of leather instead of one. Amazingly, talking about the things in the dungeon took the edge off her fear, though she knew that wouldn't be the case when she was tied down somewhere and he had one of these things in his hand.

"That's not a whip. It's called a flogger."

"How bad is it?"

"I usually start a sub off with that. Floggers can be very pleasurable, even on someone who doesn't consider themselves much of a masochist."

Faith wrinkled her nose. "How can it be pleasurable?"

"It's hard to explain, but I'll show you. It can be made to hurt, of course. Any implement with enough force behind it can hurt. I could hit you with a vibrator and it would hurt. Though I wouldn't do that. Pleasure toys are for pleasure."

His expression was sexually hungry, and Faith was sure she hadn't imagined a double *entendre* when he'd used the phrase *pleasure toy*. No doubt that was how he saw her, now that she'd signed the last shred of her life over to him.

He could have taken anything from her at any moment, but her verbal agreement had removed any remnant of guilt that may have otherwise held him back.

Faith stared at the flogger for a good thirty seconds and said, "Make that the least bad one." She caught the ghost of a smile on his face as he wrote it down.

"What's this?" She pointed to a leather strap that was split down the middle about halfway so that one end formed a fork.

"That's a tawse. They were used in Scotland for corporal punishment in schools. Only, they rapped a student's palm with it. I can't promise I would limit it to that. They sting quite a bit."

Faith filed that away and looked back over the wall. There were several whips with one tail that were

smaller than the bull whip. And there were a few floggers and paddles, and the tawse, and a belt. She
quickly rated everything ending up with bullwhip as
worst, followed by canes, the belt, clamps, then the
smaller whips, then the tawse, paddle, and the flogger.

He seemed surprised by the belt ranking so high
on her list. She held her breath, waiting for him to
demand an explanation on why a belt should be so
terrifying, but he simply noted it in the leather journal.

The flogger, she was going to try to trust Leo on. If
he was lying, she would never make the mistake of
trusting him again. Not that trusting or not trusting
him mattered, but it was one thing she could still
control. The clamps made it pretty high on the list
because of the uncertainty. She'd had a difficult time
deciding whether the smaller whips or the clamps
would be worse, but the clamps were so foreign that it
made little sense to put them low on the list.

In the event that he intended to slowly work her up
going by her list, she wanted to move the clamps
further into the future. Given that, should she have
listed the belt as the worst?

Leo observed as Faith went through each item on
the wall and in the tray. They'd yet to catalog
everything in the toy box. There were still many things
in the large box she might find fearful—things she may
not have gotten a good look at on their previous tour.
He was sure she thought the violet wand was another
vibrator and that the concept of playing with electricity

would send her over the edge. It would be months before he could introduce it.

And then there was simply the matter of how certain things—even meant for pleasure—might humiliate or scare her because of how much they would expose her to him. He'd seen her naked once in those fleeting moments the first night she'd been in his home—in his room, and briefly in his bed. He'd gorged himself on the look of her, the lush, soft curves. The unmarred flesh. He'd held the memory in his mind for weeks as he'd jerked off in the shower.

He'd been new to her then, but he wasn't foolish enough to think her shyness was all about newness or the circumstances of them being thrown together. It was something innate that he wanted to exploit.

Leo could practically hear her heart trying to escape out of her chest as he peeled his sweater off and laid it over a spanking horse. He crossed to the far end of the dungeon to stand in front of a large, leaner mirror, typically a tool used for humiliation, and it would be again—most likely in a few moments. But for now, he looked at the scars on his back. It was true he'd hired a dominatrix to come to his dungeon when he'd first created it. But the marks were about so much more than that.

Since puberty, he'd had the fantasies: tying women up, hurting them, fucking them, sometimes kidnapping and forcing them. The latter fantasies disturbed him the most. He'd tried to be good. He couldn't understand what evil had possessed him or what he'd done to deserve these thoughts and feelings that wouldn't leave him no matter how often he went to church or how much he prayed or tried to be good.

For a long time, it had only been thoughts and masturbation. He'd avoided the fairer sex, fearing he'd hurt someone. But once he'd made his money and everything became possible, he'd started collecting. The estate had been built from the beginning with what he'd originally said was going to be a large and extensive wine cellar. And true, he did keep wine down here, but not nearly the collection so vast a space demanded.

Over months he collected the toys in the box and the implements on the wall and in the sliding tray, as well as all the furniture—both kinky and standard. As he'd put the room together, he'd told himself comforting lies. It was a simple extension of a fantasy. He'd never bring a woman down here. He would never hurt anybody for real.

Even if it was consensual, women like that . . . they must be as fucked up as him, maybe more. Surely they had some history of abuse or trauma that he was merely capitalizing on. He wouldn't cross that line.

But then he did cross it. Instead of bringing a masochist or submissive to his pristine and untouched dungeon, he'd brought a dominatrix. He'd wanted to know what it was that he fantasized about doing to someone else. He didn't want to sugarcoat it. He needed to use the pain to jolt himself back to reality and convince himself to stay away from this fascination.

But the sessions with the dominatrix only made his desires stronger, awakening the beast inside him, making it hungrier and determined to surface—angry that someone else got to play but he didn't.

Later sessions—the ones that had created the scars on his back—had been about something else. Punishment. He wanted to punish himself for what he was and couldn't erase and for what he knew he would act on soon. He was never sure if Esmeralda—pretty sure that wasn't her real name—suspected that the increased intensity wasn't about learning or about a secret masochistic tendency he must feed. It was pure penance. Though he was sure the Church wouldn't approve of this makeshift form he'd created for himself.

Leo turned from the mirror to look at Faith. Far too young and innocent. Not someone into this. He'd fallen this far, but even so, he knew a hundred harsh visits from the dominatrix could never stop what he was going to do to the terrified red-haired beauty in front of him.

She was his type in every way but one, and it was time to change that one incompatibility.

He went to the wine cellar and brought back a bottle of pinot noir. He collected wine glasses from a cabinet in the kitchenette and placed them on the counter.

"Faith?"

She detached herself from the wall by the whips and sat on one of the bar stools he indicated while he poured them each a glass of wine. He should have chosen white. Something fruity and light like a Riesling or sauvignon blanc. The red was too strong and dark and made him think of blood and pain. It made him more eager, so that the gesture of trying to relax her would only come at a price to her later.

He watched while she sipped more slowly than necessary, postponing what was coming. He indulged her until he'd finished his own glass, then he took the wine from her and set it on the counter beside the sink.

"I think that's enough, don't you agree?" There was no amount that would be enough for her right now. And he knew it.

"Yes, Master." She stared at the counter. Her lovely red hair fell in front of her shoulders and covered part of her face, making her look more demure and sweet. That sweetness was going to be the death of him. Or her.

Leo helped her off the stool and led her to the large mirror, then crossed to the chest of drawers beside the bed and pulled out a black T-shirt. He slipped it on because, while he enjoyed her discomfort at his state of partial undress, he enjoyed the power imbalance of himself clothed and his slave nude even more.

As comfortable as he was with his own nudity, there was vulnerability in it, and minimizing his vulnerability while maximizing hers was the goal of the evening. While one side of him wanted to make this about trust and bonding and some long-forgotten romantic ideal which society had hammered into him long enough that it should have taken, another part of him burned to take and use that which he'd acquired.

"Last chance to back out, Faith." His better nature insisted he give her one more exit door.

If she took it and walked up those stairs, he might chase her down and take all her choices away. He wanted her to soothe his guilt by not saying no.

"And then what happens? We go back to how things were? You barely speaking to me? Those women coming over here? I told you, it hurts too much."

He had to give her points for bravery and determination. They were qualities that had been mostly lacking in the other women he'd brought to his lair. After all, how much bravery was required to face what you got off on?

"Maybe you're a bigger masochist than I thought," he taunted. But she didn't respond to the bait, she just watched the ground like a criminal waiting for sentence from some high and lofty monarch.

He took her by the hand and guided her to the mirror, then stood behind her and pulled the sweater over her head. As the fabric fell to the floor, her gaze followed it and stayed there.

"No. Watch." He raised her chin to force her to look in the mirror. Even in the dim lighting he could see the flush on her cheeks that spread down her throat and over the tops of her breasts, exposed by the pale-green, lace demi-cup bra she wore.

He cupped the feminine mounds of flesh as her chest rose and fell. Her fear seeped into the air like poison. She wouldn't make it up the stairs if she tried to run, assuming she could wriggle out of his grasp.

Looking into her eyes, he could see she'd calculated those risks and had chosen deep breathing exercises over any rash escape attempts. Smart girl. A predatory urge rose inside him, and running would excite him more.

His hands smoothed over the soft skin of her belly, and he smiled at the goose bumps that broke out over her skin. He pulled her flush against him and brushed the hair away from her throat, then kissed the side of her neck. She let out a muffled sound of pain as his teeth pressed into her flesh. He sucked on the skin where he'd bitten to soothe the discomfort away.

Leo reached to the button on her jeans, unbuttoned them, and slid them down her legs. "Step out," he growled when they were on the floor. Red-polished toes peered out from under the bundle of denim.

He supported her while she did as he asked. A few moments later, the scrap of matching lace joined the jeans on the floor, and Faith rushed to cover herself.

"No," he said, forcing her arms to her sides. When he removed her bra, he felt her struggle as she fought to obey his demands neither to cover herself, nor to look away from her reflection.

For a moment she was hypnotized by the seduction as his fingertips grazed her flesh, like he was memorizing a raised relief map. He massaged her scalp and stroked her neck and shoulders, moving down her arms, then over her stomach, her breasts, and between her legs. For this small window in time he had her, locked inside his spell.

He went to retrieve a rattan cane. She tensed, but he ignored it. She'd have to learn to trust him by his actions. She'd labeled the cane as one of the worst things on her list—a fairly accurate assessment, particularly in his hands, but he wasn't going to hit her with it every time he picked it up.

He allowed the lightweight wooden rod to trail over her skin, mimicking his fingertips of moments before. He did this until she relaxed again. Then he took a step back and pushed her to her knees.

"Spread your legs."

She hesitated and he smacked the cane against a nearby piece of bondage furniture. It had the desired effect, and she quickly assumed the position he'd demanded.

"Stay exposed, with your eyes on your reflection until I give you permission to move."

He crossed to an old-fashioned record player and thumbed through several albums until he found a collection of somber classical music that started with the first movement of Beethoven's Moonlight Sonata. The round, vinyl disc settled on the turntable like a spinning quarter, finally coming to settle. The needle hissed and sputtered against the grooves as the haunting music groaned to life.

Leo sat near the leaner mirror, arms crossed over his chest, appraising. His focused observation unnerved even the most experienced sub.

She was a delicate rose petal about to fall off the flower—so graceful and beautiful, even while falling and dying.

Her gaze strayed to him, and a cold smile crept up his cheek. "Did I give you permission to look away?"

"N-no, Master. P-please don't hurt me." Her eyes hadn't gone back to the mirror, but instead were on him . . . imploring. How long until she learned mercy came from obedience? And not begging or pathos?

"Hurt is what sadists do, my dear. But punishments hurt worse. Do you want to be punished tonight?"

"N-no, Master."

"Then don't take your eyes from your reflection until I say you can."

She flinched at the snarl in his tone.

As her eyes returned to the mirror, her situation clicked into place. There were so many things he could do to feed his urges besides hitting her.

How much would she sacrifice for him—how much could she give before he emptied her out?

Leo moved behind her, peeling his shirt off and tossing it into the pile of clothing behind him. He didn't wear shoes in the house, so it was quick work removing his jeans and boxer briefs.

He peeled a condom from a wrapper and pushed her forward so that her hands braced her against the floor. Her gaze went to his in the mirror for the barest moment of uncertainty and pleading, but he shook his head. "Eyes on your reflection," he growled.

When she obeyed, he thrust into her. The condom was lubricated, but not enough. Irrational anger gripped him. *She's not aroused.* Any other woman would be dripping from need, excited by his fucked-up brand of seduction. But Faith was only enduring.

The anger rose steadily, climbing to more extreme heights the more she cried. His hands bit into her hips marking her as his. How dare she not be turned on by this! How dare she cry when she asked for this, practically begged, her pouting mouth and doe eyes undoing him as she pleaded to be together? Well, this was together. This was how it was. How he was. If she couldn't fucking take that she should go back to her room where everything was bright and sparkling and safe and clean. The guilt chased him while he chased release, her tears eliciting twin feelings of shame and excitement.

The orgasm was empty, choking the air from the room. It felt like the icy grip of death instead of pleasure. It was supposed to be a kind of forgetting, where the drab world faded into a sharper, more pleasing reality, but this was cold and dull and lifeless, and he couldn't escape the feeling fast enough. When he was spent, he pulled out of her, removed the condom, and tossed it in a nearby trash can.

She doubled over on the floor, her sobs ringing in his ears. Had he broken her in one visit? What the hell was wrong with him? She hadn't said no. She hadn't tried to fight him, and yet it felt ugly, the evidence of his savagery painted on her thigh. The thin line of blood making her look like a spoiled virgin.

A sick thought slid into his mind. Had she lied on the questionnaire about her sexual history?

"Were you a virgin?"

"N-no, Master. You know I wasn't."

She could barely push the words out. In the space of minutes, he'd destroyed her. He'd never broken a woman's trust like this, not ever. His play things had all gone home happy with secret smiles on their faces, their bodies relaxed and loose and confident. But those women had consented, not just with words—with their whole being.

It wasn't a verbal transaction. It was bodies and trust and communion. He'd known where Faith was mentally, and yet . . . he hadn't stopped.

He'd meant to protect her. Was there no leash that would hold him back?

Leo moved slowly closer as she drew back.

"Faith?"

"Y-yes, Master?"

What was he going to say? *I'm sorry?* For what? How did one apologize for this? Words couldn't fix the brokenness. They weren't going to laugh over this later.

The surgeon side of him rose to the surface, intent on fixing her. Still not a person in his head, but at least something he wanted to heal rather than harm. How could such two disparate instincts reside in one soul without ripping it apart?

He knelt behind her and pulled her into his arms. She didn't fight him; she went limp like a rag doll, as if her spirit had vacated her body.

This was worse than if he'd taken a bullwhip to her unmarred back and sliced her open. He held her forever, stroking her hair, shocked by how she clung to him in spite of what had happened. Against his better judgment, he found himself kissing her, and she responded to his lips on hers, kissing him back. He should give her privacy and space, but he knew if he left her, she'd fall down a deep hole she couldn't climb out of. He wanted to paper over the last few minutes with tenderness. *Fix it. Fix it. Fix it.*

"Don't move. I'll be right back," he murmured against her mouth.

He left to retrieve the medical bag from the den. When he returned, she'd stopped crying, but she still huddled in a ball, her eyes vacant and staring.

"Faith, are you with me?"

"Yes, Master," she whispered.

He carried her to the bed and laid her down gently, then dug through his bag for a flashlight and a speculum. Playing doctor was a game one of his subs had been into, and he'd happily collected all the necessary tools to be a convincing gynecologist. It came in handy now as he lubricated the piece of metal and carefully inserted it and flicked on the flashlight. The physical damage was minor. But the physical damage wasn't the problem here, and they both knew it.

The eerie music played on as they lay in bed. Some of the songs she recognized, some she didn't. There couldn't be more than an hour on the record. Hadn't they been down here months? Years? But it must have been less than an hour. Was time even real? The curtain had been pulled back to reveal the void where every second was eternity, and there was no way back out again to where time marched on like obedient linear soldiers.

She'd tried to prepare herself for the hitting, but when Leo bent her over and fucked her instead while she was too scared to be turned on, it brought everything home. She was his property. She didn't want this, but he'd been in the grip of something she didn't feel strong enough to break through. The Leo that acknowledged her wouldn't be the one she thought she'd fallen in love with.

Whatever romantic fantasies she'd had of love between them scattered and faded into the empty air. Why did it have to be like this?

And to allow him to kiss her like that . . . to return the kiss . . . to want to after . . . what was wrong with her? But the moment he'd switched to kindness, as if there could be an apology wrapped inside his kiss, she'd drunk it up like a parched animal at a stream— desperate to hold onto *this* version of Leo just a little while longer.

Those other women . . . She'd seen them happy afterward, and Mei Lin was happy to return. Another sob escaped her throat, and Leo swallowed it up in another kiss that felt like flowers blooming after the storm.

She couldn't stop her body from responding to the careful, yet passionate way he kissed her as he held her in his arms.

"Close your eyes."

Closing her eyes was a sign of trust. How could she trust him now? But she couldn't fight him, so she closed her eyes, hoping to go some place safe.

His weight lifted off the bed. A lid opened and closed. *The box.* Her mind screamed. The music continued to play, filling every space of the room, the notes foreboding. He returned a moment later and slipped a blindfold over her eyes, then he took her wrists in his hands and bound them with rope to the headboard of the bed.

She let out a desperate whimper. "Please, Master . . . "

"Shhhh. I'm not going to hurt you again."

Again.

His voice was softer and kinder, and though she knew she was stupid for it, she believed him. He pushed her legs apart, and she tensed. He'd already hurt her down there, and he'd promised that he wouldn't . . . but his fingers went to her clit. They were cold and wet with lubricant, and even after everything that had happened, her body opened to him and awakened under his touch.

She was ashamed when she came, moaning and squirming under his hand. It should have taken longer. He should have had to work more for it. He should have had to drag her kicking and screaming to pleasure after hours of endless stimulation. His hand should have cramped. And yet . . . minutes. Mere minutes for her surrender.

Could he do anything to her, then change course and make her pant for her treat like a well-trained dog? She flinched as his greedy mouth engulfed her nipple, and he ran his hands over her, assessing his property, feeling every curve and contour of what she'd foolishly given him.

He inched down her body, and his expert tongue brought her to a second orgasm in only a few minutes more. Everything pleasurable and gentle he did was tinged with the memory of the savage way he'd taken her. If he thought he could erase that with orgasms, he was wrong.

Without a word, he untied her wrists and removed the blindfold. She kept her eyes shut, unable to look at him. If this was day one, what would the rest of her life be like? How could she walk down an aisle and marry such a man? How could she fake happiness on that day? And how badly would he punish her for failing?

She thought about Christmas morning when Angelo had almost shot her. She wasn't sure she'd have the heart to beg for her life again.

Leo was not her Prince Charming riding in on a horse. He'd killed her more expertly than Angelo ever could have. And what's more, he'd done it without leaving a speck of evidence that she was dead. A living, breathing, corpse no one suspected was long gone.

The light clicked off, pitching her into blackness. The music played. Faith felt the weight of him again as he wrapped her in his arms and his breathing smoothed into the peaceful rhythm of dreams

The record reached its end, and the needle scratched against the empty space, creating a white noise that lulled her finally to sleep.

Sixteen

Faith woke to an empty bed in the dungeon. With only a small lamp that had been turned on and no sunlight, the place was creepy. She started up the stairs, but stopped herself. Was she allowed to leave? She wasn't sure. And if she was, did she want to see Leo right now? Or ever again?

She showered for half an hour, scrubbing until she was raw. She wasn't sure if she was scrubbing off what had happened in front of the mirror or the later orgasms. Both were equally horrible.

When the water ran cold, she got out and dressed, then checked the cabinets and fridge. But there was no food. Just the wine. Getting drunk might help erase the memories—at least for a while—but it wasn't worth the sickness that would follow.

Faith took a glass from the cabinet and poured water from the tap. She huddled back in bed, propping the pillows against the headboard and wrapping the blankets around her. She waited to be hurt again.

Around noon, Leo came down. "Aren't you hungry?"

"Yes, Master." As soon as his feet touched the bottom step, she looked away.

Max came down with him, the golden retriever hopping on the bed to comfort her, which reminded her she needed to clean the litter box and feed the cats. Snowball had been litter trained for two weeks now, which was a blessing because the box she'd arrived in was becoming too small for both of the cats to cuddle up together. Snowball and Squish were no doubt in the bright, window-filled room, lying in patches of sunlight like they'd gone to cat heaven.

"I can restock the kitchen down here if you want, but you don't have to stay here. Your room is still your room. Nothing's changed."

Everything's changed.

Well past dark that evening, the doorbell rang. The Christmas decorations had been taken down the preceding week, so there was nowhere for Faith to hide except a nearby parlor. A woman's voice filled the entryway.

"Good evening, Demetri."

"Ah, Esmeralda. Mr. Raspallo is expecting you. You know the way, of course."

"Of course." Her voice was smooth honey with a bite of bitter chilled wind. Her words were clipped and precise—nothing like the other women who'd come before. None of them would have dared to clip a word.

For the others, each word had been a modest question, practically an ascetic's prayer. This was the person they prayed to.

When Demetri returned to the formal dining room to polish silver, Faith slipped through the entryway and stole to the back of the house where the dark hallways led to the dungeon.

Leo had ordered her never to eavesdrop on him again, and maybe this woman wasn't here for that. Maybe it was some kind of business thing. Leo *did* run a business. It was easy to forget he actually worked in that office of his and wasn't off being mysterious and unavailable for the sake of intrigue.

She crept to her normal hiding spot, determined to pay attention so she could escape in time if things went quiet for too long.

"What's this really about, Leo?" the woman asked.

"I'm paying you not to ask questions."

"And I don't need your money," she replied, more honey than bitter for the moment. "Are you sure you aren't a masochist? Perhaps a switch? A lot of men have some submissive tendencies. It's nothing to be ashamed of. It doesn't make you less of a man. Running such a successful business and practice with so many people to keep happy is stressful. It's okay to surrender sometimes."

"It's not about that. Business is great. I told you, I'm not a sub, nor a masochist. I get no pleasure out of this."

"Well, you've learned everything I have to teach you, so what are you punishing yourself for?"

Silence filled the space below. It stretched long enough that Faith worried she'd made a sound. She was poised to make her escape when he spoke.

"Are you going to do it or not?"

"This is the last time, Leo. If you call me again, I'll expect a full explanation of why my services are required by a man who doesn't get off on being whipped."

"Make sure the ropes are tight so I can't get out, and don't hold back. Don't stop until your arm gives out."

"That's the last order you'll be delivering tonight, Mr. Raspallo. Undress. We wouldn't want to ruin your fine clothes." The bite was back.

Faith couldn't imagine Leo ever allowing a woman to tie him up, to render him so utterly helpless and defenseless. He was all powerful, holding her life in his hands, capable of doing anything. The contrast was too stark.

What followed was an endless number of sickening cracks as the whip made contact with Leo's flesh. Eternity passed and then circled in on itself before he howled in pain, as if he'd held it all in, fighting through the misery until he couldn't take it any longer. And from there, the sounds got worse—the cracks and screams mixed together into an unholy symphony. Faith hadn't once imagined he could ever be anyone's victim, the tormented instead of the tormentor.

She wanted to make it stop, but if she interrupted, he might punish her. The thought of the whip across her own back made her stomach turn and destroyed any small sliver of bravery before it could assert itself.

Crack. Scream. Crack. Scream. Like a horror movie. Each time he screamed, Faith prayed it would be the last time, but it kept going . . . until all that remained was the sobbing of a broken man.

"Have you had enough?" the woman asked, sounding weary.

"It'll never be enough for what I did," he choked out.

"What did you do?"

"It's personal. It doesn't matter."

"I can't do any more without doing damage you might not recover from, and I'm not that kind of sadist," she said. "I don't care what you say, you might not be getting sexual pleasure out of it, but there are fewer things more masochistic than what you asked for tonight."

"I knew it wouldn't erase it, but I had to try."

"Do you need me to call a doctor? Someone discreet?"

"I'll be fine."

"So the cliché is true," she said. "Doctors make the worst patients."

Faith realized suddenly that she'd been crying, and belatedly tried to muffle the sound, but Leo must have heard that she'd disobeyed. And she couldn't leave him down there like this—alone and injured and helpless.

"You can go," he said. His voice was weak when he spoke, as if it took the last of his life force to form the words. "Demetri has your check."

"Are you sure I can't call someone for you?" Her voice had gone softer, all honey and concern now.

"Just go, please," he said. "And thank you."

"I'm sorry it didn't fix anything."

"There was no other way."

"You're Catholic. There's confession."

He made a disgusted sound. "A few Hail Marys and Our Fathers? A promise to be a good boy from now on? Not for this. I couldn't even make myself say I was sorry."

Faith didn't bother trying to hide when she heard those high-heeled leather boots making their way up the stairs. When the dominatrix reached her, understanding flashed across her face. Then she was gone.

Music drifted up the stairs. That same damned record. He was torturing himself with it. Faith wanted to burn it so he couldn't play it again. The music was vile and evil, and shouldn't be heard by the good people of the world.

"I know you're there." His voice faltered as it tripped over words like some drunken sailor.

When she reached the bottom of the stairs, she gasped and the tears came harder. He sat on a piece of bondage furniture, naked, his back to her. The whip had cut him into strips of so much meat. Ribbons. Blood. She was surprised he'd kept consciousness.

"Why would you do this?"

"You know why."

Faith got him some water so she could be useful instead of just staring as if he were a traffic accident. Leo drank it down, his hands shaking like an old man's. That was when she noticed his wrists. The ropes had cut into him when he'd struggled, rubbing them raw. When the water was gone, he handed the glass back to her.

"More?"

He shook his head and stared at the ground for a long time. "I broke your trust."

Compared to the scene before her, last night was barely anything now. A small blip. A misunderstanding. Like a date that hadn't gone well.

"What can I do? This is bad. You need a doctor."

"No doctors!" his voice cracked. She refilled his glass with more water.

"What can I do?" She wouldn't leave him in this state.

"I keep a backup medical bag down here, but I put it back in the den earlier . . . next to the bookcase."

It didn't take long to find the bag. She peeked inside to make sure she had the right one and rushed back to the dungeon. Faith had just reached the door again when she heard him cry out.

He'd managed to make it into the bathroom to take a shower, dragging a trail of blood over the concrete and carpet. The trail ended at the base of the tub. Faith sat on the closed toilet seat, staring at the floor, trying to hold herself together until the water stopped.

When he shut it off, he said, "Take several towels, and lay a couple over the table."

It was a leather table with metal rings around the sides to loop ropes or cuffs through. The ropes still hung from the rings.

"Yes, Master."

She was surprised to hear herself say it. All she wanted to do was please him and ease his suffering.

This was more than a gesture, more than an apology. To do something like this . . . his own mental anguish had to match hers. Regret and agony balanced the scale between them even if he couldn't believe in such miracles.

"Master?" she said at the door.

"Yes, Faith?"

"If I'd begged you to stop, would you have?"

"Yes."

He could be lying, but with the shattered way the word came out, she knew he wasn't.

"It's not your fault. I knew. I should have stopped."

She went to the other room and laid out the towels as he'd asked. He came in a few moments later, still dripping, naked and beautiful—at least from the front. The marble perfection of his chest hid the macabre truth of his back.

He lay on his stomach and took several deep breaths.

Faith became aware of the music again. The music that frightened her the night before was haunting and sad and lonely now.

Leo guided her through sterilizing his wounds and applying the bandages. She worked as quickly as she could, bracing herself against his cries of pain as he gripped the edge of the table, his knuckles going white each time. Tears blinded her eyes as she worked. When it was done, he resembled a mummy.

Ropes had cut into his ankles as well. It was hard to believe anyone could do this to another human being. Whatever she'd thought of Leo, whatever fears she'd had, she knew he'd never hurt her like this.

He struggled to get up.

"Wait, we didn't do anything about your wrists and ankles."

"They're fine. It's not a big deal."

She couldn't stand the idea of the bed covers irritating the raw skin. It had been hard enough not to vomit as she'd worked on his back.

"Please, Master."

He relented, and she applied salve gently to his wrists and ankles, then loosely wrapped strips of gauze around them.

"I'll stay down here for a few weeks while I heal," he said, his voice tired, aged thirty years. "Ask Demetri to bring down my meals . . . and my phone. I'll need to make a few business calls. And I'll have to reschedule surgeries."

"No. I'll get them." She'd do anything to delete from her mind the images of what he'd suffered trying to make things right.

He nodded, relenting to her request as she helped him to the bed and tucked him in.

"I'm going to make you some stew," she said. He needed something with meat in it, something to help him get strong, but nothing so heavy he'd vomit it back up. "D-do you have any painkillers?"

"No painkillers," he said.

"But . . ."

"I should suffer."

The dominatrix was right. He was a masochist even if he didn't get off on it. It made Faith wonder if perhaps she was, too, because she found herself continually drawn to him, willing to put herself in the path of pain for a brief glimpse of approval or affection.

Leo had almost drifted to sleep when she brought the stew down. The record needle was doing that obnoxious scratching thing at the end, so she lifted it off, thankful to have the silence.

"Master?"

"Yes, Faith?"

"Can we never listen to this again?"

"Okay."

She helped him sit up and sat on the edge of the bed to feed him the stew. He stared stubbornly at her for several minutes before finally opening his mouth.

After the stew was gone, she got up to leave, but he gripped her wrist, his hold on her still impossibly strong.

"Stay." It didn't feel like a request. "It's late. Get in the bed."

Faith got in, but his voice stopped her.

"Naked."

She hesitated, unsure. It was impossible not to forgive him after his penance, but the request was so wrong.

"I'm hardly in a position to do anything to you," he said. "I-I need your body heat, that's all."

"W-will you please not look?"

He closed his eyes without protest.

She felt briefly stupid for her fear and stripped off the clothing. His arm went around her, the gauze from his wrist brushing against her waist.

Somehow she slept soundly.

Weeks passed. Leo healed. They returned to the world upstairs.

He watched her across the table at dinner—her cheeseburger special. He didn't know how she made them taste like they'd come right off a restaurant grill.

Faith pretended to be consumed with the task of swirling a steak fry in a giant glob of ketchup on her plate.

"I'll speak to Angelo. He might agree to release you if I convince him you aren't a threat to the family. And I'll smooth things over with Uncle Sal so you won't have to worry about him, either. To everyone else, I'll say we broke off the engagement."

Faith's ring glittered in the kitchen light. Leo hadn't insisted she wear it all the time, but she had. And every time he saw it on her hand, he became more convinced she wanted their engagement to be real.

But her happy ending came at a dark price . . . a price Leo felt increasingly guilty asking her to pay, no matter how much he wanted to keep her locked away in the glass room. If that night in the dungeon hadn't happened, he could have eased her into his kinks slowly, conditioned her to want them . . . if for no other reason than her deep desire to please him.

But now . . . the gulf was too great.

"Do you want to leave, Faith?"

Her eyes stayed trained on her food. "I can't leave, Master."

"Why can't you leave? If it's money, I can give you money. I'll set you up some place nice. I'll pull a few strings and get you a good job." He wanted to stuff every word out of his mouth back in.

"Do you want me to go?" she asked, chancing a glance up from her plate, searching his face for the answer.

"You know I don't."

"Then I won't go."

She'd killed his attraction to fear. But he needed to hear cries and whimpers and begging and see tears and hear cracks and smacks and watch red burst out over flesh. He needed it like a drug addict needed meth.

Even while he held Faith at night and wanted to protect her, he wanted to make her cry. He wanted her to cower and tremble at his feet, and he couldn't simply wish that desire out of existence.

"Faith, you know what I'll do to you. You've seen the things in the dungeon. Take your chance and go. For your own safety, please."

He could make her go. He could take her out of here as easily as he'd brought her in.

Her jaw set in a determined line. "I'm not going."

"Why not?"

"You know why not! Don't make me say it."

"Say it." He'd seen all the signs. The way she'd looked at him before that night, and then again after Esmeralda had come. She had fallen for him and couldn't make herself leave no matter the threat. Just like a battered wife. Just like Gemma with Emilio. He'd killed the bastard, now he *was* the bastard.

"I love you," she whispered. "I wish Angelo had killed me."

He knew this time she meant it. If he brought his brother in with a gun, she wouldn't fight them again.

"It's better for you to go. I can't give you what you need, and I don't think you can give me what I need. And after that night . . . I don't know how we could ever . . . "

She reached out and laid her hand over his. "I know you're a good man. What you did for me . . . I know we haven't talked about it but . . . it was everything. Y-you saw the gravity of what happened and you paid a price higher than I ever would have asked just to try to make it right."

"It can't ever be right."

Leo's muscles went rigid when she left her chair and knelt at his feet. He could barely breathe.

"I want to be with you. I want to please you. I'll be your slave. I'll be whatever you want."

His suspicions about her being a sub were right. Just not a masochist. One out of two? A strong one out of two wasn't bad.

"I'm going to my office to do some work. When I'm finished, you will be in one of two places, either in your room with your bags packed and ready to go, or in the dungeon naked in front of the mirror. Like that night."

She flinched, and he knew she'd be packed in an hour.

Faith knelt on the kitchen floor as Leo's footsteps faded from the room. She could go back to her life. Not her exact life, but a better life. She trusted when he said he'd give her a nice apartment or house and help her find a job. But the idea of going back to cats and no real family made her feel cold inside. If she took his offer, she knew she'd never see him again, and despite everything, she couldn't stand that ending. Let him kill her if he didn't want her. But tossing her away after all this?

If she were wise, she'd take the offer, go to her room, and pack her things. But she loved the way he smelled and his warmth and the way he held her. She loved how he'd protected her so many times, and despite how wrong it all was, she loved him for the scars he'd always carry for her.

It shouldn't have been, but the decision was easy.

When she got downstairs, she turned on the lamps and removed her clothing, folding them and placing them carefully on a chest of drawers beside the bed. She paused in front of the record player, thumbing through the cardboard sleeves until she found the dreaded record. They'd agreed never to play it again, but nothing would let him know she was serious more than playing this collection of music, resetting everything exactly as it had been. It was the only way she could prove she was his, and the only way he could ever hope to rewind and redo that night. If she didn't trust him to make a different set of choices, she should be upstairs in her room packing.

The record player had a setting to restart the needle at the beginning when it reached the end. She didn't know how long he would be, so she set it and the music started—that deep, haunting tone. Frightening and sad. Everything she'd found her experience with Leo to be.

Faith went to the mirror and knelt in front of it, spreading her legs, committed to the outcome.

Leo sorted through mail, mostly wedding bills and deposit receipts. Then he checked email. He wanted to put off the moment when he'd go upstairs, find her ready to go, and have to keep his end of things. The idea that she'd go to the dungeon was too far outside reality to hope for, especially after he'd asked her to relive that night. It would push her the final bit to wake her up and take her out of his life for good where she'd be safe and could find some happiness.

When she was gone, he'd call Mei Lin. If she hadn't gotten back with her Master, perhaps there was something they could build on in this life after all. If it ended up being a rebound, that might be ideal, a short fling to scratch each other's itches and help heal each other's losses. Faith felt like she belonged to him, like she was his responsibility to care for and keep safe, but keeping her safe from himself meant she couldn't be under his roof.

As he closed the browser window, his cell rang. He recognized the number.

"Hello, Caprice."

"I miss you." She sounded as if she'd been crying. He doubted it was over him. Most likely some other love affair had gone sour and he was the first person she thought of when she was alone again. Lucky him.

Leo glanced at the calendar. It was about time for a Caprice call. He should have known a few quick sessions during the holidays weren't going to end with her meekly going off to Vegas and never contacting him again. But his dick could tell convincing lies when necessary.

"I told you it was just during the holidays," he said.

"Why are you marrying her? I don't get it. Honestly, I don't. I mean she's pretty enough, I guess, but she's not what you need, and you know it. I'm what you need."

Caprice wasn't what anybody needed. Least of all Leo. But he held on to that retort. He also wasn't about to tell her the engagement was broken off. It would send her into his arms faster than anything, or else it would start the rumor mill going. When it came out, he needed the family to hear it from him, not twisted in with Caprice's jealousy and half truths.

"I need to be going," he said. "I have somewhere to go with Faith."

She made a disgusted snort over the phone. "Dinner and a movie? Maybe she'll get the courage to hold your hand. Maybe you two can share a tub of popcorn and look longingly into each other's eyes during the romantic comedy and come home and fuck in the missionary position with the lights out and roll over and go to sleep."

"Don't ever call here again."

He was about to disconnect the call when her words stopped him. "Maybe I should tell your naïve fiancée what you were sneaking off to do during Christmas. Would she marry you then?"

"If you come near her, I will kill you. Is that clear enough? Stay the hell out of our lives." He disconnected the call before she could reply.

No, Caprice wouldn't meekly go home, and there was no telling what havoc she could bring to his life. Even without Faith, he didn't want her, because at the end of the day she always came back to manipulation and nastiness to get what she wanted. He couldn't train it out of her using any moral methods, anymore than he could train kink into Faith.

Leo took his time walking to the glass room in the east wing. He didn't know if he could stand to see her sitting there, waiting with her bags packed.

He knocked, but there was no answer. He tried the knob, and it gave freely in his hand. When he stepped into the room, Snowball and Squish meowed and wrapped around his legs briefly before darting out the door. Faith must have forgotten to let them out. Normally they spent some time here, but otherwise had the run of the house.

The room was empty, all of her things still in their normal spots.

"Faith?"

Silence.

Snow fell outside the windows, the last gasps of winter creating a heavy blanket. He didn't want to drive in this right now. And where was he going to take her until he found a permanent living solution?

He found himself irrationally irritated that she wasn't packed yet. He'd been in his office for an hour at least. He searched the normal places she frequented: the kitchen, the game room, the family room where she liked to sit with a book beside the fire with a mug of cocoa or tea, even the pool.

He refused to consider she could have taken the other option. As obvious as it was, it felt like the kind of thing one would fantasize about and convince themselves of, only to be disappointed in the end. He couldn't take any more disappointments. And he didn't deserve a stroke of fortune. Despite this, when he was out of options, he made his way down the back hallways to the metal door at the top of the stairs.

He slid it open and pushed the flat switch that turned the LED lights on. He was halfway down when he heard the music. He hadn't mentioned the music. Even he couldn't be that sadistic.

Though he knew what he should expect, he still couldn't believe it when he reached the bottom. Faith was in front of the mirror, watching her nude reflection, her legs spread as he'd requested.

He sat in the chair he'd been seated in that night. Her gaze never strayed. He glanced to the record player to find it on repeat, and he wondered how long she'd been waiting. Could it have been this whole time?

"Are you sure about this?"

"I'm not leaving," she said, not looking away from the mirror.

It was practically an engraved invitation. If she was teasing him, she'd picked the wrong man to do it with.

"Come here."

She crawled across the carpet to his feet as he unzipped his pants. "I think you know what I want."

Even as he said it, he berated himself for expecting she'd rush to please him with her mouth.

Leo let out a soft hiss and gripped the arms of the chair when her lips wrapped around him, her warm, wet mouth engulfing his stiff member. The way she gave a blow job was the way she did everything else. There was something tentative and sweet and almost innocent in the act as she sucked on his hardened flesh. It was clear she'd done this before and knew her way around a man's anatomy, but she was still shy. It was the most deeply erotic thing he'd ever experienced. He became more convinced that, with patience, he could remake her. His fingers tangled in her hair as she pleasured him.

When he came, he didn't allow her to pull away. He wasn't going to scrub cum out of the carpet. If she was letting him use her mouth as a receptacle, she'd finish the job. His breathing deepened and then stopped for a moment as he came. She swallowed without fighting the degradation, and when he pulled out of her and tucked himself back into his pants, she remained on her knees with her gaze cast down at the ground, waiting, her breath coming out in short flutters.

He lifted her chin. Her eyes held a glazed expression that contained equal parts fear and longing, and a foolish sort of love that danced around the edges. He helped her to her feet and took her to the table he'd been strapped to a few weeks before with Esmeralda.

She panicked like a spooked deer and tried to pull out of his grip. Leo would never comprehend the level of fear she must feel when this wasn't her kink, especially after the gore she'd witnessed when he'd been on this same table. But it was time to jump in or run, and she'd refused the chance to run. He wouldn't keep offering freedom, and he suspected if he did again, she'd begin to see it as a sort of threat that he'd throw her away. If she'd made this choice with such resolute certainty—adding the music on top of everything—then to continue to question her desire to obey him, no matter how great the fear, disrespected her and what she offered. Whether he deserved it or not.

"I understand you're afraid, but you knew what was down here, and I gave you a chance at your freedom. Not staying in this house and watching while I take other women, but real freedom away from me. And you chose to stay. I won't be vanilla for you. I can't. It's not who I am."

"I know, Master, I'm sorry. I'm just scared."

He took her into his arms, feeling her heart pumping against her chest, beating into his, practically throwing his own heart off its normal rhythm.

"Get on the table, on your stomach," he whispered, pressing a kiss to her temple.

He went to the wall, expecting she'd do as he'd asked and selected a couple of the less scary items: the flogger and the paddle. Then he went to the toy box to retrieve the last coil of fresh rope.

When he returned, she was on her stomach on the padded table, shivering with her eyes squeezed shut. Leo dragged the thick blanket off the bed. He made it snug around her torso as if she were being tucked in for the night. Her eyes remained closed, but were squeezed less tightly. He took a knife from a drawer and began to cut lengths of rope, knowing exactly how long each should be.

The endless metal rings attached to the table, allowed for extensive and intricate rope bondage in all imaginable positions, but he was content to tie her down in a standard spread eagle. It was convenient and secure, while being the least distressing form of bondage he could use to start. Tying her down wasn't just about his own pleasure, but for her safety.

If the ropes hadn't kept him so tightly bound in place when Esmeralda had whipped him, he could have moved in such a way that the whip would have injured him much more severely than it already had. He didn't plan on doing anything that sadistic and cruel to Faith, but it was safer for her to stay as still as possible so he could strike the places he intended and nothing else.

He changed the record to something more peaceful: Chopin. The first piece was the third Nocturne for piano. He left the player on repeat and went back to the box for massage oil and a few pleasurable toys, as well as a blindfold. If he intended to train her to want what he wanted, he must make sure that all pain came with a sharp dose of pleasure so the lines would blur and she wouldn't know which she was getting. Her body would eventually respond to both.

It wouldn't matter how she was wired or what her brain wanted. He could remap that, reprogram it to his liking so that her body did what he wanted it to do. She'd be aroused and ready when he demanded.

Leo didn't anticipate she'd open her eyes, but he wanted to be sure. She let out a soft, almost begging whimper as he tied the blindfold around her head, but she didn't seek to remove it.

He gently took one arm and then the other, and looped the rope through the metal, tying her arms so they were stretched over her head in a V. Then he repeated the process with her legs. She was still covered with the blanket. He let her lie like that for a few moments as he carefully stroked her back through the fabric.

"Faith, did you know that a lot of what we call pain is about expectation? When you expect something to hurt a lot, and you tense all your muscles, it hurts more. If you can relax and flow with it, it hurts less. Think of yourself like a stream flowing softly over rocks. The jagged edges of the rocks don't hurt the water, it just flows." He allowed his voice to drop an octave as he spoke, becoming softer and less harsh, lulling her into a sense of safety.

The music he'd selected fit well with the imagery he fed into her mind. He spoke quietly about water and flow and relaxing while he let his hands trail over her back, still wrapped in the warm cocoon of the blanket.

He continued to speak as he went to the thermostat to raise it a couple of degrees. As the room warmed, he took the blanket away. She tensed, but not as much as before, so he poured some oil onto his hands to allow his skin to slide more easily against hers.

He started at her neck, then worked down her back and her arms and hands, then her waist, and over her bottom, and legs and feet. He tenderly massaged until each muscle group unclenched in turn, until her body became limp and receptive.

Seventeen

Faith hadn't thought it would be possible to relax. After what she'd heard with the other women, and after the first night the way he'd lost control and taken her in such a cold, heartless way . . . this was different.

He was right about relaxation and pain, and yet, she'd been determined to stay tense, as if it could magically protect her from him. Or maybe she didn't want him to see the signs of her trusting him again, not after how he'd misused that trust the first time and she'd sworn to herself she wouldn't give it again. To relax under his touch when he promised pain was shameful.

The blanket caught her off guard, and then the music changed to something more soothing, and . . . his hands and the massage. She fell into the illusion he'd created. His voice wrapped around her as the blanket had and the music moving through her like the energy that sustained her. His hot breath was on her ear when he leaned in and spoke again.

"Remember you are water."

His voice was hypnotic velvet. It had the same power as when it was darker and more demonic. She thought back to Catholic school where the nuns had told her the devil came disguised as an angel of light. It was enough to make anybody paranoid because you didn't just have to worry about the things that were overtly evil and scary, but about the things that appeared innocent and warm and loving.

Like Leo right now. She'd already seen the beast underneath this mask, and yet the spell he cast with his words and touch made her forget.

His hand came down across her bottom, jolting her from the drifting thoughts back into a more visceral moment. The smack stung, but it wasn't as painful as the first night he'd spanked her when she'd been more tense, when her only thoughts involved how long she might live.

Fear for her life had disappeared, and after Leo's sacrifice, fears he didn't care or didn't understand the damage he could cause or that maybe he *did* understand and wanted to cause it—those fears had left as well. Now it was fear of the unknown and how much pain she might have to endure to be with this man who she shouldn't love or want to please.

After each strike, he caressed her flesh, soothing her so that her muscles stayed loose and receptive to more pain. Faith jerked against the ropes when a smooth, thin piece of lubricated glass slid inside her pussy. Despite her tension, the penetration wasn't painful. She'd been tightly clenched—another piece of unconscious self protection. But he'd been prepared for that defense and had chosen something smaller to press inside her.

"That's it, move with it. I like that. Exactly how my good little whores act."

Heat crept up her neck and into her face. She hadn't realized she'd raised and lowered her hips, her body begging for the toy as he moved it inside her in an achingly slow rhythm. The brief pain of the spanking was forgotten as she moved, grateful that he'd switched to something that could feel good and wouldn't overload her so soon. But he was far from done.

She whimpered in protest when he extracted the toy and resumed the spanking. Her skin heated with each strike, the pain blending with the other sensations: the caresses, the light throbbing that moved from deep inside her skin. At the peak of discomfort— almost enough to beg—he backed off again.

Leo pushed the dildo into her, cold from fresh lubricant. She gripped the edges of the table as he fucked her harder with it this time. The force and momentum were enough that she could come if he'd keep doing it just like this at just this angle. He stopped too soon.

"Please, Master," she found herself saying. She struggled in the ropes, knowing it was pointless, and a few tears slid down her cheeks. *I'm not ready for more pain.*

"Shhhhh." He stroked her back, and a moment later, another lubricated phallus was inside her. This one larger than the first. Her walls expanded to accept it, and she moved, rocking against the cold toy as he slowly fucked her with it.

But slow wasn't enough now. Faith struggled and pulled against her bonds, not caring as the rough rope dug into her wrists, tearing at her skin. She needed to push back harder, to force the dildo to be seated more deeply inside her, to fill her.

He pulled it away and she let out a frustrated cry.

"Eager is okay, demanding is not. Do you understand?"

"Yes, Master."

He waited until her pelvis had lowered onto the table, until she was calmly spread out, relaxed and docile, before he slid the toy back inside her again at that sadistically idle pace. Her pussy throbbed against the glass. It would take very little to make her come. If she was patient and calm, then maybe . . .

"It's time for a choice," he said, breaking her concentration. "I can stop everything for the night and we can go upstairs to bed, or I can move on to the paddle and the flogger and let you have your orgasm when I'm finished."

Normally, Faith's choice would have been easy. *Stop the pain and scariness, and let's go to bed.* But he knew her body like a poem he'd memorized. He knew how to play nerve endings in both good and bad ways. It wasn't a secret how close she was, or how desperate, given the rope burns she would likely wear around her wrists for the next several days.

"Master, please . . . "

"Choose or I'll choose for you. Maybe this is all too much too soon. We should go to sleep. Or maybe you should sleep down here alone tonight. It'll give you some space away from me to think and feel safer." The honey in his voice was a trap, but it held such possibilities that she couldn't resist entertaining the new option.

Yes. She could stay here for the night alone and masturbate and take care of this ache he'd caused with the toys he kept fucking her with. She'd have her orgasm and be spared further escalation.

"O-okay," she said. "W-we should stop."

"Of course, you'll wear a chastity belt so you can't touch that sweet cunt. That's mine. You don't get to touch it without my permission ever again." He chuckled at the shock that must have been on her face. "Did you think your body was still yours to control? It's *mine*." The last word he whispered in her ear, his voice animalistic and guttural. "Does that change your answer?"

During all of this he hadn't let up on his assault of her body. He removed the toy and she almost lost her mind, but then his tongue was on her. She squirmed against his mouth. A few more strokes and she could come.

He backed away seconds before her release. "Well? Alone with your chastity belt, or pain and an orgasm?"

"Please . . . I need . . . " If she could manage the self control, she could be spared one more night.

"I know what you need. Answer me. Say the words. I want to hear them fall sweetly from your lips. And say please again. I enjoy how polite you are."

"P-please, Master, I need to come."

"So you want to move up to the paddle and the flogger then? A bit more pain?" As he spoke, he pressed two fingers inside her.

"Y-yes, Master, please."

"I told you I could make you wet when we did this."

They both knew it wasn't the pain that caused her arousal, but if he mixed everything up like this often enough, would her brain and body become so jumbled that she wouldn't know the difference? It was certainly a better outcome than simply *enduring* it to be with him. She thought about the looks of satisfaction and peace on the faces of the women as they left his dungeon, and wondered if that look would soon be on her own face. For the first time, it felt like a real possibility.

He removed his fingers and her heart sank into her stomach, knowing what was coming next. She gripped the edge of the table, bracing herself, but his hand stroked gently over her back. His mouth moved close to her ear. "Water," he whispered.

She tried to focus on the music and relax as the paddle came down across her bottom. Harder than his hand, but less intimate. She was suddenly a school girl being sent in for discipline. His power over her was absolute.

After a few moments, the tears started rolling down her cheeks. She didn't know why she was crying. The pain was greater, but she knew he was holding back, his intent not to damage or traumatize her. She cried for everything and nothing, but physical pain was the least of it. She cried for her lost little life that hadn't been glamorous but had been comfortable. She cried for the things she hadn't realized were such big holes until she had the facsimile of the thing—family. And love. She cried for the fake engagement she wished meant something, for her love for Leo that she didn't think he'd ever return, for how low she'd sunk to be so desperate for him after everything—to allow him to do these things to her when he'd given her a chance to take her freedom and go. For the shame of knowing she would allow him to debase her in any way if there was some small chance he might later love her in return.

"Let it out, sweetheart. You need a good cry." He switched from the paddle to the flogger. She jumped when the leather cords snapped across her back, and immediately her mind went to Leo's scars, and she tensed again.

He must have guessed where her mental trail was going because he said, "It's not a bull whip. Relax. I won't break your skin."

Water. The thought stole into her mind, with his voice attached. Though he hadn't audibly said the word, she knew he must be thinking it. For this moment she felt as if she could read his thoughts, as if some magic now flowed between them and connected them in a way that made telepathy not only possible, but pedestrian.

The sting of the flogger didn't feel pleasant, but it wasn't a kind of pain that a person winced and pulled away from. It was a kind of pain you moved closer to, tested and pushed, more curious to experience the sensation without judgment because it wasn't bad enough to seek to avoid right away. The hypnotic, repetitive strikes created a sense of space around her, a solitude where she could allow the rest of her tears to flow out in safety.

By the time she'd let everything out, things she hadn't realized she was holding in so emotionally, her back and bottom were warm and almost pleasantly numb. She still didn't fully understand the appeal—at least not in a sexual way—but it was cathartic. She got that part. And despite the fears that had lurked in her subconscious in a place she hadn't been able to access them before, now she knew, it wasn't like the beatings she'd taken as a child, and never could be. Leo wasn't him.

When she realized the pain wasn't intensifying or angry, but instead leveled out and faded, she faded with it, flowing along the sensation, allowing it to wrap around her, floating. She didn't notice when he'd stopped until she felt the coldness of new lubricant on glass. Her body responded more quickly this time to the pleasure, grateful for it, lapping it up—desperate to please him.

He used the wider phallus again and increased the pace, pressing down on her back so she couldn't rise up. His message was clear: he would be controlling the exact sensations she received. She would come on his terms or not at all. That realization sent an uncharacteristic flutter of something warm and electric through her stomach.

"Please . . . please . . . please . . . "

He stopped and untied her.

"No . . . please . . . " She thought untying meant he was done with her. Was he breaking his promise? Only teasing her again?

He chuckled but rolled her onto her back. Having the leather press against her back and bottom, stung, but she took deep breaths until it dissipated.

"Spread your legs," he growled.

She obeyed the command, thankful and eager to have him touch her more. He fucked her with the toy as he lowered his mouth to her clit, licking and sucking on it until the dual sensations built to the point of explosion.

Faith moaned as she came against his mouth, squirming despite how sensitive her back was. He pulled away from her as her orgasm ebbed. She lay trembling from the force of it until he picked her up and carried her to the bed.

"Lie on your stomach."

She didn't have the will to do anything else. He rummaged through the black bag and came out with a salve that he rubbed onto her wrists and gently massaged into her back and bottom. When he was finished, he pulled her into his arms and she lay against his shoulder, sobbing.

She'd thought she'd been done. She didn't know where more tears had come from, or why. There were too many feelings and emotions to name. She was beginning to see why this appealed to those women, why Leo being like this had appealed to them. The feeling of complete helplessness and fear followed by a rush of endorphins and safety activated some primal code that made no sense to her but worked with the same reliability as the rising and setting of the sun. It was the code that activated bad boy attraction and the desire for the most inappropriate and doomed romance to work.

He stroked her back while she cried and continued to hold her when she was finished.

"You did very well, sweetheart. I'm so proud of you."

She flushed at his words and knew she really had walked through the door this time. Though it hadn't physically hurt as much as she'd thought it would, it *had* overwhelmed her. And these were the baby steps. The beginning. She shuddered in his arms at that thought, and he held her more tightly.

After a few minutes of silence, he helped her stand and guided her across the room. When he removed her blindfold, she was in front of the mirror. He stood behind her, his hands on her shoulders, urging her to take a look. Her face was like the faces of those women. Serene. Older. Wiser. Peaceful. Satisfied.

He turned her body to show her the marks he'd left: mostly redness with a few light stripes from the flogger. She ran her fingers over the still-warm flesh and stared, mesmerized. She felt his absence when he stepped away to turn off the record player, but was grateful to feel his hand in hers again as he wrapped her in the blanket from the bed and led her up the stairs.

What if Demetri or other members of the household staff were lurking around? They would know what she and Leo had done. It was obvious she was naked under the blanket. Why else would she be wrapped in it? But their trip to his bedroom was uneventful. It was late and the staff had retired to their part of the house, and Demetri with them. Most of the electricity was off, with only a few strategic lamps left on to light their way.

When they reached Leo's room, he took the blanket off her and helped her into bed, tucking her in. He kissed her lightly on the forehead. "I'll be right back."

She nodded.

The way he looked at her . . . she resolved she would allow him to do anything he wanted without complaint if it meant he would always look at her like that. She'd seen desire in his eyes before. She'd seen kindness and anger and sadness. But she'd never seen this look he had now. She didn't want to be foolish and call it love, but it was a strong fondness and affection, the kind that made her melt inside at being the recipient of such a gaze.

Leo returned a few minutes later, the cats and Max slipping in behind him before he shut the door. He held a tray with water and some cheese and crackers and fruit. He got in bed and shoved the food toward her.

"Eat something. It will help you feel more grounded."

The light snack did help to bring her back to reality and the world of solid three-dimensional things. He set the tray on the table beside the sofa, undressed, and climbed into bed with her. She assumed they would sleep, but he was erect again—no doubt from everything they'd done in the dungeon.

He guided her down the length of him, and she took him into her mouth again, pleasuring him until he was satisfied.

Eighteen

Leo's erection had grown physically painful, but he'd gagged her and wasn't ready to replace the gag with his cock yet. Tears streamed down her face as he laid down lines of welts across her ass with the cane. He needed to make her cry more. She had to earn her pleasure with tears. Enough time had passed for that to be the price.

The gag frightened her, still, which drove him harder to use it. She needn't fear. He knew when enough was enough with her. He'd been careful and exercised restraint. Each time the cane came down, she winced in a way that both made him want to comfort her and hit her again to watch that reaction . . . the intense expression of pain on her face, the tears that rolled down, and the lovely welt as it bloomed so quickly into those sharp red lines with the groove he loved to run his tongue along.

He knew what the cane felt like. Though, used properly, it didn't often break skin, the hard rap of a thin dowel of rattan or steel always left a profound impression on the recipient. It was a kind of pain that bound them more tightly together each time he utilized it. He wasn't sure if she realized how she'd grown softer toward him, more happy to please him, more relaxed outside the dungeon, more natural in all of their interactions, as if she'd been born and shaped in the fires of creation to be his slave.

If he could read her mind, every thought would be of him and how to please him. Something in these exchanges made her so vulnerable that even while he was crushing her, he wanted to preserve and protect her. He'd destroy anything that came between the two of them. Anyone. His obsession toward her was of a character unlike what he'd felt with others. Even Mei Lin. Mei Lin was a wonderful sub and a masochist, but the chemistry between them was nothing like the chemistry that came alive when he touched Faith and she melted beneath him.

They'd been together like this for months. The snow had melted and fled as winter had edged into spring, and spring was beginning to be oppressed and wilted by the heat of the coming summer. Faith was on the phone with his mother nearly every day as June loomed nearer.

She was still less than excited about the wedding. Did she see him as a monster, forcing her to marry him on threat of death or horror? She'd said she loved him. Wasn't marriage what all women fantasized about? Wasn't he giving her the right things? She'd promised to stay with him; what difference did jewelry and a piece of paper make? Maybe she didn't want to lose her identity inside his as Jacobson was exchanged for Raspallo. After all, he'd never allow her to keep her name, or hyphenate. She was his, and she'd wear his name like a brand across her flesh.

Leo let the cane fall once more, this time going across the tops of her thighs, which made her jump as if he'd sent a bolt of electricity through her. Some day. He hadn't yet been able to bring himself to use the violet wand. Electrical play could be scary. She wasn't ready, and he wouldn't risk damaging her trust in him again. They had all the time in the world together to get there.

She cried around the gag, nearly spent, almost at the breaking point that might send her into insanity if he didn't stop soon. He set the cane on the tray and went to the medical bag with the salve. She whimpered as he rubbed the cool cream into her skin.

He tried not to go this intense every day, certainly not across the same expanse of flesh. Sometimes he was softer with her, more gentle. Some nights it was about humiliation, devising ways to make her uncomfortable for the sheer joy of watching her obediently carry out his demands. He'd used toys of every stripe: vibrators and dildos and anal plugs, gaining great amusement when he made her wear a plug for hours during the day. He'd enjoyed watching the blush come over her face when she'd encountered Demetri or another member of the household staff, afraid someone might realize there was a smooth, lubricated piece of glass being held between her cheeks.

He had slowly moved up in the size of the plug . . . preparing her body for a use he knew she was smart enough to know was coming. Each time he went up a size he could feel the anticipation that hummed through her as she closed her eyes and took slow, even breaths. Each time the toy inched in, an expression of pleasure lit her face.

He'd been shocked by her pleasure. Not every woman reacted to it that way.

And yet, he'd held back. He had to be sure he wouldn't damage her physically or emotionally when he did it. Since the night he'd had to atone for, the night he couldn't think about too long, or give the ugly name that he knew the event deserved, he hadn't penetrated her in the normal way. He wouldn't fuck her until she begged him for it, and so far, she hadn't. He'd contented himself during that time with the use of her mouth and her tiny hand wrapped around him, jerking him off when he demanded she join him in the shower.

Some days he tied her up and tortured her in other ways—with teasing and orgasm denial. Sometimes he used the clamps on her nipples and on her labia, adding small weights until she couldn't take it anymore. She'd obeyed him in everything, her body slowly becoming as confused as he'd known it would until her nerve endings responded to his cues instead of those coming from her own brain.

He slipped a finger inside her to find the wetness he'd known would be there. He doubted she would ever be a true masochist, but the desire to please him had transmuted into physical arousal like lead into gold.

He had thought the catalyst for her body's full capitulation would be more physical pleasure, but desire was desire, and her need for his approval had moved between her legs to express itself in the way she knew would gratify him most. It was more sweet than if he'd only plied her with pleasure.

He continued to finger her as her body rocked to keep rhythm with him, then he replaced his fingers with a vibrator until she came screaming around the gag. He pushed her beyond the point of pleasure and waited patiently for her second and then her third orgasm before finally allowing her the mercy of a space without sensation in it.

Leo left her tied down as he removed the gag. She remained quiet, the tears sliding silently down her cheeks.

"Are you all right, sweetheart?"

"Yes, Master," she whispered.

But she wasn't all right. He raised her chin to look into her eyes and was struck by the painful sadness he found there. He was ruining her. And yet, her body responded. She was desperate to make him happy. If he offered her freedom again, it would only upset her more. She was addicted to him, unable to be without him but clearly disgusted with what she'd become at his hands. He was disgusted with the things he'd done to her. And yet . . . he couldn't stop. The more disgust he felt, the more desire, the more unyielding the urge to keep going and never stop.

He'd planned to use her mouth, but couldn't now, not with so much pain and sadness in her eyes. This

wasn't the cathartic crying of a good session. It wasn't
the bittersweet pain that melted back into pleasure. It
was genuine distress. He untied her and rubbed the
salve on her wrists and ankles, then sat on the table
with her, holding her in his arms.

Leo was glad for the integrity of the furniture that
allowed them both to use it at once. He stroked her
hair and fought the urge to cry with her.

"Do I make you that unhappy?"

"N-no, Master." Her voice was muffled against his
shoulder, but he heard her. And he didn't believe her.
Part of him wanted to punish her for her lies, but the
sadness was so deep that to punish her further might
break him past the point from which he could recover.

"Can you stand?"

She nodded and got off the table.

"Let's go have a shower," he said.

Faith was shaky as she walked. He stayed behind
her, guiding her so she didn't fall.

In the bathroom, he laid out towels for them and
turned the water on, waiting for it to heat to the right
temperature. "Would you be happier if we called off
the wedding?" His family would give him hell for it,
and he'd have to hide her during the holidays . . . but
they wouldn't be happy with the lack of children
produced, either. And frankly, none of it was their
business in the first place. This had all gone too far. He
wouldn't sacrifice Faith to keep his family relations
humming along.

"No! D-do you want to call it off?" She looked so
fragile and broken, as if he were doing anything but
trying to find the right thing to do to take away the

pain. As if he would call off the wedding to hurt her in some way or to use as emotional blackmail to keep her in line.

"No," he said. "But with how I feel about the sanctity of the institution, what it means to the Church . . . to force you into marriage . . . whatever our arrangement otherwise, I can't do it if it's going to torment you like this."

She looked away, her eyes studying the black and silver pattern on the shower curtain. "Please don't call it off."

Leo pulled her back into his arms. He pressed his lips against her cheek. "I won't."

They got under the spray together, and he gently washed her. She leaned against the wall, quiet and still as a trophy as he ran his hands over her with the soap, not moving until he pulled her under the water to rinse her.

He put the soap in her hands and groaned as she lathered him. Faith lingered on his cock, stroking and squeezing with her soapy hands. She didn't slow down until he came. He hadn't asked her to do it. She'd seen his raging erection and had taken care of matters because she understood it was her duty to keep him satisfied. He gripped her shoulders as he rode the fading strains of his orgasm.

Then she went back to washing him as if nothing had happened. When she reached his back, she started crying again. Tears she couldn't stop or control.

The scars.

When he'd asked Esmeralda to make him pay for what he'd done, he hadn't thought about how the scars would be a permanent reminder, not just to him, but to Faith, and not just about what he'd done to try to make it right, but what had precipitated the event to make it necessary: that night that could never be erased, no matter how much blood flowed to cover it.

But Faith's words surprised him. "Your poor back. How could you let someone do this to you?"

Her fingertips traced over the scars as his silent tears blended into the falling water.

Nineteen

F aith sat in front of a mirror in the many-win-
dowed room in the east wing. Her wedding
veil lay before her on the vanity table. Gemma
had offered to help her get ready, but it was only a ruse
to try to talk Faith out of marrying her brother. It was
anathema to her that Leo should be happy after killing
her husband.

"I know my brother is very charming, but you
know what he did to Emilio. What makes you think
you're safe with him?"

As if Faith needed more things to fear. Though Leo
hadn't harmed her since that one night, it always existed as a possibility now.

"Leo loves me," she said. It hurt to say it because
he'd never uttered the words, and she had no reason to
believe it. But people assumed marriage was about
love, and if she didn't speak in terms of romance and
candy that his sister could relate to, someone might
see through the whole ploy. And they were so close to
the end.

"Leo loves Leo."

Faith held back the urge to cry as Gemma gave voice to her greatest fear.

"He *is* hurting you, isn't he?"

Faith looked up suddenly, her eyes going to Gemma's reflection in the mirror. "No! Of course not. He would never . . . "

"Mm-hmm. It will only get worse. You think a man who hits you before your wedding day stops after it?"

Gemma didn't know about Leo's kinks. She only assumed run-of-the-mill domestic abuse like what she'd suffered with her husband. There was no room for nuance in her world.

"It's not like that."

"Whatever you say. I think you're quite foolish." Gemma buttoned the last of the long line of buttons on Faith's dress and took a step back.

"I'd really like to be alone for a few minutes before the wedding," Faith said.

Gemma shrugged. "If I were you, I'd slip out the back door. But you already know how I feel about it."

When Faith was finally alone, her fingertips trailed over the delicate sapphire necklace at her throat. It had been in Leo's family for years. Gina had lent it to her, counting it as something borrowed, something old, and something blue. Was it all right to do three parts of the tradition in one object? What did it matter? It was still a sham. None of it was real. It wasn't being sanctioned by the Vatican. It was why they were having the wedding outdoors and not inside St. Stephen's.

Leo had decided they would join a different parish to avoid further questions about the marriage. He must not want to marry her if he was going to flee his childhood church to avoid making it official in the eyes of God.

He'd offered to call the wedding off, but that was worse. With a legal marriage, even if it wasn't sanctioned, she felt safer. She held onto the hope that as the years passed she could make him love her in the way she hoped for. Maybe then he would get a priest to bless their marriage so it would be real.

She couldn't stay in the dungeon every Christmas. She couldn't give up the illusion of a family. Aunts and uncles and cousins and brothers and sisters and grandparents and parents. These had all been foreign concepts for much of her life, except on TV.

Even if Leo couldn't give her all the things she needed, he could give her family holidays. That by itself was almost worth going through with this. She had to get through today, then she could have a breakdown privately behind closed doors.

She ran her fingers over the intricate beading of her gown. It was simple with thin straps and a satin wrap to go over her shoulders. The veil was more ornate. She felt like Cinderella, right before everything turned to rags, when it was easy to fall into the illusion and believe it could be real.

Months had passed since she'd agreed to truly be his slave, and though the cane and whips and clamps never stopped hurting, and though she never stopped being afraid of what was coming next, she went through it all because each day her need to see that look of pride and devotion remain in his eyes grew stronger. The more she became his creation, the less it mattered if she was like him.

When he'd realized he couldn't fully transmute pain for her, instead of being disappointed, she'd seen the look of triumph on his face, as if this were better because it fed his sadism. She was his perfect doll, giving everything he wanted, and yet there was a piece missing, things he hadn't taken or done since the very first night when she'd thought she was broken. Since that night she still couldn't give name to because making it disappear into the mists of falsely reconstructed memory was better.

It didn't matter what he did. As long as she survived it. As long as he held her and whispered soft words to her at the end. That was all that mattered. She'd gone with him to hell each night and been his toy and the object of his sadism. She'd had her cathartic moments punctuated by nights where it was more pain than catharsis. Yet the peace he had by the end gave her peace, as if he'd gotten the demons out that tormented him—at least for a while, and in doing so, he'd slain some of hers as well.

There was a soft knock at the door, and she looked up, her heart beating faster in her chest, desire rippling through her stomach. She knew that knock. Nobody knocked on a door quite the same way as Leo. A moment of superstition pushed into her mind. It was bad luck for the groom to see the bride before the wedding. But did that matter if the whole thing was a farce anyway? How much worse could her luck get?

"Come in."

Leo strode in like a dark, fairy-tale prince, his hair slicked back in a way that made him appear even more debonair than normal. More polished and in control, and she melted beneath the power of him a little more.

He stood behind her, his hands on her shoulders, his gaze meeting hers in the mirror. Her breath caught as his fingers trailed down her throat to slide over the necklace Gina had lent her.

"My Ma's?"

"Yes, Master," she said.

"No. Leo today. You must call me Leo, even in private, until all the guests are gone. I don't want you to slip by mistake."

"L-Leo." The word tasted strange in her mouth, almost unpleasant. It made her feel like his equal. In another time she might have longed for that, but now, if she couldn't have the true love she'd heard stories about, at least she could belong to him.

The bond between them had grown thick and tight. Nothing could break it. It had been forged in the fires of betrayal and redemption, of suffering and pleasure and secret moments below ground. It was stronger than normal love, more sure. Whatever happened, she would always be his.

His fingers brushed her throat, unclasping the necklace and placing it on the table. Her eyes searched his, but he was already pulling a large, velvet case from his inside pocket. He set the box on the vanity in front of her, her veil framing it like a hazy dream.

"Open it."

She lifted the lid and let out a gasp. A circle of platinum lay against the velvet. Glittering sapphires went fully around the choker.

"Do you understand its significance?"

Faith shook her head. Besides it replacing her something blue, she had no idea.

"I'll give you a wedding band today at the ceremony to wear with the diamond, but this is what's real between us. It's a collar. It's my commitment and promise to you that you'll always be mine. I'll always protect you, and you'll always obey me." There was an edge in his voice at the end that sent a thrill down her spine. There was no question, no doubt, only a command.

"Do you understand these terms?" He didn't ask if she accepted them, just if she understood them. As far as he was concerned, gifting her with this symbol was a formality. She'd given herself body and soul to him long ago, and true to his word, the door had closed behind her after that choice.

She nodded, unable to force a reply from her mouth. She watched, mesmerized, as he lifted the jewelry from the box and put it around her neck.

"I never want to see your throat bare again. You will always wear this. You may take it off to shower or swim, but then it goes right back on."

The weight of the collar around the base of her throat felt like his hand on her always. He didn't need to worry she'd take it off.

He went to the door. "The ceremony starts in thirty minutes. I'll see you down there."

"Leo, wait."

He stopped but didn't turn around. "Yes?"

"Will we ever . . . I mean . . . don't you want to . . . "
She was flustered and couldn't get the words out, but

their lack of consummation of the relationship since that one ugly night, had nearly burned her soul into oblivion. Didn't he want her? Was she crazy for wanting him to go there again? Was it better to let it go and be content with the moments they had? But . . . didn't he want her?

Leo turned, his expression intense. "Don't I want to . . . what?"

He was going to make her say it. Her gaze went back to the empty box sitting on the veil. "We've never . . . made love." She cringed as she said it. It sounded like the thing a high school girl would say. What adult woman called it "making love" anymore? Was she trapped in 1952?

Wasn't it more sophisticated to call it sex or fucking? Don't make it too romantic. Don't make it mean too much. Just let it be a physical act that sits alongside any other feelings but doesn't define them, because that nonsense is for movies and books. Not the life of the three dimensional. Even if those weren't her feelings and thoughts, she was sure they must be Leo's. With their age difference, his world had always struck her as much more adult than the world she'd inhabited, as if she'd been surrounded by children wearing adult costumes.

"Is that what you want?" His voice was soft when he asked, so soft that she almost didn't hear it for all her inner turmoil.

Yes. No. Maybe. I think so. I don't know. It needs to happen. It's a bad idea. It'll happen eventually, or maybe it won't. Can I be with him if it never happens? Or if it does?

She heard the lock click into place and then felt more than saw as he came closer. Did she know what she was asking for? Would he hurt her? Would he be cold like before? Would it feel like rape? What if she couldn't have normal sex again? Crossing this line meant they couldn't uncross it. He'd left her body alone in that one way for months. Wasn't that mercy? He could have taken it at any time but he hadn't. And now . . . if he did again, did that mean that safety was gone forever? Was it okay to love him? Did it matter when she couldn't make the feelings die anyway?

Leo pulled her up from the vanity stool and spun her around, swallowing her fears and mental screams with his kiss. She whimpered against his mouth as he took her hand in his and guided her to the bed.

"T-the windows," she said.

Bright light poured into the glass room.

"Everyone is outside behind the house. No one can see in up here," he said as his mouth moved over hers.

He spun her away from him to undress her. The dress didn't have a zipper. It was all buttons down the back—at least a hundred tiny buttons. It took several long minutes to get the gown off and would probably take longer to get it back on. They were going to be late to their own wedding. Even the fastest coupling would have their guests wondering at the delay.

Faith blushed at that, but she was too far in. She had to finish this. She couldn't stand in front of God and all their guests and marry Leo, no matter what the ceremony meant or didn't mean to him, unless she knew. She had to know if she could do this with him and not feel like she was dying inside.

He growled in frustration when he came to all the hooks on the corset. "All these damned buttons and hooks. Why not lock yourself in a chastity belt?"

She sucked in a breath as he squeezed the corset tighter to release her from it one small hook at a time. When she was nude, he worked quickly to get out of his own clothing.

Though the clock ticked impatiently to their wedding, he took his time. His mouth on her stayed gentle, his hands moved over her the same. When his body was inside hers, tears flowed down her cheeks with such force that she couldn't remain quiet.

"Are you all right?"

"Yes." She gripped his back, her fingers pressing against the small indentations of the scars.

He searched her eyes and must have found the truth because he kept going. The tears were relief. It was nothing like that night, and in that moment with the sunlight streaming in and their guests waiting, she knew she could face anything with him.

Faith stood at the back of the rows of chairs with her veil in place, a bouquet of white roses in her hands. The wedding was all white. White chairs. White flowers. White candles. A white runner on the ground for her to walk on. The only thing besides the tuxedos that weren't white were the clothing of the guests and her bright red hair.

The reception, by contrast, had been planned under large tents with Japanese lanterns and bright jewel tones. It reminded Faith of the Wizard of Oz where everything went from black and white to color, and it gave her the smallest shred of hope that her life with Leo would be in color.

Uncle Sal had offered to walk her down the aisle. He stood next to her looking more like an aging body-guard than a father figure.

He leaned close to her ear. "I think you know a lot more about this family than you should."

Her back went rigid. Uncle Sal was the type of man who would shoot you on any day of the year, be it your birthday, your graduation, or your wedding day. So the occasion might not save her.

He let out a short grunt. "That's what I thought."

She kept her voice low. "I don't care what anybody is involved with. I want to stay out of it."

Sal nodded, displaying a sinister half-smile. "Keep that attitude. It's safer for everyone." After a beat he said, "You really have no family?"

"What little I have, I don't want here," she said. Then possibly foolishly she added, "There's no one else you can threaten."

Pachelbel's Canon in D started, and the brides-maids began to walk down the aisle wearing white sundresses and carrying daisies. They were followed by two of Leo's nieces, Mariella and Noelle, in fluffy dresses that made them look like colorless cotton candy. They took their time scattering white rose petals on the ground, causing the orchestra to have to loop the music. The ring bearers wore white tuxedos and carried a white satin pillow on which was tied the ring.

Faith glanced back at the house, then at the wedding stretched before her, and Leo standing at the front waiting for her. Even if it wasn't the full fairy tale, wasn't it more than what most women got? Did it matter if he returned her love? Was it enough that she loved him and that he wanted her?

It had to be.

Sal offered his arm, and she gripped it like a lifeline as the orchestra changed to the traditional wedding march. Some of the guests she recognized—family she'd met over the holidays—but there were many more people she didn't know. She wondered how many of them thought it odd that the entirety of the guest list was composed of Leo's family and friends with nobody there for her.

When she reached the front, Sal lifted her veil and kissed her on the cheek before handing her over to Leo and returning to his seat. She gripped Leo's hand as tightly as she'd held Sal's arm. She felt as if she might pass out and wondered if it was the wedding or the corset or hunger that had put her in this state.

She tried to ignore everything but Leo. Even the priest's words blended and mixed with the warm summer breeze. It was only because she'd heard the marriage rite many times that she was able to keep up. Her eyes widened when she heard "obey" had been slipped into the bride's wedding vows. How Leo managed to get the priest to deviate from the traditional Catholic rite to include "obey" she didn't know, but if the ceremony was merely legal and not a sacrament, perhaps he'd decided they could do what they wanted.

Leo smirked as she repeated the obey part. She glanced out at the guests, but no one noticed the addition. As she recited her vows, her fingers strayed to touch the platinum at her throat, and Leo smiled a secret smile meant for her.

When rings were on fingers and vows had been exchanged and the kiss had been shared, they were announced as Mr. and Mrs. Leo Raspallo. They turned as the reprise of the wedding march began. Faith looked into the sea of smiling faces and something low in her gut twinged in panic. Her gaze was drawn to the left side of the crowd, the face that didn't fit.

A man dressed in a dark suit stood at the back. Faster than seemed possible, a gun was out of his jacket and aimed at Leo. Faith didn't think; she just moved in front of her husband.

A spray of gunshots rang loud and hollow in the air, silencing the orchestra and bringing screams from the guests. The roses escaped her grasp and fell to the ground, and then she fell, barely feeling the hands around her waist that cushioned her as she hit the ground. Vaguely she could see color in her wedding now. Drops of red on her roses, on her dress, on the white runner she'd walked upon.

Black, red, and white were very elegant colors for a wedding.

Leo had been looking at his mother when Faith suddenly jumped in front of him. Then those terrible sounds and the surreal gasp from the guests. He looked up in time to see a man running from the scene, most people too hysterical to go after him. Except for his brother.

Angelo shot him a brief, black look and followed after the gunman with Davide in tow. Leo moved quickly, his hands barely spanning Faith's waist in time to catch her.

"Sal, call my blood guy! I need a lot. I don't know her blood type. Have him bring everything." That panicked, out-of-control shout had come out of his mouth.

"But Leo, on short notice, I don't know if . . . "

"He's got access. He will bring me the blood or he'll spend the rest of his life running from me. Be sure he gets that message."

Sal pulled out his cell phone.

Uncaring of how it looked, Leo ripped the gown apart to find where the bullets had hit. One had grazed her head, another had gone through her shoulder, a third had embedded in the muscle of her calf. Terror froze her features as she gripped him. He tore his coat off and wrapped it around her to hold off the shock.

"Why would you jump in front of a gun for me?" But he knew the answer. She'd confessed her love for him a long time ago. The words had never made it past his own lips. But she had to know. How could she not see it?

Her voice came out shaky. "I-I thought some day you might love me back." The last part faded out as she said it; she was already getting too weak to talk.

"You think I don't love you?" Perhaps what he did to her downstairs was too confusing for her to ever hope it could happen inside love.

The nurses rushed toward him to offer assistance.

He held up a hand. "No! I've got her. A through and through and a graze and one in her calf muscle. Nothing vital hit. It's the blood loss. Set up the operating theater. Get the machines and anesthesia and the IV fluids ready to go. Bring all the artificial blood from the lab. And prepare for a live transfusion." He'd never been so happy to be a universal donor.

The women scrambled toward the house.

It was risky doing a live transfusion and then operating. He'd have to be careful not to weaken himself too much. He had to hope the blood guy got there in time.

He couldn't stop this bleeding, he had to get her to the operating theater *now*.

Leo flung her over his shoulder, fireman-style, and strode with grim determination to the separate entrance at the back of the house. Family and friends jumped out of his way, looks of horror and pity on their faces. Looks that said, *poor bastard doesn't realize she's not going to make it.*

Faith's blood ran down his back, soaking his linen shirt as she went limp.

Twenty

L eo sat in his den with Angelo over copious amounts of alcohol. "Well?" Since the previous day, he'd been a crazed lunatic, intent on revenge and blood and death for the bullets that had been meant for him but had hit the woman he loved instead.

"It was Emilio's cousin. When I caught up to him, he wouldn't talk. Davide and I had to overpower him and tie him down. It took hours before I got the full story."

"And?"

"You won't like it. Caprice told him what you did to Gemma's husband."

Leo paced the floor, regret and the weight of responsibility crushing him. Caprice should never have been at their family Christmas. But even so, if he hadn't played with her, used her body and screwed with her mind, she might not have gone to Emilio's cousin set on instigating violence.

"I know Vinny is your best friend and you and Caprice have history, but she's a loose cannon. She's dangerous to all of us. I have to . . . "

Leo finished the sentence, " . . . kill her." Something wild and evil rose from the depths of his soul, single-minded and obsessed. "Yes, I know. But don't just put a bullet in her head, Ange. Make her suffer first. I don't care what you do, but make sure she suffers. And before you kill her, tell her the order came from me."

Angelo's eyes widened before his face went back to its normal, cold perfection. They embraced and kissed, then his brother set his glass on the side bar and started toward the door.

"Ange?"

His mirror image turned back to him. "Yeah?"

"Vinny can never know."

Angelo gave a short nod.

When his brother was gone, Leo went to the east wing. The pain and memories rose in his chest, a physical thing threatening to take his breath. The memory of her lifeless in his arms.

As she'd gone still, he'd snapped into focus, like a robot, seeing her no longer as the woman he loved, but as a broken piece of flesh to fix.

Leo leaned his forehead against the door to Faith's room and took a long, shuddering breath, to pull himself together. Thinking of all he could have lost was pointless torment. He hadn't lost her. No thanks to his own foolish choices that had put her in harm's way.

He'd thought it best to keep her in the glass room during recovery. The sunlight would do her good. Leo knocked, then turned the knob without waiting for a reply. She was still too weak to call out. A nurse sat on the sofa reading a book, and his ma sat in a chair beside the bed, watching over Faith as the machines beeped away.

The room overflowed with balloons and flowers and stuffed animals from all of the family. If Uncle Sal or Uncle Bernie, or even Angelo had doubted Faith's worth, they were her biggest fans now. The word *liability* would never cross their lips again.

Max sprawled across the foot of the bed, guarding her, while the two cats cuddled into her side. The animals kept their vigil, and no power on earth would have removed them from their stations.

Faith's eyes fluttered open as he approached the bed. He took her hand and leaned in to kiss her forehead.

"I'm going into town. Do you need anything?"

Her heart rate beeped erratically on the machine. "No! Don't go out, you might . . . he might . . . "

"Shhhh, sweetheart. Angelo took care of it. It's safe. It was personal. It was one mistake. I have no other enemies."

After a few moments, she released her death grip on his hand.

"Now, do you need anything?"

She shook her head.

Leo turned to his mother and the nurse. "I need to speak with my wife in private."

Looks were exchanged, but the two women removed themselves from the room. When the door clicked shut, Leo said, "As soon as you're better, I'll take you to the church so Father Joseph can bless the marriage properly. Then we'll have the reception. I'm flying everyone in. They all want you to have your party."

She gripped his hand tighter than her strength should have allowed. "You'd have the marriage sanctioned?"

"I was so busy thinking of it as a sham and you as an unwilling prisoner, that I didn't stop to consider how both of our feelings had changed. I don't want it to be a lie."

"Me either."

"Then it's settled, and we'll attend St. Stephen's."

"Thank you."

"But Faith, being my wife doesn't change our relationship."

She touched the collar at her throat almost unconsciously. "Yes, Master."

He squeezed her hand. "Good girl. I'll be back soon. I promise."

The day had been filled with rain and gloom, the perfect, bright sun of the wedding refusing to return. Leo drove to St. Stephen's and sat outside the building for a long time.

He pulled his cell phone from his pocket and stared at Angelo's name in his contact list. He knew he couldn't stop his brother from killing Caprice, but he could remove his blessing. He could stop the rest, whatever Angelo would do to her that would go far beyond a quick shot to the head. He could be merciful and make sure she never saw it coming.

He closed the phone and cursed when the call went to voice mail.

Inside, the church was quiet, but Leo knew someone would be there. He opened the door to the confessional booth and sat. Cloaked in the warm, tight darkness, he breathed in the smells of the incense and candles.

"Forgive me, Father, for I have sinned."

Other Titles by Kitty Thomas:

Comfort Food
Guilty Pleasures
Tender Mercies
The Last Girl
Submissive Fairy Tales
Big Sky

Lightning Source UK Ltd.
Milton Keynes UK
UKOW01f0400150218
317900UK00003B/127/P